TESTED BY FIRE

C.J. PETERSON

This book is dedicated to my loving husband and dear family, who love and support me. You all mean more to me than you will ever know. Thank you! I love you!

Also, a special "Thank you" to Author Patty Wiseman for the story idea! To learn more about Patty and her work, check out her website: https://www.pattywiseman.com

A portion of the proceeds from **Tested By Fire** *will go to "**Jenny's Hope**."*

"No one should ever have to grieve alone. There is healing found when we share our stories, our fears, and our memories. In 2017, we discovered Wise County Christian Counseling had 59 families with children needing grief counseling on the wait list. We could hardly bear it that 59 sets of parents were on the edge of their seats waiting for a call for help. We prayed, we dreamed, we sought advice. We decided to open Jenny's Hope, a free grief center for children and adults."

To find out more about Jenny's Hope, go to: https://jennys-hope.org

To learn more about C.J. Peterson, you can find her online at: http://cjpetersonwrites.com/
'While the stories are fiction, the journey is real!'

Summary

Robin Flynn's life was one firestorm after another. With the tender heart of an artist, she learned at a young age to take life as she saw it. She continued to get back on her feet after being knocked down time after time. She loved art, painting, and particularly working with metal. It was her escape when her life took turns for the worst. She was a welder, by trade, like her father, and an artist by heart. Unfortunately, she found herself in a precarious position. She accidentally burned down an abandoned warehouse. What she thought was going to be horrific, the firefighters seemed to be grateful. So, she continued to cleanse the town of Hemlock of its abandoned warehouses.

Nate Mitchell always wanted to be a fire marshal. He was getting everything he ever wanted. Dating the girl of his dreams while in training to be a fire marshal. What could go wrong?

What happens when a fire marshal falls in love with an arsonist before he finds out she's the arsonist? Find out in *Tested By Fire*.

1 Peter 1:7 (NIV) *"These trials will show that your faith is genuine. It is being tested as fire tests and purifies gold--though your* *faith is far more precious than mere gold. So when your faith remains strong through many trials, it will bring you much praise and glory and honor on the day when Jesus Christ is revealed to the whole world."*

CHAPTER 1

FIRE IS NEVER A GENTLE MASTER

"Ben? Ben?" Andrea said, jostling her husband. "Ben, wake up!"

"Honey," Ben mumbled in his heavy sleepy state. "Please quiet down so you don't wake Robin again."

"Ben, I'm serious. Something's wrong. There's..." Her voice faded as the color drained from her face. "Ben, there's smoke coming under the door," Andrea said, jumping out of bed. Looking to the window she remembered the bars on the outside of all of their doors and windows. The realization of their situation hit. "Ben! We have to get to Stevie and get out of here!"

"What do you mean?" he asked, groggy.

"There's a fire! Get up!" Andrea's hand sizzled when she touched the doorknob. "It's in the hall! Ben! Get up now!"

"Stevie!" He jumped out of bed. "Robin, you need to go with Mommy," he said, wrapping the eight-year-old in a blanket, who had come to the bed earlier due to a nightmare. Turning to Andrea, he instructed, "Keep her face covered until you're outside." He snatched a couple shirts from the hamper. "Cover your face. Once I open this door, you need to run!" he said, securing a shirt around Andrea's face. Then he put one on him, as he added, "I'll get Steven and meet you outside."

Andrea nodded.

Once the door flew open, the fire rushed in. It headed for the ceiling before tackling the room.

"Go!" Ben ordered. "Go now!"

Andrea bolted from the room into the flames. As she ran, she stopped for a moment to look for Ben. When she saw him duck into Steven's room, the flames chased him in.

"Mommy! It's hot!" Robin complained from inside the covers. She coughed, gagging on the smoke.

Andrea pawed at the fire that was trying to eat the blanket wrapped around her daughter. Passing the kitchen, Andrea's head began to spin. Coughing, she dropped to the ground. Robin almost fell from her arms. Andrea could see the door in the living room which led to the freedom and fresh air. Struggling to catch her breath, she cleared her throat and shook her head. She *had* to get Robin to safety.

"Come on, baby, we need to get out of here."

Stumbling into the living room, the flames surrounded them. *How will I get us out of this?* "God, please help!" she begged, tears streaking down her face as panic took over. "I don't want my little girl to die!"

The fire-engulfed living room looked like literal Hell to Andrea. As she fought her way to the door, the fire consumed the bottom of the bookcase, causing it to fall. It caught the bottom of Andrea's leg.

Tugging on her leg, the fire closed in on Andrea. In that instant, she realized their horrific reality and knew what she had to do. Andrea unwrapped Robin and threw the blanket into the fire. "Honey, you need..." Andrea knew she would not make it out the door, but Robin could. "You need to get out of here! Quick! Get outside!"

"You need to come with me, Mommy!" Robin pleaded, tugging on her mother's arm. "You have to come with me!"

Andrea pushed Robin toward the door. "Go!"

"I can't!" Robin sobbed. "You have come with me, Mommy!"

"Go, Robin! Go get help!"

Running to the door, Robin fumbled with the bolt for a moment before she finally got it, and the door unlocked. Turning to her mom to tell her the good news, she saw her mom's body being consumed while she screamed in terror. Their entire home was fully engulfed by the flames. Wide-eyed, Robin stared at her, unable to form any thought.

The door burst open, and a fireman filled the doorframe. She saw them in school, but never this close up. He snatched her out of the house, hugging her to his body. She watched over his shoulder as the other firemen ran into the burning house after her family.

Never taking her eyes off the house, she was enthralled by the way the flames devoured her home. They almost seemed to wave at her.

"Come here, sweetheart," a paramedic said as the fireman handed her off before running back to the house. The paramedic carried her to the ambulance.

She tried to see around him, but he blocked her view, which was good because it was at that moment one of the firemen brought her mother's charred body out of the house. When he placed her on the ground another fireman covered the body with a sheet.

"The fire originated in here," Fire Marshal Ian Mitchell said to Lieutenant Tucker after the fire was out and the firemen were cleaning up.

"That's what we were thinking, too," Tucker agreed. Going to the curtains in the little girl's room, he pointed. "It started over here."

Cocking his head to the side, Ian then went across the room

and knelt next to the curtains. Out of the corner of his eye, he saw something under the bed. Pulling it out, he held up the votive candle. The glass was almost completely melted due to the intensity of the heat. "Why would a little girl have a candle in her room? How old is she again?"

"She's eight. She lost her three-year-old brother and both of her parents."

"Wow. That's rough," Ian said, sick to his stomach. He had a daughter, Jenny, who was the same age. He could not imagine what Jenny would be going through if she were to lose her entire family. "What's going to happen to the little girl?"

"According to Children's Services, she will be living with her grandmother and grandfather. They live about twenty minutes from here."

"Has she left yet?"

"Yes. They took her to the hospital for smoke inhalation."

"I'm heading to the hospital to talk to her," Ian said, sliding the candle into an evidence bag as he left the room. At the doorway, he instructed, "Make sure to tape everything off until I can get back here."

"Will do."

Walking out into the darkness of night, his eyes were blinded by the flashing red and blue lights from the emergency vehicles up and down the road. After stepping over the maze of hoses and various household belongings, he sloshed through the puddles of water to get to his truck.

Days like these broke his heart. An entire family, save one, was taken in a matter of minutes. Their lives, their homes...all gone. He sighed heavily as he started his truck.

When he was about to leave, a fireman ran up to the truck with a small welding helmet in his hands. Ian rolled his window down. The fireman explained, "Tucker mentioned it started in the little girl's room. We found this in the garage in the back. LT said you were going to see her in the hospital. Not sure if it's a good thing or not, but it looks like something her dad made her. His is in the garage, too. This may bring her comfort."

Ian accepted the helmet. "Thank you." The helmet was considerably smaller than the average. It was purple with a white candle on the side that was lit. Robin's name was painted on it, with blue and purple flames surrounding it.

Ian set it on the seat before heading to the hospital. He did not want to hurt the little girl, but there were some questions that needed answers.

When Ian walked into Robin's room in the emergency room, the social worker was sitting in a chair next to the bed. The tiny eight-year-old little girl with big brown eyes and long black hair sat on a bed that was too big for her. She was lost in her own thoughts. The little girl nervously sat there with a blanket around her and an oxygen mask on her face.

"What's her name, Kara?" Ian asked the social worker, setting the bag he carried in onto the end of the bed.

"Hey, Ian," Kara said. They had run into each other multiple times over the last several years. "This is Robin Flynn."

"Hi, Robin. My name is Ian," he introduced himself. He sat on the end of the bed. "Can I talk to you for a minute?"

Robin nodded in response.

"Here. Let me lower this a bit so I can hear you. Is that okay?" he asked. When she nodded, he pulled the mask down a bit and she held it in place. "Can you tell me how old you are?" he asked.

"Eight," she responded quietly.

He had to strain to hear her. "Did you say eight?"

"Yes."

"Good. Robin, I need your help with a few things." When she

nodded in response again, he continued. "Were you in your bedroom by yourself?"

"No. I had a nightmare, so I went to Mommy and Daddy's room."

"Okay. Where were your brother and your parents?"

"Stevie was in his room across the hall from mine, and Mommy and Daddy were in their room next to his."

"Good." Tossing around several ways to ask the next question, he finally decided to put it off after a few more questions in order to keep her relaxed. "Robin, what did your mommy do for a job?"

"She works at my school."

"Was she a teacher?"

"Yes."

"Good. What grade?"

"Second."

"Why are you –"

"Trust me," Ian said, cutting off Kara. When Kara nodded for him to go ahead, he asked Robin, "What did your daddy do for a job?"

"He welds."

"He was as an offshore welder," Kara explained.

Turing back to Robin, Ian asked, "Did you get to watch your daddy as he welded in the garage?"

She nodded.

"Did you like doing that?"

"Yes."

"What did you like about it?"

"Being with Daddy."

Chuckling, Ian said, "I'll bet! Every little girl enjoys spending time with her daddy. Did you know that I have a little girl who is your age? You may know her. Her name is Jenny Mitchell."

Robin shook her head.

"Jenny likes pretty things. She loves to dress up. This year she wants to be a firefighter for the harvest party. She said it was so she could be just like her daddy. Do you want to be like your daddy when you grow up?"

"Yes."

"Why?"

When she didn't respond, he opened the bag he brought with him and pulled out her mask. "Is this yours?" he asked her.

"Yes. Daddy made it," Robin said, reaching for it.

As he handed it to her, Ian asked, "Do you like candles?"

"Yes. Mommy lights one for me every night. When it burns out, I have to go to sleep. I get to look at books until it goes out. That's our deal."

"I see. I'm sorry you had to go through this, Robin," Ian said, resting his hand on her shoulder. "I pray for peace for you," he said before he stood up.

When he went to leave, Kara ran after him. Closing the door partway behind her so she could still hear Robin, but speak quietly with Ian, she asked, "What was that all about?"

Pulling out the evidence bag with the candle in it from the bag he brought with him, he explained, "The fire originated from this candle. It must have fallen onto the floor and caught the carpet and curtains on fire. I needed to know why it was lit in the first place. Looks like the candle was lit, and when she left for her parents' room with the nightmare, she forgot to blow it out. Unfortunately, that oversight seems to have been the cause of the fire and the loss of her entire family."

"I see," Kara said. "So, is she safe to place with her grandparents?"

"I don't see a problem. From what the firefighters told me about where the bodies were found, it looks like the dad went to run for the son when they discovered the fire, while the mom ran with the daughter for the front door. Unfortunately, with the bars on the windows, they didn't have a choice of going out the windows. The dad died in the son's room with the baby in his arms, and the mom collapsed in the living room. There was no way for Robin to get her mom out. There was a bookcase on her legs. By some of the burns on her arms and legs, Robin was lucky to get out herself. This was an extremely unfortunate accident."

"I only pray she'll recover from the trauma of this. I'll have her meet with the counselor until I'm comfortable."

"Sounds like a plan. I'll tell my wife about her, and we'll keep her in prayer."

"I would appreciate it," Kara said, grateful.

"I'll make sure you get a copy of the final report."

"Thank you," Kara said. "So, do you feel it was an accident?"

"I do. A tragically horrific, unfortunate accident," he said, and left the hospital.

Seven Years Later

"Robin!" Liam Rodgers called to Robin in the middle of the hall at their high school. "Robin! Wait up!"

"Hey, Liam!" Robin greeted him with a smile.

"Your art project is amazing!" he said. "Mr. Samuels has it on display. I know why you got first place. The way you drew that fire was incredible! It is so realistic! I almost felt like I was standing next to real fire!"

"Thank you!"

"You're going to Jenny's house for the bonfire tonight after the Homecoming game, right?" Liam stood to about six feet, with medium length light brown hair and brown eyes. He was a receiver for the football team and played basketball and baseball, too. He excelled at all the sports he enjoyed due to his competitive nature. To his opposite, his girlfriend, Robin, had dark brown eyes, and raven hair that reached several inches below her shoulders on her thin frame. She excelled in art but often felt like a klutz when it came to sports. They were an odd pair, but they worked for going on three-and-a-half years.

"I don't know." Robin shook her head. "My grandma's being strict lately. She says it's great that I'm doing so well in English, Literature, and Art, but my math and science grades are a lot to be desired."

Liam leaned against the locker next to hers. "She loves me. I could ask her?"

"You're going to milk that for all it's worth, aren't ya?" Robin shook her head. "Ohhh, those big brown eyes kill me."

"You love me too," Liam said, wrapping his arms around her. Leaning down to kiss her cheek, he said, "I'll pick you up at five for the game." Liam was two years older than Robin, but there was only a one-year difference between them in school. While Robin was a sophomore, Liam was a junior. Her grandparents didn't like the age difference but tolerated it for sake of harmony within the home.

"Then *you* are talking to Grams," Robin agreed. Turning toward him, she ran her fingers through his light brown hair. Sighing, she asked, "How did I get so lucky to be your girlfriend?"

"Well," he said, snuggling closer as kids moved all around them in the hall. It was the end of the day, and everyone was trying to get out of the school. "It could be because of those gorgeous deep brown eyes of yours," he said, stroking the side of her face. "Or that stunning long black hair that flows down to your mid-back. Or this baby smooth skin all over your body," he said, kissing her neck.

"Will you two go take a cold shower already?" their friend Drew said, walking up to the pair with his girlfriend, Mia, and her friend Jenny. They were sophomores like Robin. Mia and Jenny were new to their friend circle since mid-summer when Drew and Mia started dating.

"Jealous?" Liam asked, leaning down to kiss her neck again before sliding off to the side of Robin, keeping his arm at her lower back.

"Are you guys coming to my house after the game?" Jenny asked. "My dad's going be there to watch the fire for a bit, and then he'll take off."

"What about your brother, Nate?" Zoey, another friend of theirs, asked as she met them at Robin's locker. "He's hot!"

"He'll be there, but he has given me strict instructions to keep my friends away from his friends," Jenny said, crinkling her nose in disgust. "With his friends being seniors, he doesn't want my friends to annoy them."

"We're not all that different in age," Liam said, wrapping his arms around Robin's waist from behind her. "Some of us are even on the same teams he's on. That's kind of a –"

"Some of you aren't," Jenny cut Liam off, pretty sure where he was headed with his language, "but some are. We've tentatively divided the yard in half to keep the peace. I'm not allowed to mess up Nate's senior year."

"Big, bad Nate." Drew rolled his eyes. "Captain of the varsity football and basketball teams."

"Yeah, it'll be a bit rowdy tonight with all of the team, along with the cheerleaders and all their friends, too." Jenny rolled her eyes.

"Sounds loud," Drew said.

"I can have a few girls spend the night...if you're interested?" Jenny asked Robin, Mia, and Zoey.

All three girls got a smile on their face and nodded.

"Tonight's going to be sick!" Drew grinned. "We're going to kick some wildcat behind and then party into the night!"

"And with Homecoming tomorrow night, it'll be a weekend to remember for sure!" Mia said.

The Rangers beat the Wildcats 37-30. The noise level in the stadium was deafening as Robin and her friends made their way to the parking lot. Stopping to pick up soda and chips on the way to Jenny's house, they still managed to beat most of the football players there.

By the time they walked the six acres behind Jenny's twenty-acre home to where the bonfire was, the group was more than ready to relax.

"Homecoming tomorrow night is going to be great!" blond-haired, blue-eyed Jenny said, excited.

Her parents were opposite in looks. While her dad had blond hair and brown eyes, her mom had jet-black hair and blue eyes. This made for an interesting mix when she and her three brothers came along. She was closest in age to her older brother, Nate, who had jet-black hair and sky-blue eyes. He was only a year older than Jenny, but they were two years apart in school due to how their birthdays fell within the calendar year. They had two more older brothers as well, Brad and Scott. Brad was the spitting image of his dad, while Scott had black hair and brown eyes. While they each looked different, they were extremely popular in their schools, even the two in college.

"Can't wait!" Mia grinned. Then looking at Robin, she asked, "Robin, please tell me you finally found a dress?"

"Not yet." Robin shook her head. "I'll find it in the morning."

"How are you supposed to match her?" Drew asked Liam.

"Easy. I know Robin. It'll probably be red, right?"

Blushing, Robin nodded.

"Or black," Zoey teased. "Those are pretty much her colors."

"I wear white and royal blue, too," Robin defended herself.

"Not often," Zoey said.

"Can you believe Sara and Matt are going together?" Mia asked. "He tries to control everything she does. I can't believe she's still with him."

"It's because she loves him," Zoey jumped to her defense.

"That's not love." Robin huffed. "I'm going to get a soda." She got up, hoping the subject would change by the time she returned. So far, the conversation steered toward her least favorite subjects. She hated being the topic of conversation. And small talk and pathetic drama irritated her. It's not that she did not enjoy the high school experience. It's that after the loss of her parents at such a young age, she just wanted to get out on her own. She loved her grandparents, but they often smothered her, trying to love her almost too much to make up for the loss of her family.

As she grabbed a can of soda, she heard cheers behind her. She turned to see the football players, cheerleaders, along with a lot of older high school kids noisily coming into the back half of Jenny's parent's yard. When he saw them, Jenny and Nate's dad lit the bonfire in several places. It burst into flames as it reached toward the sky. The flames stretched higher than Robin had ever seen. Mesmerized by the sight, she slowly wandered over to the bonfire, soda in hand.

The fire intertwined itself deep into the stack of wood, clinging to every branch, devouring the bark as it headed deeper into the pile. Stepping closer to get a better look, Robin watched the stunning colors of red and orange, morph into blue and white. The heat was intense, but she felt drawn to it.

The flames reminded her of her father. He would let her be in his workshop behind the house with him as he welded. He even made Robin her very own welding mask, which she still had in her room. When the light sparked, it molded the pieces of metal, forced by the immense heat. The intensity of fire fascinated her. The colors were almost enchanting.

She then remembered the candle that always burned on her nightstand. Her mom lit it each night. She would watch it whirl in the breeze of the fan in her room until it fully melted the candle to the bottom of the glass. At that point, she would drift off to sleep with visions of flames swaying in her dreams. Her grandparents allowed her to continue the tradition as long as it was kept on a dresser to stop it from falling.

She wasn't afraid of the fire, as most in her position would be. On the contrary, she was fascinated by it. She wanted to study it, understand it. It mesmerized her, almost charmed her, enticing her to attempt to control it. She almost feared, in the end, it would control her.

"You get too close, and you'll catch fire," Jenny's dad commented as he threw a couple more pieces of wood onto the fire.

"Oh, I'm fine, Mr. Mitchell," Robin said. "I've been around fire since I was a little girl."

Slightly taken aback, he asked, "Are your parents firefighters?"

"No, sir. I lost them when I was young."

"Then, what do –"

"What's a pretty little thing like you doing so close to the fire?" Jenny's brother Nate asked Robin, cutting off his dad. "I *think* your friends are looking for you," he said, turning her back toward where her friends were sitting around a small fire pit. There were three fire pits strategically placed around the yard, so everyone could enjoy the warmth of a chilly fall night in the deep east Texas town of Hemlock.

Hemlock used to be more than an oil town. The town used to manufacture chemicals and electronics. There were several skeletal remains of plants, buildings, and warehouses that showed the once-booming town's history. There were still a few food manufacturing and oil refinery plants in the area that employed a good portion of the town.

"I'll get to them eventually. We have plenty of time," Robin said. "I was just watching the fire for a bit."

"Really?" Nate asked, intrigued. "Why do you like fire? Are you some kind of pyromaniac or something?"

"No. I just think it's pretty."

"Pretty scary," Nate remarked. "Did you know that I'll be going to school to be a fireman."

"Really?" Robin smirked. "Trying to impress me?"

"It's true," his dad confirmed. "I'm the fire marshal. He intends to follow in my footsteps."

"Don't they come in *after* the fire is out?" Robin asked.

"Not at first. He needs to figure out fire before he heads into the big leagues," his dad teased.

"Figure out fire?" Robin questioned.

"You need to locate the point of origin," Mr. Mitchell explained. "Once you find that, you need to find the ignition source...or the cause if it isn't immediately evident. The fire sometimes consumes the evidence, so it can be tricky."

"The cause? How can you be sure of the cause?"

"There is usually one of five general causes. Faulty electronics. Flammable or combustible materials. Human error. General negligence. Or outright arson."

"Interesting."

"Look, I understand fire more than plenty." Nate waved him off. "You see," Nate said, resting his arm over Robin's shoulder, "I've grown up in firehouses. I've even shadowed my dad multiple times. The cool thing about being a fire marshal is that it's like being a combination of a police investigator and a fire fighter. They figure out the why. They go deep –"

"*This* is getting pretty deep." His dad chuckled. "You want a shovel, young lady?"

Robin giggled before she asked, "So, you *like* figuring out the why?"

"No, he just likes to talk about it," his dad teased. "He'll get there soon enough."

"Robin, what are you doing over here?" Liam swooped in right next to her at seeing Nate put his arm over Robin's shoulder.

"I'm fine," she dismissed him.

"No," Liam insisted, grabbing her wrist. "You need to come over here with me."

"No, I don't," Robin said, getting herself released from Liam's grip.

"Yes," he said, tightly grasping her arm. "You need to come with me."

Feeling a bruise forming under his grip on her upper arm, she tried to pull away, but he held tighter. "No, I don't!"

As Mr. Mitchell peeked over the burn pile, Nate immediately appeared at her side. "She's fine with us," Nate said, prying Liam's fingers off her arm.

"No!" Liam snarled. "Go get yourself another girl. This one's mine!"

"I'm nobody's property!" Robin snapped, appalled at how quickly it escalated. She backed into Nate, who protectively put his hands on her shoulders.

"Get your hands off her!" Liam growled, fists to the side.

"I think you need to leave, young man," Mr. Mitchell said sternly.

"I'm *not* leaving without her."

"I'm staying," Robin insisted.

Grabbing her wrist, Liam went to pull Robin away from Nate, who wrapped his arm around her waist. "She's not going anywhere she doesn't want to go," Nate said, glaring at Liam.

"Boys!" Mr. Mitchell snapped, moving between them. When he did, Liam let Robin go. Turning to Liam, he said, "You need to leave. You can do it calmly, or you can be forcibly removed. The choice is yours."

"You'll regret this," Liam narrowed his eyes at Robin. "If you don't come with me now, you can forget tomorrow night!"

"Fine." Robin crossed her arms in defiance. "Go to Homecoming by yourself!"

Hands in the air in surrender when five other football players suddenly appeared behind Nate, Liam backed away. "Fine. I'm leaving."

"Do not come back here tonight," Mr. Mitchell warned. "I will have the police keeping an eye on the house."

"Yes, sir," Liam said, and left the party, fuming.

"Are you okay?" Mr. Mitchell asked Robin.

"Yeah. I'm fine," Robin said, hugging herself as Nate let her go.

"You okay, man?" one of Nate's friends asked. "I can go kick his –"

"That won't be necessary, Brent." Mr. Mitchell shook his head. "It's been handled. Please just do me a favor and make sure that young man actually leaves the property?"

"Yes, sir. C'mon guys," Brent said, and the guys with him followed Liam to the front of the house, leaving Robin, Nate, and Mr. Mitchell still by the fire.

"Has he done that before?" Mr. Mitchell asked.

"Yes, but I usually just go with him so he doesn't get mad," Robin explained.

"Did he say your name was Robin?"

"Yes," she said.

"Robin, you need to understand that real men don't treat women as property."

"I do," she said, looking down.

Lifting her chin so she would look at him, he said, "You are a priceless treasure to God. You are worth more than you know. If any man does not treat you like the princess you are, then you don't need to be with him."

"Thank you," she said, wiping the few tears that escaped her eyes. "I don't believe in God, though."

"Someday you may. When you do, you will then truly understand your value. Now, Jenny's over there. Why don't you go join her?"

"I will. Thank you," she said, and left the pair standing next to the fire as she slowly made her way back to her friends.

"Poor thing," Nate said, shaking his head as he crossed his arms.

"She's lost in more ways than one," Mr. Mitchell said. "I pray she finds her way soon."

Later that night, the girls camped in Jenny's basement for their overnight. Robin ran upstairs to grab some chips and go to the bathroom. While she was upstairs, the other girls paused the movie and talked about the game and what fun Homecoming was going to be Saturday night.

When Robin went upstairs, it was around two-thirty in the morning. The house was completely silent except for the giggles coming from the basement. The storm that started about an hour ago, did its best to wake the entire house. With the storm raging, she didn't think she had to be all that quiet, so she walked over and grabbed one of the bags of chips off the counter. A flash of lightning lit up the back yard. When she looked up, she saw a person standing in the rain outside. She gasped, dropping the chip bag on the floor, frozen in place, unable to form any words.

When the lightning lit up the sky again, thunder crackled and rumbled across the sky. When the lightning struck, she saw a face staring at her. After finally catching her breath, she cocked her head to the side. "Liam?"

He nodded, and then pointed to the back door.

Looking toward the basement to see if she alerted anyone when he startled her, she noted the complete silence in the house except for the talking coming from the basement. Setting the bag of chips back onto the counter, she went out of the kitchen through the garage, out the door off the other side of the garage where Liam was waiting for her.

As soon as she quietly closed the door behind her, Liam grabbed her shoulders and shoved her against the wall of the garage. "Why did you embarrass me like that?" he demanded, ramming his arm against her neck. "When I tell you to come with me, you come with me! If you're going to be with me, you *will* do *what* I say, *when* I say! Do you understand?"

Pushing him away, she growled, "Do *not* talk to me like that!"

Grabbing her wrists, he turned them into her body, pushing them against her chest.

Robin wiggled, struggling to get free. "You're hurting me!"

"Good! Now you know what will happen to you if you do that again. I'm a junior. My family has run that school for generations. I will make you pay if you ever consider going against me again the rest of this year and into the next. Destroying your next year too."

"Get-off-me!" Robin snapped, trying to shove him away. He held on tighter, causing bruising on her wrists. "Liam, I don't like you like this!"

Less than two inches from her face, with water dripping off him, he sternly warned, "You *will* be ready for Homecoming at five-thirty tomorrow, and you *will not* disobey me again. Do you understand?"

Robin stared at him, wide-eyed.

Looking at her lips for a moment, he leaned in and kissed her. Not sure what to do, but not wanting to make things worse, she kissed him back. She just wanted him to leave, but she didn't know how to make him go. As the kiss intensified, he released her wrists and grabbed her waist, getting closer to her.

Within a moment, he suddenly bit her lip. She pulled back and pushed him away at the same time. He grabbed her wrists again, pulling her to him. "*You are mine.* Do you understand that?"

Struggling for only another moment, she knew he was too strong for her. "I'm going to scream," she warned. Lightening lit up the sky once again, sending thunder rattling immediately after.

"You scream, and I *promise* you will regret it. Do *not* push me."

"Then let me go. *You're hurting me.*"

Slamming her into the wall, he leaned down, kissing her neck, trying to force himself on her.

"Let me go!" she growled, pushing him away. "*Let-me-go!*"

"I'm *never* letting you go."

Feeling like she didn't have a choice, she let him kiss her for a few more minutes until he seemed to calm down. "I need...I need to get inside," she said weakly.

"And tomorrow, you are going with me to Homecoming, right?" he said, moving so he could see her eyes in the darkness.

"If you leave now, yes," she relented.

"Good. We'll finish this tomorrow night," he said with a sly smile.

"I-I need to go," Robin insisted.

Seeing a light turn on in the kitchen, Liam quickly kissed her. "Do *not* tell anyone about this," he warned.

"Fine," she said on a sigh. "Just go."

Watching him until she was sure he was gone, she then headed back into the house. Coming in from the garage, she was surprised to see Nate standing in the kitchen wearing a t-shirt and shorts. "What are you doing up?" she asked.

"The storm," he said, eating a chip he had dunked in dip. Looking up at her, he studied her for a moment. "You're drenched. Why were you outside?" he asked. A look of realization crossed his face, and he looked out the window. "Is that guy here?"

"Who?"

"Your boyfriend. Is he here?" he asked, searching the darkness.

"Not anymore," she admitted.

Tearing off a paper towel, he dampened it before handing it to her. "You're bleeding. The girls will see it in a heartbeat if you go down there like that. You're also soaked. Just stay here for a moment," he said before he disappeared downstairs. When he returned, he explained, "I told them we needed to talk about what happened with your boyfriend tonight and that you'd be down in a bit. I also told them to go ahead and start the movie back up."

"Thank you," Robin said, grateful. As he handed her a towel to dry off, she asked, "Why are you being so nice? I'm just one of your sisters annoying friends."

"Well," he said, leaning against the counter with his arms crossed, "despite what the everyone says about me, I actually *do* have a heart. I just choose not to date until college. I don't want to mess up my future."

"At least you have one," Robin said.

"Who says you don't have a future?"

Robin held up her wrist to show the bruises forming on them. "I can't get away from him. He won't let me. At this rate, I'm pretty sure my lifespan will be short."

"Has he done this before?" Nate asked, examining her wrists.

Robin looked at him with her big brown eyes, hoping he would understand.

When he looked back up at her, his heart softened. "Seriously? Why are you still with him?"

"Honestly? Because no one else will have me. I'm a poor little orphan who lives with her grandparents. We're not well off by any stretch of the imagination. I'm not athletic, nor am I a brain. I'm not even sure what I'm going to do after high school. And I would be surprised if I don't end up pregnant before high school is over."

"How long have you dated?"

"Since I was in seventh grade and he was in eighth."

"How did you meet?"

"We met through friends. It started innocent enough. Sure," she shrugged, "he had a bit of a temper. He said it was to protect me. He said I needed to listen to him, and he would keep me safe. Safe felt good for a while. Then, when I started to buck him, he would get physical with me. It only happened once and a while. Lately it's a bit more frequent."

"Has he done anything to you? You know, like –"

"Yes. I felt I had to," she admitted, blushing.

"Wow. You really *don't* know your value. Do you?"

"He's going to make me go with him to Homecoming. Then afterward, he's going to make me –"

"No, he won't," Nate said, resting his hands on her shoulders.

"I will take you tomorrow night if you want to go. If not, we can go to a movie, bowling, or whatever *you* want to do."

"It's your senior year. It's your last Homecoming. It wouldn't look good if you weren't there. Besides, I heard you're Homecoming King."

"I don't care about some silly Homecoming dance. I care about *you*."

"Why do you care? Why are you doing this?"

"Because you shouldn't feel that you need to do anything you don't want to do. No one should have someone else control them. Look, I'm not looking for anything with you, only to help you get away from him."

"Then what happens next year when you're gone, and he's a senior?"

Thinking for a moment, he said, "I'll have some of the football players look out for you and protect you. They owe me. We often have each other's back, *and* that of our friends."

"Is that what I am?"

"I think you're a nice girl who needs to know what a date with a real man should look like. Wanna do something else, or do you want to go to Homecoming with me?" Nate asked.

After a moment's hesitation, she nodded. "What if we go putt-putting or to a movie?" she offered. "Something fun. That way, you won't be embarrassed for taking me to Homecoming."

"I wouldn't be embarrassed to take you." He waved her off. "Have you ever shot bow and arrows?"

"No."

"What if we go to dinner and then we can go putt-putting under the lights when it gets dark? Does that sound fun?"

She smiled. "Very much so!"

"Wow!"

"What?"

"You *do* smile! You have a pretty smile. You should really do it more often."

"I'm the sullen artist type," she joked.

"I know."

"What do you mean?"

"Jenny showed me your first-place art project. I loved the way the fire looks so real. You have crazy talent!"

"Thank you." She blushed. "Look, I should probably go back downstairs to the others."

"You're still soaked," Nate said.

"I can't stay up here all night."

"Here," he said, going into the living room. Picking up one of the throw blankets, he wrapped it around her before handing her the bag of chips. "There. That should help hide your wet clothes until they dry."

"Thank you. You're being very sweet," Robin said, grateful. "You don't fit your reputation at all."

"Oh really?" Nate raised an eyebrow. "What's my reputation?"

"Well, while you like girls, you steer clear of them. It's no secret you are a Jesus person."

"A Jesus person?" Nate chuckled. "What does that mean?"

"You know. One of those religious people," Robin said. "One of those type people who believe in Jesus, or whatever."

Nate smiled, trying to put her at ease. "You were closer when you called me one of those Jesus people."

Robin was struggling inside. While she was with Liam, Nate seemed really sweet and kind. He had a great smile and was easy to talk to. His beautiful blue eyes stood out with his jet-black hair. She knew a lot of girls who liked him, but he chose not to date. This intrigued her, and she decided to ask more questions, "Why are you a Jesus guy?"

"Because of what He did for me."

"What did He do?"

"Robin! Come on!" Jenny said, running up the stairs. "We're waiting for you."

"I told you to start the movie," Nate snapped. He was visibly upset that Jenny interrupted them.

"You're not my boss," Jenny said, sticking out her tongue at Nate. Then she grabbed Robin's arm. "Come on."

"Coming. Give me a second?" Robin asked.

"I'm coming back up in exactly one minute," Jenny warned. "You're missing out on the fun!"

"Okay," Robin agreed. Once she was out of earshot, Robin grabbed a piece of paper off the refrigerator and a pen from the counter. She wrote her phone number and address on it. "Please pick me up by five tomorrow?" she asked, handing it to Nate. "Liam's supposed to pick me up at five-thirty and I want to be gone."

"Done," Nate said, accepting the paper. "I'll see you tomorrow night."

Taking one last look at him, she then bolted down the stairs before Jenny came back up after her again. Once downstairs, she settled in across from Jenny.

Furrowing her brow, Jenny asked, "What happened to your lip?"

"I slipped and fell," Robin said, wrapping the blanket around her tighter to hide her wet clothes. She didn't want to answer twenty questions. She wanted to have fun.

"And why is your hair soaked?" Mia asked, flipping Robin's wet hair.

"Look, you guys got me down here. Let's just have fun!" Robin said. "I'm in the mood to have a good time."

"About time!" Jenny grinned. "Let's turn the lights off and watch the movie," she said. She lit candles through the room before turning on the movie again.

"A good horror flick is always a great way to keep us up all night," Mia said with a smirk.

"Yeah, we won't be sleeping for days," Zoey added.

While the movie played, Robin propped up her head with her hand and watched the three votive candles on the coffee table instead. The flames danced in front of her, taking Robin back to a good point in her life...far away from where she was now.

CHAPTER 2

BURN YOUR BRIDGES

"Robin, honey, your friend is here," Robin's grandmother called to her.

"Thanks, Grams," Robin said, coming into the living room in jeans, boots, and a turtleneck shirt. She grabbed her jacket out of the closet on the way by. After introductions were made, Robin kissed her grandmother's cheek before she disappeared out the door with Nate. "Thank you," Robin said, as they walked out to Nate's truck.

Just then a silver sportscar sped down the road. The driver slammed on the breaks just behind Nate's truck. "What do you think you're doing?" Liam demanded, as he got out of his Aston Martin, slamming the door behind him.

Robin groaned. "Liam," she on a sigh.

Nate held open the door on his truck. "Get in," he said to her.

"He's not going to let me leave with you," she said, tears in her eyes. "I don't want to go with him."

"If you don't want to go with him, you don't have to." Nate pulled his cell phone from his pocket. Dialing 9-1-1, he then handed the phone to Robin. "Only dial if I tell you," he instructed. "I don't want to if I don't have to, but if we need them, we'll call."

"Agreed," Robin said, positioning her thumb over the dial button.

Liam walked purposely over to Nate and slammed him into the truck. "Where do you think you're going with my girl?"

"Take your hands off me. I'm not some little girl who can't defend herself. Be careful who you lay your hands on," Nate said grabbing Liam's wrists. He twisted Liam's wrists away from Liam's body, and Liam went to the ground. Nate continued, "You *will* leave Robin alone. You will not disrespect her ever again. If I hear otherwise, we're going to have a very long, extremely *painful* conversation you will not be happy about."

"Are you threatening me?"

"Nope. That's a promise."

Liam swung his leg around, kicking Nate's legs out from under him. Once Nate was down, Liam jumped up and punched Nate. Nate took the cue and grabbed Liam's fist when he went to punch him again. Slowly getting off the ground, Nate tightened his grip on Liam's hand, bending it toward his body, causing Liam to whimper.

"You're hurting me!" Liam said, stunned.

"Now you know what it feels like when you do this to Robin," Nate growled.

When Liam went to punch him with his other hand, Nate grabbed it as well.

"You had better change your mind, or Robin is going to dial that phone. Then you can explain to the cops why she has a fat lip and bruised wrists. You can also explain why I have a mark on my cheek," Nate warned.

"You going to tattle on me?"

"No. I would much rather let you know what it feels like to get your behind kicked, but I'll let Brent and the other guys handle *that* one," Nate said with a smile. "They enjoy that sort of thing. When they find out what you did, you might as well change schools."

Liam glared at Nate. "I *own* that school!"

"You only *think* you do. Keep it up and I'll have her dial."

"If you do this, we're through!" Liam said to Robin.

"We're through anyway. I'm walking away," she said, closing the door of the truck.

Liam got loose from Nate and slammed his fist into the window of the truck. He let out a loud howl as he heard the bones in his hand crack.

"Go ahead and dial," Nate told Robin, as he chuckled. "He needs medical. I also don't want him coming after you again."

"This is *not* funny!" Liam snapped.

"Actually, it is, dude." Nate couldn't stop laughing. "I can't believe you really thought you could break a window with your hand." Nate shook his head. "You are not anywhere near strong enough."

"You'll pay for this!" Liam seethed.

"No, I won't. You, on the other hand, will...for about six to eight weeks. Your writing hand, too. Dude, could you be more stupid?"

Liam let off with a string of swear words, until Nate finally told him to shut up, which was about the time the police pulled up. Robin feared what Monday at school would look like for her. She knew whatever was coming, she would do her best to stay strong. She wanted to be done with Liam. Nate gave her the courage to do it. She only hoped he would follow through with the protection or she was in trouble.

"Robin!" Jenny ran up to her that Monday, closely followed by Mia and Drew. "What happened? Liam's ticked!"

"Nate didn't tell you?" Robin asked, surprised.

"Tell me what?"

"Liam got himself in a bit of trouble on Saturday with the police."

"Is that why you guys weren't at Homecoming?" Mia asked.

"Yes."

"Wait. What does this have to do with Nate?" Jenny asked. "Why would he know anything?"

"Nate and Erin were Prom King and Queen," Drew added. "Erin was furious Nate wasn't there. She danced with Skylar for the King and Queen Dance instead. Pretty sure she'll give him an earful this morning."

Still trying to figure things out, Jenny asked, "Does Saturday have anything to do with the mark on Nate's..." her voice faded as it dawned on her. "Did Liam hit Nate?"

"Yes," Robin said.

Narrowing her eyes, Jenny pressed, "Why?"

"Because he wouldn't let me leave with Liam, and Liam didn't like it," she quietly admitted.

"Nate doesn't get involved in other people's relationships unless –" She stopped short and looked at her wide-eyed. "What did Liam do to you?"

"What do you mean what did Liam do to her?" Drew asked. "Liam loves her."

"Liam? Do to her?" Mia asked, confused. "They've been together since seventh grade!"

"My brother would only stop you from leaving with Liam if he thought you were in danger," Jenny continued, ignoring Drew and Mia. "What happened?"

Robin couldn't push herself to physically tell them. She set her backpack down and pulled up the sleeves of her shirt to show bruising on her arms. The group was stunned silent.

"When did that happen?" Jenny asked, finally putting everything together. "Did he do this to you at my house? Is that why my dad kicked him out?" When Robin nodded, Jenny asked, "Was Nate with you Saturday night when Liam was supposed to pick you up for Homecoming?"

When Robin nodded again, Mia asked, "Were you out with Nate during Homecoming? Is that why he wasn't here?" Again, Robin nodded. Mia furrowed her brow. "Are you dating Nate?"

"No. We're just –" Robin was cut off when Liam burst through Drew, Mia, and Jenny, and slammed Robin into the lockers. He slammed his arm into her neck, hitting her head against the lockers.

"I *told* you that you would regret Saturday night!" he said, spitting in Robin's face. While Drew tugged on Liam to get him off, Jenny ran to find Nate, and Mia ran to find a teacher. Slamming her against the lockers again, he smacked Robin's head on the locker, causing her to see stars. "Do *not ever* let that happen again! Do you understand? You are mine!"

"No, I'm not," she squeaked out, struggling to remain conscious.

Pulling her away from the locker, he reached back and punched her, slamming her into the locker, knocking her unconscious. Just then, Nate, along with several other football players ran up and jumped on Liam.

It took multiple teachers to separate everyone. The police were called, and since Robin did go unconscious, she was taken to the hospital via ambulance once it was over. Liam was arrested, and the other guys got detention. While it was chivalrous, it was still against school rules to fight.

Checked out and released to her home, Nate, Jenny, and their dad stopped by Robin's house later that night. "Hi," Mr. Mitchell introduced himself to Robin's grandparents, "I'm Ian Mitchell. This is my son, Nate, whom you met on Saturday, and my daughter, Jenny, a friend of Robin's."

Hearing them at the door, Robin came out of her room. As soon as Jenny saw her, she pushed passed her dad, and ran, grabbing Robin in a hug. "I'm so glad you're okay!"

"Pretty sure you are all the talk of the school," Robin's grandpa said. And then added, "And *not* for a good reason, either."

As Nate and his dad came in, everyone was ushered to the table to talk. While her grandma got everyone coffee or milk, and a piece of pie, Ian started, "I've heard all sides, and I wanted to assure you that Liam will not be in school for the rest of the year." Turning to Robin, he said, "The police will be by later to talk to you. There are some things they want to discuss with you, so I thought I would give y'all a head's up." Looking to her grandparents, he asked, "Were you aware that Liam was abusing your granddaughter?"

"I...what?" Robin's face immediately flushed. "No! I deserved —"

"No one deserves what he did to you," Nate cut her off. "I told him everything."

"You *what*?" Robin looked at him, mortified. "How could you?"

"Told him what?" her grandma asked, sitting down at the table after serving everyone. "What is he talking about?"

"There was more than what happened at school. Wasn't there?" her grandpa asked her.

Robin just looked at him wide-eyed, vigorously shaking her head.

"Dad already knows," Nate told her again.

"I...I..." was all Robin could get out.

"What am I missing?" Jenny asked. "Why do I feel like I'm more than just a chapter behind? Like not even in the same book?"

"He raped her and caused bruising on her," Nate clarified.

As tears brimmed Robin's eyes, her grandma set her hand on Robin's and asked, "Is this true, dear?"

Closing her eyes, Robin only nodded in acknowledgement as a tear slid down her cheek.

"He did *what*?" Jenny asked, horrified. "How do *you* know this?" Jenny demanded from Nate. "How do *you* know and I don't?"

"Why didn't you say something to us?" her grandpa asked.

"A.J., honey," her grandma lightly tapped her grandpa's hand, "that is not something a woman wants another person in the entire world to know." Giving Robin's hand a gentle squeeze, she asked Ian, "What can we do to keep him away from her for good?"

"A restraining order is a good place to start," Ian suggested. "The officer will talk to you more about it. It'll be tricky since they share the same school. Then, with social media the way it is nowadays, that will make it even more challenging. You may want to consider staying off it for a bit."

Robin nodded.

"Trust me, if the other football players have anything to say about it, he won't make it within a hundred yards of her," Nate said.

"You're gone next year," Robin whispered, wiping her tears away. "He can also get me when I'm not in school."

"That's what the restraining order is for," her grandma said.

"It's only a piece of paper," Robin pointed out. "Look, maybe I should just make up with him, and –"

"No!" the entire table of people said in unison.

"Rob, this isn't right," Jenny said. Moving her chair closer to Robin, Jenny explained, "He doesn't have the right to do any of that to you, no matter how long you've dated."

"I-I pushed him to it," Robin stammered.

"Do you have any idea how messed up that sounds?" Nate asked. When his dad went to object, Nate stopped him, "Seriously? You think you could push someone to the point of him hurting you, or of him forcing himself on you? That is *their* choice. He made a choice to hurt you."

"I *can* be kind of infuriating," she admitted.

"No. I *will not* let you put this on yourself," Nate said. "As your friend, I am telling you his lack of self-control is not brought on by your behavior *or* attitude...no matter how bad a day you're having." When she went to object again, Nate continued, "Trust me when I tell you he will not get near you again. You have my word, and that of the team. Coach even said he's off the team."

"Great! There goes his scholarship," Robin said, throwing her hands up in surrender. "He can hold that against me too."

"No, he can't," Jenny disagreed. "He's the one who hurt you. He made the choice. Please tell me you won't go near him again, and you'll block his number on your phone and social media accounts?"

"How will I know what he's saying?" Robin asked. "I can't defend myself if I don't know."

"He punched you, unprovoked in front of the entire school. That's the main reason why we didn't get into more trouble," Nate pointed out. "The entire school knows what happened. If he's smart, he'll change schools."

Robin shook her head. "He'll be back on the team by next year." Looking up to stop the tears from falling again, she blinked. "Why can't I just escape this nightmare?"

"You can. Let us help you," Ian offered. "Let the police help you."

Taking a deep breath, she finally relented. "All right. I'll do whatever you need me to do."

Ian said, "What we need you to do, is figure out your true value. We'll start with the restraining order, though."

That day seemed so long ago to Robin. Nate and his friends looked after Robin for the rest of the school year. The team teased her that she was the football team's mascot. During the following year and Liam's last year, the football team still ran interference for her. It wasn't until he graduated that Robin finally felt safe enough to go to school without worry.

For her last two years, she actually enjoyed school. She continued to get awards for her drawings and even picked up her science and math grades to acceptable levels for her grandparents.

On graduation night, once they got home, Robin's grandparents sat her down for a deep discussion. "Robin, I wish we could say we'll pay for your college, but we can't," her grandfather admitted.

"We were able to set aside some money for you each year. Unfortunately, that's all we can spare," her grandmother explained. "Your parents didn't have life insurance. So, this is the best we could do," she said, handing Robin an envelope.

"How much is in here," Robin asked, jaw-dropped, as she thumbed through the hundreds in the envelope.

"There is only ten thousand in there. It's enough for you to start," her grandfather said. "We wish it could be more."

"You both have done so much for me." Robin started to cry out of happiness. Hugging her grandparents, she said, "Thank you for everything!"

"Take the summer to figure out what you want to do," her grandfather said. "Come September, though, your grandmother and I will be moving to a retirement home. We have to sell the house and a good portion of our belongings to pay for it."

"Seriously?" Robin asked, sitting back on her chair.

"I'm sorry. We're not getting any younger," her grandfather apologized. "Your grandmother's health has been deteriorating for quite some time now."

"I know. I just..." her voice faded as she realized she would be completely on her own come September. "This is just..."

"We put it off until you were out of high school. I'm sorry we couldn't do more."

"It's okay. Really. I appreciate you both more than you know," Robin said as she stood. Giving her grandparents each a kiss on the head, she then went to her room, closing the door behind her. Setting the money down on her nightstand, she picked up a match and lit the candle on her dresser.

This September would mark a new chapter in her life. While most kids her age would be heading to college, or working for their parents, she was truly on her own. She would have to figure out a new plan of attack...and she only had ten thousand dollars to do it. Getting lost in the motion of the flames, she used the candle to escape her new reality, even if it were only for a few moments.

Chapter 3

Adding Fuel To The Flames

After searching through the summer, Robin finally found an economy apartment that would fit her budget. Once she was settled, she spent the next week getting her grandparents settled into their new retirement apartment.

"Thank you, Robin," her grandmother said, giving her a hug. "You have helped us out a lot."

"As you both have helped me. Know I will always be around and will come by at a minimum of once a month," she promised. "Maybe more," she added with a wink. "You'll get tired of seeing me."

"Never. You have been a tremendous blessing to us," her grandfather said, giving her a hug. "Take care. And, Robin? Please look for something better for you. You are better than just a waitress."

"Thank you. I will do what I have to do to survive," she said, and left.

As she was in her car on the way back to her apartment, she had a sick feeling in her stomach. Reflecting on the good times she had in high school where she was protected, she realized with no uncertainty that was on her own. Her friends were either in college, in vocational education schools, or at their jobs or internships.

Stopping by the library on her way home, she looked up the cost for vocational schools. Not sure what she wanted to do, she was online for over a half hour before it hit her. Her fingers couldn't work fast enough for her as she typed in what it would take to become a certified welder, just like her father.

Stunned by not only how little it would cost but also by the amount of time it would take, she quickly signed up, invigorated at the possibilities. She knew it was far from safe work, but it would be great money!

Over the next few years, Robin saved a lot of money. During her spare time, she started working more on her art, creating metal sculptures and signs. While doing so, she started to sell them online. Once she generated enough clients and her sculptures and signs were selling well enough, she left offshore oil rig welding. To supplement her income, she was a part-time waitress. Once again, she had to start over with her friend circle.

"This job will get you good tips if you're good," her trainer, Kent, explained. "Now, you've been here for about a week. Tonight, you're on your own."

She smiled. "Gee, thanks."

"You got this. You've done amazingly well this whole time."

"If you say so," Robin said.

"How are your grandparents doing? I know you said they weren't doing well."

"Grams is in the hospital, and Gramps is running himself down going every day. I kind of hope this is going to be one of those situations they have in movies where they go together. They've been together since junior high."

"Being together that long is a rare occurrence anymore," Kent said, shaking his head. "I wish it happened more often, but it doesn't."

"Tell me about it." Robin rolled her eyes. "I'm not even in contact with anyone I knew in high school anymore."

Kent pointed to a table of men. "Oooh! You're first table is here."

They all wore firefighter shirts and were in turn-out gear bottoms.

"Oh girl," Sandra said, walking up to Robin, "you got a table full of hotties!"

"Geez! Get a grip," Robin teased securing her apron around her waist. Going up to the table, she said, "Good evening! Welcome to Rousseau's. May I get something for you gentlemen to drink while you look at the menu?"

"Robin?" Nate asked, stunned. "Robin Flynn?"

"Nate!" Robin grinned. "I see you finally made part of your goal."

"Yep! Been a firefighter for a few years now. I just started training as a fire marshal apprentice with my dad, too."

"Nepotism," one of the guys with him grumbled.

"Oh, come on, Wright." another guy playfully shoved him. "It's not like you want it."

"No," Wright confessed. "It's too much extra work."

"Wow! I feel like it's been forever," Nate ignored his coworkers as he looked at Robin.

"Been about seven years," Robin clarified.

"Unbelievable!" Nate shook his head. "You look great!"

"Thank you! I am a certified welder now and sell my metal art as well as make signs. I just do this to supplement my income."

"Do you still draw?"

"Yep. Sell that too."

"You guys should see her art! It's amazing!"

"Anyway," Robin said, turning their attention back to the menus, "what can I get you guys to drink?"

After taking their drink orders, Robin went to fill them. When she did, she could still hear the guys at the table.

"How do you know her? She's hot!" one guy said.

"I went to high school with her. She was a good friend," Nate explained.

"A girl who looks like that? Just a friend?" Wright pressed. "Really? What's the story?"

"Guys, she's the same age as Jenny."

"Doesn't mean she's not hot," another guy pointed out. "The girl welds, she's pretty, and she's artsy. What's she like?"

"She's funny, sweet, quiet, kind, pretty..."

"And *why* are you not dating her?" Wright asked. "Seriously, I'm going to ask her out if you don't."

"Yeah. Why aren't you dating her?" another guy pressed.

"I just found her again," Nate said in his defense.

"Then ask her out!"

"No, guys. She's like a little sister to me."

"Tell me another one, Mitchell," another guy said, rolling his eyes. "It's the Christian thing, isn't it?"

Nate nodded. "As far as I know, she's not a Christian. So, yes."

"And if she were?" Wright asked.

"Maybe." Nate shrugged. "I don't know what she's like anymore."

After loading up the drinks onto her tray, Robin took the drinks to the table. As she passed them out, she asked, "Do you guys know what you want to eat, or do you need a few minutes?"

"We have a few questions," one guy said.

"Go for it," Robin said, resting the tray under her arm as she pulled her ticket pad and pen out of the pocket of her apron.

"Do you have a boyfriend?"

"Patterson!" Nate slapped his arm in reprimand.

Blushing, Robin asked, "Is there – are there any questions regarding your food choices?"

"Sorry, Robin," Nate apologized. "No more questions. We'll just have four large supreme pizzas, along with three orders of breadsticks."

Wide-eyed, Robin exclaimed, "That's a lot of food!"

"We're working men," Patterson said. "We eat hearty!"

"Okay, then." Robin wrote it down on the ticket. "Four large supreme pizzas with three orders of bread sticks coming up."

"Thank you," Nate said, his face bright red. Before she left the table, Nate mouthed, *I'm sorry.*

As Robin walked away, she couldn't stop thinking of how Nate looked now. He filled out very well, and even had some stubble on his face. Her best guess is that the group had just finished their shift. Nate was cute in high school, but he was downright handsome now.

"Robin," the manager, Rick, walked up to her in the kitchen as she put her order into the system.

"What's up?" she asked, concentrating on putting the order in.

"Robin," Rick said, slowly taking the notepad from her.

"What's going on?" She furrowed her brow. "Am I fired already?"

"No. You need to go to the hospital. A nurse called."

"What happened?"

"You just need to get to the hospital. Let me know if you need some time off."

"For what? What's going on?"

"Trust me on this. I would take you if I could. You need to get to the hospital now."

"All right," she said and clocked out before grabbing her purse. Running out the door, she glanced back to see Nate watching her with a concerned expression on his face.

"I'm sorry, Ms. Flynn," the doctor said as he met her in the waiting room, "I did the best I could, as did Dr. Hall. Your grandparents didn't make it through the accident."

Her world spun around her. She sat in the chair, dazed. "I'm alone now," she gulped, terror grappling her so tightly within she thought it would tear her in two. "All alone."

"Dr. Hall has another emergency patient, or he would be here, too. When the other vehicle impacted your grandparent's vehicle..." As he droned on, Robin looked around in a fog. She remembered something about internal bleeding, hemorrhaging in the brain, along with broken bones. She didn't really care what he said. The only words that mattered to her were, *"Your grandparents didn't make it through the accident."*

There would be no more Christmas around the tree or Thanksgiving sitting around the table. She would never be able to hear them call her name or wrap their arms around her in a hug. Holding herself, she rocked in her seat, distraught.

"I could have one of the caseworkers come talk with you if you'd like?" the doctor offered when he finished.

"No. No, I..." her voice faded. Looking for the exit, she got up to leave.

"I'm sorry, but you need to wait," the doctor said. "There is some paperwork you have to fill out."

"Are you serious? I'm twenty-four years old," Robin said, still in a fog. "My grandparents were the last family I had on this planet. I need to go home right now."

"Let me set up an appointment for you with a caseworker. They can help you with all the proper steps."

"Fine," she relented.

After he set it up, she left the hospital, shaking. Papers in hand, she struggled to find her car. Setting the papers on the passenger's seat as she got in the car, she then looked toward the sky, and said, "You! People tell me that You love me. If You really loved me, why do You continue to take the people I love away from me?" She slammed her hands on the steering wheel before dropping her head onto it, tears streaming down her face.

When she finally got home, she went straight to her living room. Sitting on the floor in front of the coffee table, she lit the five votive candles on the long candle-holder in the center of the table.

With each one she lit, peace overwrote the terror and anxiety. Once they were all five lit, she propped her head on her arms and inhaled the apple pie scent as it drifted into the air. Apple pie reminded her of her grandparents, while the flames themselves reminded her of that horrific night so long ago. The night that took the lives of her family.

CHAPTER 4

───────

WHERE THERE'S SMOKE, THERE'S FIRE

Early that morning, around three, Robin woke up. She had fallen asleep with her head resting back on the couch. She let out a long sigh. The tears threatened to return, but she pushed them back. Looking up at the ceiling fan, she noticed the dust starting to form. "Well, no one else will clean it," she said, getting off the ground.

After she cleaned the fan, she looked around. Her house was clean. She was too antsy to go back to sleep, so she grabbed her gym bag. Throwing it over her shoulder, she left her home, walking out into the night.

Her grandparents were thrilled when she let them see her new house about a month ago. Her intention was to have them come and live with her. Grams had to come out of the hospital first. With her just getting out the week before, she hoped to get them out of that depressing home where they lived. Now, she would have to go get their stuff in the next week due to the facility needing the room for other residents. She did not look forward to that trip.

While she walked, she pictured the design she would create. Her bag contained various spray paint cans, a myriad of chalk colors, a candle, a lighter, and a small bottle of water to drink.

Depending on what she used for a canvas would determine which medium she would utilize.

The town was almost silent at three in the morning. Even those who closed the bars were home by that point. The silence was calming and peaceful to her. Being a female in the dead of night should have scared her, but she was far from afraid. This was her town.

Shoving her hands in her jacket pockets, she continued until she walked out of town. Just past the outskirts of town was an area Robin nicknamed the graveyard of Hemlock. There were multiple skeletons of warehouses and buildings of businesses long forgotten.

She often went into these remains and created her works of art on the walls. Usually, it was during tough points in her life. She was pretty sure the rats and mice enjoyed her art, but that was about it. With broken windows and holes in the walls, it was not a good place for people to live who did not have a home. There was not much protection from the elements.

Heading up to the office of the former clothing warehouse, she set her bag on the desk. Pulling out the tall glass jar candle, she lit it. Its light awakened the office, exposing her new canvas.

Pulling out the white chalk, she drew the outline of the design of the fire. She then pulled out her water and drained the bottle as she studied the design. "Okay," she said aloud. "I'm thinking spray paint for this one."

She grabbed two paint cans, one red and the other yellow. With that, she got lost in her work. She was so invested in her project; she did not even hear the raccoon who crept into the office. He climbed onto the desk.

It happened in a matter of seconds, but to Robin, it was in slow motion. "No!" she shouted as the raccoon scampered off the desk, pushing the candle off in the opposite direction. Before Robin could get to it, the glass broke and lit the floor and desk of fire. The wood from the floor and desk was so dry it lit up beyond her control in no time. She tried to stamp it out, but it spread like wildfire. Deciding to save her bag, paints, and chalk, she grabbed her bag and ran for the stairs.

By the time she reached the bottom of the stairs, she turned and saw the office in flames. The glass melted. The wood getting eaten by the second. She almost wanted to stay and watch, but the smoke was already crawling all over the entire building. The fire climbed out of the office window and raced for the ceiling and the outer walls.

She let out a slow breath of air. Tugging the bag further up on her shoulder, she ran out of the building. Ducking into the woods, she turned and saw the fire poke through the roof, almost waving good bye to her. She debated in her head whether to call the fire department, but someone else answered that for her as she heard the sirens in the distance.

Ducking further behind some bushes, she crouched down and watched as the firefighters funneled from their trucks and pulled hoses off the back of the truck while being shouted at by the one in charge. While some set up, others ran in to make sure no one was in there. Robin marveled at the way they attacked the burning building. It was as if they were on a mission to conquer it. After clearing the warehouse, they kept the buildings on either side wet down while they let the warehouse burn to the ground.

Robin stayed around watching the entire scene unfold. She admired the firefighters and their skills.

"Someone did this town a favor in taking this one down," one of the firefighters said loudly to his buddy.

Another one shook his head. "We still had to get out of bed at this ugly hour to take care of it, *and* it cost the city and us time and resources."

"But it's gone. Hopefully, they will build something that will bring jobs to this area. Maybe the person should burn the other three warehouses and do the city a favor," another one mentioned.

"Phillips, that's not even funny!" another snapped.

"I'm not laughing!" Phillips said in his defense.

"Why would you wish that on us?"

"On us? This town needs a boost. These empty buildings are not helping in the least," Phillips explained. "If it were my choice, I would turn them into control burns, but the city won't let us."

"Phillips, Garza, Reynolds, quit gabbing and roll the hose!" the lieutenant snapped. "That is unless you want to do probie's work for the next month?"

"No, sir!" the three said in unison.

Robin slowly ducked back into the woods, keeping an eye on the scene to make sure she wasn't followed. After a few minutes, she turned around and headed home, secure in the fact that she was by herself.

Going into her house. She set her bag down in the kitchen, sat at the table, and dropped her head down on her arms. She groaned.

Looking toward the ceiling, Robin said, "I'm sorry. I didn't mean to burn it down." She got up and paced the kitchen. "I mean, some of them were grateful, but I know it's actually wrong. I don't know what to do. It was an accident. Do I report it?"

She continued to pace as she ran her fingers through her hair. Letting out a slow breath of air, she said, "I guess I need to figure something else out. Or maybe I'll just forget it even happened. Yeah! That's it! It never happened! It wasn't me. I can just go to bed and let everything sail away." She resumed her pacing. "Except that it did. My grandparents are going to –" She stopped short. Shoulders sagging, she couldn't help the tears that fell onto her cheeks that slowly built into a stream.

She dropped to her knees. "They're gone." She shook her head. "I'm by myself. They're gone."

Robin continued to sob for several minutes. She lay down on

the floor of the kitchen. "I'm alone in the world. I-I burned down that building," she said in between sobs. Rolling toward the ceiling, she looked up and moaned, "I'm such a horrible person! I-I don't know what to do!"

She cried into the early morning until she cried herself to sleep right there in the middle of the floor of her kitchen.

When she woke the next morning, she was still on the floor of her kitchen. She groaned. The achiness from sleeping on the floor reminded her of the previous night's events and the memories hit her mind like a freight train.

She slowly sat up. Letting out a breath of air, she then pulled herself up by the counter. She reached forward and pushed the button for the coffee maker. Resting her head on her folded arms, she watched the water flow through the filter, creating the precious blend of life-giving sustenance...coffee.

She knew she had a lot to do in regard to making arrangements for her grandparents. Unfortunately, there were no other family members to help, nor were there any to notify in the country. She did have family, but they were on her mother's side, and they were in Mexico. She highly doubted they would be able to come or even want to come for her father's parent's funeral. Her dad was an only child, so there were no aunts, uncles, or even cousins to speak of on his side. She was truly alone.

After dealing with the funeral home, paying for her grandparents to be cremated per their request, she set up to have their ashes buried in the plots they purchased over thirty years ago. She did not need a pastor or a priest to attend since it was just her. Once the funeral home notified her everything was ready, she would go visit them at their gravesite. She did not need, nor want, an actual funeral. She would remember them in her own way.

In the meantime, her grandparents' insurance company got ahold of her. It seemed, per the police report, the driver of the other vehicle was at fault. Therefore, as the sole heir to her grandparent's estate, she would be due financial compensation. To her, she would much rather have her grandparents. No amount of money would bring her family or joy for the holidays or birthdays. No more precious moments together. Her reality seemed dark.

"Why are you here today?" her manager Rick asked as she walked in two days after losing her grandparents.

"Honestly? I need the distraction," she admitted. "Please tell me you need someone today?"

"But you just lost your grandparents," he said, eyes softened.

"It was either sit at home twiddling my thumbs, lost in memories of my only family, at least the only family I know, or come to work. Which would you choose?"

Rick rested his hand on her shoulder. "I'll make room. Don't worry. I got your back. Give me a few minutes to do some creative shuffling with Sandra regarding the stations."

"Thank you," she said, relieved.

Kent walked up to Robin. "Girl! What are you doing here? Rick said you lost your grandparents."

"It was either sit at home by myself or come here."

"Fair enough. Is Rick taking care of you?"

"Yes."

"Oh! Hey! Your *friend* came in yesterday looking for you," he said, wiggling his eyebrows.

"Who?"

"The hot firefighter," Kent said with a wink. "Girl! You'd better take advantage of that situation."

"Or what?"

"Or I will disown you."

Robin couldn't help the laughter that escaped her. "I needed that. Thank you."

"Good. Then, you'd better take advantage, or I'll make good on my threat," Kent said, turning her toward the door to see Nate standing there in jeans, a t-shirt, and a leather jacket.

"Dang!" Robin said in a whisper.

"I know, right?" Kent said from behind her.

Nate walked up to Rick and Sandra and said something. Rick turned toward Robin and nodded, and then showed him to a table for two. Afterward, Rick went to Robin and Kent and explained, "He asked for your section."

"Got it. Th-thank you," Robin mumbled.

"Go get him," Kent encouraged.

"Right," Robin said, taking a deep breath. "I got this."

"You go, girl!" Kent shoved her forward a few steps.

Robin brushed her hands on her pants before putting her apron on. Then, she headed over to the table. "Hey, Nate!" she said, doing her best to put on a good face. "What can I get you today?"

"I have a confession," he said, his dimples in full view as he smiled.

Oh! Those dimples! "What's that?"

"I found out from your manager about your grandparents the other day. I wanted to know if you were okay."

"I am. Well, I will be. It's fine. I'm fine. I'll be fine. Everything's fine."

"I'm sure. I-well, I also wanted to know if you, well, wanted to go to dinner with me? It's eleven now. What time do you get off?"

"I-I don't. Are you sure?" she asked.

"Look, I liked you in high school, but I wanted to focus on the firefighting. I don't take things for granted, nor do I see things as a coincidence. Saying all of that, I don't think it was a coincidence I was at your table a couple days ago. Running into you after all of these years makes me think maybe, just maybe, there is something there we should explore. What do you think?"

"I think," she tucked a piece of her hair behind her ear, "I think that's a sound thought process. If you're serious, I would love to go out with you tonight."

"Great!" He grinned. "What time do you want me to pick you up, and where?"

"Um, what about –"

"Robin." Kent skirted up next to her. "Why don't y'all go right now? I'll have Sandra shift everything back to the way it was. You could use a good day off."

"What will Rick think?" Robin asked.

Kent gestured toward Rick, who stood by the kitchen door. "He's the one who sent me over here."

When she turned, Rick winked and waved her off.

"All righty then. Looks like I'm off work," Robin said to Nate.

Nate grinned again as he stood. "Then, shall we?" he asked, putting his arm out.

She looped her arm through his and said, "We shall. Thank you," she said to Kent and then mouthed *thank you* to Rick.

"Have fun! Can't wait to hear the deets!" Kent said as they left the restaurant.

"They seem like a fun bunch," Nate commented while they walked toward his truck.

"They are. I like them."

"What do you want to do?"

"You mean in the booming metropolis of Hemlock?"

"Well, I was thinking of heading toward a bigger city if you want?"

"We can."

"There's that new movie if you want to do that? Or we can go putt-putting."

"Kind of a remember when?" Robin asked.

"We can also go shopping?" Nate offered, opening her door for her.

"Let's start with food," Robin suggested.

"Good plan." He started the truck. While he pulled out of the parking lot, he mentioned, "Italian sound good?"

"Perfect!"

As they pulled out of the parking lot, he walked up to Robin's car. Reaching under the car from the bumper area, he placed the tracking device and then slipped out of the area on foot.

CHAPTER 5

———

FIRE, WATER, AND GOVERNMENT, KNOW NOTHING OF MERCY

Robin and Nate had a great time together. They went out to eat and then headed over to the bowling alley. Since most people were otherwise occupied during the day for the work week, it wasn't that crowded. This allotted them the time to get to know each other better.

"So, you're a welder, an artist, *and* a waitress?" Nate asked after an hour of them chatting.

"I am. If I remember correctly, you wanted to be a fire marshal?"

"Yep. I started training with my dad a few weeks ago," he proudly boasted.

"Is that fun? Really? Working with your dad?"

"Actually, it's not too bad. He doesn't take it easy on me, but he's also not overly hard on me. He knows I'll be his legacy, so he wants to make sure I know everything."

"Sounds interesting."

"Oh! It is! I learned a lot from a fire a few nights ago."

"Fire? Really? Where?"

"It was in one of the old warehouses just outside of town."

"What happened?" she asked, heart racing as she tried to play it off. "I thought those places were abandoned for years."

"They are. Sometimes people stay in them, though. We think someone was coming through town and used the place to sleep. They lit a candle. It broke on the floor in the upstairs office, and the place lit up. It was basically tinder. It didn't take much. My dad's concerned the others will go up pretty quickly as well. He's been worried about those places for years."

"Interesting. How do you guys know it came from a candle?"

"Some of the glass was melted, and the wax was melted and scorched around at the origination point. It lit the desk and floor pretty quickly."

"I'm sure! So, do you think it was arson since a candle was involved?"

"We're pretty sure it was an accident."

"I see."

"Thing is, whoever did this kind of did the city a favor. They're going to knock them down in the upcoming months since they *are* a danger. We tried to get the city to donate the warehouses to the fire department for control burns in order to train, but they refused. They said to burn them on purpose was a liability because it could get out of control too easily."

"I don't understand," Robin said, taking her turn with the bowling ball. After she threw it, she turned and asked, "Aren't y'all supposed to work together?"

"Man! You didn't even see that you got a strike!" Nate chuckled, shaking his head. "And, yes, we're supposed to, but the city doesn't always play nice."

"That's kind of messed up."

"It is. Well, looks like you win," Nate said, adding the points. "Good job!"

"Thank you!"

"What do you want to do now?"

"Well, we could go for round two and then head over to putt-putting?" she offered.

"Do you want to make a bet? We would need to figure out what the winner gets," Nate asked.

"Well," Robin sat down next to him, "I think it needs to be different for each of us. Maybe if you win, I'll teach you how to make a metal art project?"

"That actually sounds like fun! We'll have to do that anyway. What about if you win, I'll make you a homemade meal?"

"You cook?"

"Oh yeah! I have to. Each one of us cooks at the station. So, yeah, I can cook for the whole crew."

"Not frozen?"

"No. Not frozen. If we try to cheat, Captain gives us grunt work. He says his people need to know how to take care of themselves. Our mamas don't live there."

"Hmm. I like him already!"

"Thought you might like that. So, you get a home-cooked meal, and I'll get an art project?"

"Does that sound good?" she asked.

"Actually, it does. Okay. Right now, it's 1-0 you. Want to do bowl another game or head over to putt-putting?"

"What about putt-putting?"

"Perfect! Let's go!"

They had a fantastic time putt-putting, and he won. Afterward, they went to the shooting range for a tie-breaker.

"I feel like this may be slightly slanted in your favor," Robin said as she sat at the table where Nate was loading the bullets into the magazines.

Nate raised an eyebrow. "You don't shoot? And here, I thought you were a Texas girl."

"I am a Texas girl."

"Most Texas girls can shoot."

"I never said I couldn't shoot. This is your gun," she explained.

"Well, what if I give you a full magazine for you to get used to it," he offered.

"Okay."

"Then, we'll go with these for the bet. That's two for you – one to warm up and one for the bet. Then, this one," he said, holding up the magazine, "is mine for the bet."

"Fair enough," she said and shook his hand. As soon as they touched, she had sparks shoot up her arm, and tingles went through her body. "Um, ready?" she asked, letting go.

"Just about. Here." He handed her a set of electronic ear muffs. Then he put his on. Speaking loud enough to be heard over the ear muffs, he handed her the loaded gun and said, "Just go when you're ready."

She nodded in appreciation as she accepted the gun. Taking the safety off, she cocked the gun, aimed, and fired. The bullet landed dead-center.

"Wow! Nice!"

"Thank you!" she yelled. Then she emptied the magazine, almost all in the middle of the target.

"Great grouping!" he said as they took their hearing protection off. "Only a few off-center. Well done! I'm impressed."

"Thank you. Told you I was a Texas girl."

"Okay. Do you want to go ahead and do your turn, or do you want me to take mine?"

"Dealer's choice," she said, handing him the empty gun.

"You go first." He changed the magazine and then handed her back the gun.

They each replaced their ear protection before her turn. After emptying the weapon, she handed it to him and then took off her ear protection.

"Again, great grouping," Nate said. "It's like you fire a few dead-center, and then you venture off a few inches. That happened both times."

"Well, it happens," she said. She did not want to admit it was because her mind wandered toward him. He was standing on her left, and that's the direction they floated.

"Okay. It's my turn," he said, changing the magazine out for a fresh one.

Replacing her ear protection at the same time he did, she braced for the gun to go off. It took only a few moments for him to empty his magazine. He won by a long shot. All of his were centrally located, almost on top of each other.

"Okay. Looks like you win," she said, taking off her hearing protection. "When do you want to do your art project?"

"Well, I'm thinking..." He set down the empty gun. Turning toward her, he took off his hearing protection. "We both won."

"What do you mean?"

"You were only a few inches off. You're shooting was really good. So, this is what I'm proposing. What if I come to your house, cook you dinner, and then we work on the project afterward?"

"I think that's a good idea."

"So, second date material?" Nate asked, hopeful.

"I think that's a great second date option, if you want to?"

"I do."

"Great!"

"Okay," he said, "let's get this cleaned up and head out of here."

"Sounds like a plan."

After cleaning up, they headed to the truck.

"Do many people use this place for practice?" Robin asked.

"If they can find it, sure. There are quite a few who use it, but it's a small list."

Robin saw a car on the far side of the parking lot. It was a silver Nissan Altima. "Have you seen that car before?" Robin asked, pointing it out.

"I don't think so," Nate said, opening her door for her, taking note of the car as it pulled out of the parking lot. "Can't see the plate from here," he mentioned.

After closing the door, he ran around to his side of the truck. They left and headed to the restaurant to get her car.

"Not gonna lie. I feel a little paranoid," Robin admitted. "I kind of feel like someone is following me."

"Because there was a silver car in the parking lot?"

Robin tossed her head side-to-side. "It's just a feeling I have, but I guess you're right. Totally in my head."

"I kind of don't want to drop you off," he admitted about fifteen minutes of them chatting. "I feel like a little kid who got exactly what he wanted for Christmas."

"What do you mean?"

"Full disclosure?"

"Okay."

"I liked you way back when I asked you out for Homecoming. Then, when I saw you the other day at the restaurant, I couldn't believe my eyes. There you were, looking beautiful as ever."

"What is it about me?" Robin asked. "I'm not all that."

"You're more *all that* than you know. You're beautiful, talented, humble, sweet, and so much more."

She blushed. "Thank you."

"So, why did you agree to go out with me?"

"Because despite your reputation, I had a wonderful time that night. I wanted to see if it was a fluke."

"And?"

"It wasn't. You're a good guy," she said.

"Thank you."

"I have to ask. What about the Christian thing?"

"What about it?"

"I'm not a Christian and you are. Isn't that a bad thing? Jenny used to say that was one thing you wanted that was a non-negotiable."

"Are you open to Christianity? I mean, would you be willing to go with me to church once and a while and aren't going to shut Christ out?"

"I'm willing to go with you," she said. "Not too sold on this Jesus thing. I'm angry at God."

"Because of your parents and brother?"

She nodded. "And now my grandparents. I'm not exactly the poster child for stability. As far as people in my life, they seem to die if I get close to them. Kind of makes me feel like a black widow."

He chuckled. "I don't think you're a black widow." He straightened his face as he continued, "I think you've had some horrific circumstances in your life, but God seems to have brought you through them quite well."

"My entire family died. Most of them when I was only eight. Then, my grandparents stepped into the picture. They were my saving grace. Now, they're gone. Where am I supposed to turn now? I have zero family in the States. My mom's family is in Mexico, but I am not going to move there. This is my home. Well, it's supposed to be my home, but I don't really know if it is my home anymore."

"Don't you have a home here?"

"I do."

"Do you feel at home here?"

"I do."

"Then, it's your home."

"There's so much out there, though," she explained. "I've

traveled. However, I always come back to this place. I don't know what it is that pulls me back."

"Your heart?" Nate offered, pulling into the parking lot. "Look, if you want, we can go to your house to keep talking."

"I need to think about some things. I'm okay. I just need to process. My grandparent's memorial is tomorrow."

"Do you want me to be there for you?"

"I'm good. I think I just want to say goodbye to them by myself."

"I have to start my shift tomorrow morning at seven. If you want me to call off, I can be there for you?"

"No. It's okay. I'm a big girl."

"Okay. The offer's there. Maybe we can have that second date on Thursday?" Nate suggested, meaning in two days.

"I do have to work on that day."

"What's your shift?"

"Eleven to eight. They like to have me there for most of the day. Rick is happy with me and how I'm performing."

"Kent seems to like you, too."

"Kent and Rick are unique characters," Robin said with a chuckle. "They don't have a filter...either of them."

"Well, do you want dinner before we split up for the night? We're already at the restaurant. That way I know you are fully fed."

Robin burst into laughter. "What am I? A pet?"

"No." Nate smiled. "I just want to make sure you're okay. I know in living alone, there are times we forget to eat."

"This is true. Okay. Maybe Kent's still here, and we can be at one of his tables. He could use the tips."

"Sounds like a plan," Nate said, turning off the truck. He ran around and opened her door for her.

"You know you don't have to do that, right. I can open my own door."

"It's a chivalry thing. My mom would not be happy if I didn't open the door for you. She taught us all well."

"That she did. Thank you," she said, accepting his hand down from the F150.

When they walked in, Sandra looked up and smiled. "Hey, Robin!"

"Hi. Is Kent still here?"

"Actually, you can be his last table of the day. I don't think he'll mind," she before showing them to a booth.

As they sat down, Kent was standing there waiting for them to get settled. He had a grin on his face. "Hey, y'all. So, how was the date?" he asked, looking like he was about to burst.

"Really good...I think?" Robin said and looked to Nate for his reaction.

"Definitely! We have a second date in a few days."

Kent sat down on Robin's side of the booth and said, "Spill it! I want the deets!"

"I don't know if I can give them," Robin said, looking from Kent to Nate and back again, her face flushed.

"Well," Nate started, "we went out to lunch, and then bowling. Then we started a competition."

"Competition? Do tell!" Kent said, leaning forward. "And what, pray tell, was the prize?" He wiggled his eyebrows.

Both Nate and Robin burst out in laughter.

"The prize for her was me cooking her a home-cooked meal. The one for me if I won was her teaching me to make a metal art project."

"Ooooh! Both sound like they could end steamy!" Kent gushed. "Who won?"

"Well, she won the bowling. I won the putt-putting. Then, I think we were close enough to tie in shooting. So, instead of only one of us winning, we both did," Nate explained. "That's going to be our second date."

"Shivers! I can envision a *Ghost* moment here!" Kent said. Leaning on his arm as he looked at both of them, he asked Robin, "You *are* going to tell me *everything*, right?"

"I don't know that I can."

"If you want to, you can," Nate said with a shrug. "It's up to you. I don't mind. He's your friend. I'm not going to tell you what to do and what not to do."

"I knew I liked you! Girl, you'd better take good care of him."

"That's my intention," Robin acknowledged. "So, dinner?"

"Oh yeah! What do you two want to eat?" Kent asked.

Nate looked toward Robin. "This is your stomping ground. What do you want?"

"Hmm," Robin glanced at the menu. "Who's cooking?"

"Alfonso," Kent said.

"He makes a mean chicken parm," Robin said.

"Do you want to split one?" Nate asked.

"Actually, yeah. Can we have a chicken parmesan to split and a side salad for each of us?"

"Perfect," Nate said. "That sounds great."

"All right. I got ya. I'll be back in a few. What do you want to drink?" Kent asked.

"Do you want a soda?" Nate asked.

"Actually, a strawberry lemonade would be great," Robin said.

"I'm good with a soda," Nate said.

"What kind?" Kent asked.

"Dealer's choice. I'm not picky."

"Sounds good," Kent said. "I'll be back in a flash."

When he left, Nate looked at Robin and said, "I'm not the controlling type. While there may be some things that I would like us to keep to ourselves, for the most part I don't hide anything."

"I mean, I get it for sure. When it comes to intimate things, that's between us. Otherwise, I don't have a problem if you talk to your firefighter buddies either. I know you are a gentleman."

"That I am. You can thank my mom for that."

"I hope to get the opportunity to do just that."

While they were at their table across the restaurant, he sat watching them while he snacked on his fries and worked on his computer.

"Sir," Sara-Ann said, walking up to the table in her section, "you've been here for hours. Is there anything more I can get you?"

"I'm good. Don't worry, though. I will take care of you. I tip very well. You have taken good care in making sure my lemonade was never empty. I won't hold your table hostage for too much longer. It will be available for dinner time rush."

"Thank you."

"Thank *you*."

After the waitress left, he watched Nate and Robin interact. She was laughing at something Nate said. The more he watched, the angrier he got. She was *his*, not that guy's girl. She would relent in time. He would prove himself.

After dinner, Nate and Robin parted ways, but not before exchanging phone numbers. Robin could not help the smile plastered on her face. Nate was very much a gentleman. He even asked before he kissed her cheek.

When she pulled into her driveway in her hunter-green Jeep Rubicon, she was still on cloud nine. Her phone went off as she turned off her Jeep. She pulled her phone out of her pocket. It was Kent.

'Hey, girl! He is HOT! How was your date with him?'

She bobbed her head side-to-side, debating on what to write, before she typed, *'Great! A definite repeat!'*

In a matter of seconds, he replied, *'So jelly! You take care of him!'*

Robin laughed as she replied, *'No worries. He's really sweet. I think I'll keep him around. I knew him in high school.'*

'Girl, you let him get away? What is wrong with you?'

'It was a one-time thing, and I think it was a pity date to get me away from a complicated situation.'

'Doesn't mean he didn't like you.'

'Actually, he told me tonight that he did like me back then, too.'

'Girl! Super jelly now!'

'Get back to work! Love you!'

'Love you too! Sweet dreams of that hot thing! Dang! Firefighter and hot!'

Robin laughed as she locked her Jeep and headed into her house. She went to the front to get the mail before heading inside. As she walked up to her porch, there was a bouquet of roses by the door.

"Wow! That was fast!" she said, unlocking the door. She tossed the mail onto the coffee table and then went back for the flowers. Taking them into the kitchen, she pulled the card off the holder. After setting the vase on the counter, she opened the card. It said:

'It's been a while. I hope we can pick up where we left off.'

"Interesting choice of words," Robin said, taken aback. She texted Nate a picture of the flowers and a text:

Thank you for the flowers! Nice surprise after a wonderful day with you. Thank you!

She got his reply quickly: *I had a great time with you, too, but the flowers are not from me? What's up?*

Her heart raced. She swallowed hard. It was at that moment her phone rang. It was Nate.

"H-hello?" Robin answered.

"Robin, what's going on? Who are they from?"

"I honestly don't know. I'm really not feeling well right now. I don't know who they're from. You're the only one I have gone out with in years."

"Do you want me to come over? I can bring a couple police friends of mine to take a look."

"That's fine. I'll text you the address."

After they hung up, she texted Nate the address and then sat on the couch, hugging herself. Her heart was going a mile a minute, and she was having difficulty focusing.

She texted Kent: *I got a dozen red roses from some creeper.*

His reply was quick: *What do you mean?*

I mean, I got a dozen roses with some creepy note attached. Nate and a couple of his cop buddies are on the way over to look at them.

Do you want me to come over, too? I could spend the night so you're not alone? I could also go with you tomorrow to the memorial for your grandparents.

Actually, that sounds like a plan. Thank you!

Couching it for a friend is no big thing. I got ya, sis! he replied, and then her phone was silent.

The house was eerily quiet. The lack of sound got to her, so she turned on the television for noise. Then she turned it back off. She wanted to hear everything. She got up and paced the living room until Nate and his friends arrived.

"Robin, are you okay? You're shaking," Nate said, hugging her when she opened the door for them.

"I will be. Kent's on his way, too. He's going to stay tonight."

"Good. Do you need me to stay as well?"

"No. You have your shift in the morning. You need sleep."

"Robin, this is Brett Carmichael and Kyle Masters," Nate introduced the police officers with him. They were in plain clothes at the time. They each shook her hand and produced a badge for her to see.

"Where are the flowers?" Brett asked.

"Kitchen counter," she replied.

"Robin!" Kent ran into the house. He sat on the other side of her and hugged her. "Are you okay? Girl, you're shaking like a leaf!"

"Who is he?" Kyle asked from the kitchen doorway.

"He's a friend and co-worker of mine," Robin said. "He was at work all day. He's going to stay the night with me."

"Okay," Kyle said hesitantly. He glanced at Nate, who waved him off.

"And you are?" Kent asked.

"I'm Officer Masters, and my partner is Officer Carmichael," Kyle said and then went back into the kitchen.

"What happened to Officer Friendly?" Kent quipped.

Robin and Nate couldn't help the laughter that escaped them. "I think that's just in elementary school," Robin said.

"Then they turn into Officers Unfriendly?" Kent asked. "Dang! He needs to go back to elementary school."

Nate started laughing again while Robin smiled. "Okay. I like you," Nate said to Kent.

"Thanks!" Kent smiled. "So, I'm assuming I'm couching it tonight?"

"Yes, please?" Robin said.

"I'm not going until they do," Nate said. "Even then, I'm hesitant to leave."

"You have to work in the morning," Robin said. "I have Kent staying with me all night."

"I'm even going with her to the memorial, so she's not alone," Kent explained.

"Good deal. Thank you," Nate said. "You're a good friend."

Kent grinned. "I know."

"Okay. He's a keeper!" Nate chuckled. "If nothing else, he'll keep you laughing."

"That he does," Robin agreed.

"Okay. We're taking these with us," Brett said, carrying the vase and flowers with his hands gloved. Kyle had the card in an evidence bag. "If there is anything else, don't hesitate to contact us. We'll follow up with the florist," Brett said, handing her his card.

She accepted it. "Thank you."

"Do not hesitate to call," Brett said. "If something seems fishy, call. Okay?"

"Yes, sir," she agreed.

After they left, Nate said, "I feel like a jerk for leaving you right now."

"No. You need to work in the morning. I have Kent with me."

"Yeah. I got this," Kent said, flexing his biceps. "I won't let anyone get to her."

"Thank you. I owe you."

"Well, if there's a –"

"No!" Robin said, cutting him off.

"What?" Nate asked.

"Anything he asks, the answer is no. Trust me," Robin said.

"Fine." Kent huffed. "Use me and abuse me."

"I'll make sure to take you out to lunch tomorrow," she promised.

"With company?" Kent asked, hopeful. "I mean, if a couple of your firefighter buddies or even your police buddies want to come, I won't complain."

"Enough!" Robin chuckled. "I will not fix you up with anyone. You're on your own."

"Fine," Kent huffed. "A guy can dream."

"You are my safe friend. I know I can trust you wholeheartedly," Robin said to Kent.

"I'll own that. It's all good."

"Thank you," Nate said. "I don't want to, but I guess I have to go. We still have a date the day after tomorrow?"

"Yep!" she said, giving him a hug. "Thank you for coming."

"Anytime. I mean it. I finally found you again. I don't want anything to happen to you."

"Thank you," she said and gave him another hug.

He leaned down and went to kiss her cheek, but she turned

and kissed his lips. He pulled back. "Did I –?"

"No. I did. I wanted you to know I'm okay with that," Robin said.

He hugged her tightly. "Thank you. Please be safe."

"I will," she promised.

After she watched him pull away, she shut and locked the door.

"So, what are we watching?" Kent asked as she lit the candles on the coffee table.

"You pick." She gestured toward the DVD holders that were stacked in binders. "I'm going to go get ready for bed and get your bed together to make up the couch. Thank you."

"Look, sis, you're safe with me. I won't let anything happen to you. They have to get through me to get to you, and that ain't gonna happen!"

"Thank you!" She hugged him and then ran to her room. While she felt slightly off due to the delivery, she still felt more comfortable knowing Kent was in the next room. He was a good friend who she knew she could trust. She liked Nate, but that situation just began, and she wasn't sure about the whole God thing. Until she was more secure in the pair of them, she decided to keep him at arm's length. She knew he was a gentleman, but she didn't want to get too close without being sure where she stood with him.

CHAPTER 6

LIKE A MOTH TO A FLAME

The next morning, Robin got up and cooked her and Kent some scrambled eggs, bacon, and made toast for breakfast.

"Oh yum!" Kent said when she brought it to him in the living room. "You're going to make some guy a great wife. You need to teach me how to do this."

"Do what? Cook?"

"Yeah."

"What? You don't know how to cook?" she asked, sitting on the end of the couch while Kent sat up with his legs crossed.

"Nope. I can order like nobody's business, but I am terrible at cooking."

"Are you telling me that you literally order all of your food?" Robin asked, stunned.

"It's either that or frozen food. Yep." He took a bite of the scrambled eggs with peppers, onion, and ham in them. "Oh my! Please teach me!"

"I can do that. Can't have you starving all your life or working just to eat."

"Thank you. How'd you sleep?"

"Not great. I told Nate yesterday that I felt like someone was following me."

"Was that before the flowers?"

"Yes."

"What made you think that?"

"I saw a car in the parking lot I didn't recognize. I thought I had seen it before. I could be wrong. I was probably wrong. I don't know," she stammered. "I-I mean, who knows?"

"I would think you would know."

"I don't know. I mean, *now* I know for sure. Those flowers kind of spelled it out for me."

"They *are* a little creepy. Let's hope those officers do their thing and find the person who sent them."

"Let's hope. Speaking of which, we need to stop at the florist before we go to the memorial today."

"What time is that?" Kent asked.

"We're meeting the funeral guy there around ten."

"Can we stop by my place first? I want to change and grab a shower."

"Sure."

"Then, let's go."

After Robin got ready, they went to Kent's house, and he got ready. Then, together, they headed to the graveyard in Robin's Jeep. Together, they got out, with Kent holding the flowers.

"Thank you for coming with me. I was planning on doing this myself, but I'm glad you're here," she said with her arm looped through his.

"Hello, Ms. Flynn," the funeral parlor owner said, shaking her hand. "Everything is set. They are already buried, per your request. They're over here," he said, taking them over to the site.

After he showed them, he explained, "The stones have been ordered. They should be here in a few months. I will send you an email when they arrive and are placed."

"Thank you," Robin responded, looking at the mounds of dirt.

"Again. I'm so sorry for your loss. Losing a grandparent is tough, but losing both at the same time is brutal. If you need someone to talk to, my number is in the brochures I gave you the other day."

"Thank you," Robin said, hoping with every bone in her body that he would just leave.

After another few minutes, the gentleman got into his vehicle and left.

"Hallelujah," Robin said under her breath.

"Yeah. Thought he would never leave. So, how do you want to do this?" Kent asked.

"I was thinking of just placing the flowers. I mean, they're not really there. They're Christian. As far as they were concerned, once they died, their body was just an empty shell."

"Well, this is for you. I'm here for it, whatever that looks like."

She knelt down and placed the flowers on the dirt mound. It looked like they put both urns right next to each other and then covered them.

Robin looked up and squinted to see better. In the distance, she saw a silver sedan. It looked a lot like the one in the parking lot yesterday where she and Nate were shooting, but she wasn't one hundred percent certain.

"Kent, please come here," she asked, reaching up to him.

He knelt beside her. "What do you need?"

"Try not to make it obvious, but look around, paying attention to the path to the right. Do you see a silver Nissan Altima?"

"I see a gray car," Kent offered. "I don't know anything about cars, so I can't be sure what kind it is."

"Okay. Try to remember what that looks like in case we see it again."

"I can do that. I can't see the plate clearly. They're a little too far."

"Okay. Let's get out of here," Robin said. He helped her up, and they left.

Robin drove to the fire station, but Nate's crew was out on a call, so she and Kent headed over to the restaurant for lunchtime.

"What are you two doing here?" Sandra asked when they walked in. "Don't you get enough of us on a workday?"

"We wanted to enjoy it from the perspective of being waited on instead of waiting on people," Robin said.

"Well, at least you know it's good food," Sandra said as she showed them to a table. "Sarah-Ann is your waitress today."

"Thank you," Robin said as she and Kent sat down at the booth.

"Hey, guys!" Sarah-Ann said, coming up to the table. "You two look nice."

"Just came from her grandparents' memorial," Kent explained.

"And you really want to eat?"

"Not really. Just don't want to be home," Robin said.

"Fair enough. What can I get you two?"

"Pizza?" Kent asked Robin, who nodded. "Medium supreme pizza and a salad each."

"Sounds good. Your regular strawberry lemonade?" she asked Robin, who nodded. "And y'all both like ranch dressing, right?"

"Yes, please," Robin said as Kent nodded.

"You're a regular as well?" Sarah-Ann asked Kent.

"Thank you," Kent said.

"My pleasure," Sarah-Ann said and left. Returning momentarily with their drinks, she said, "How long are y'all planning on hanging out?" When Robin raised an eyebrow in question, Sarah-Ann sat down and explained, "There was some guy who held one of my tables hostage all day yesterday. Kind of don't want a repeat today. I lost a lot. Granted, he gave me a fifty-dollar tip to keep his drink filled and an order of fries, but it still stunk."

"No worries. We won't take that long," Robin said. "That's kind of rude."

"Kind of?" Sarah-Ann smirked. "Talk about really rude! Turn-over is how we make money. And to be honest, it was a little creepy. All he did was work on his computer all day, but geez!"

Robin looked to Kent, who was looking at her, too. "What did he look like?" Kent asked. "I don't remember someone here all day."

"He got here shortly after you and your guy left," she said to Robin. "Then, he left a little after you did when y'all came or dinner."

Kent narrowed his eyes as he looked at Robin. "You wouldn't happen to know what kind of car he drove, do you?" he asked Sarah-Ann.

"No. Why?"

"Nothing. If you see him again, point him out to one or both of us, please?" Kent asked.

Robin shuddered.

"What's going on?" Sarah-Ann asked, concern written all over her face.

"Our friend has a stalker," Kent explained. "I hope the two are not the same, but who knows."

"If he was here all day, it wasn't the Nissan Altima," Robin said. "That car was the one I saw at the shooting range yesterday when the guy was supposedly here."

"Interesting," Kent said, sitting back in his seat.

"What are you thinking?" Sarah-Ann asked.

"Not sure. Time will tell."

After lunch, Kent left Robin at her house. She was confident they were not followed, so she sent him home.

When he left, she went to her garage. Putting her welding mask on, she worked on a project she started the previous week. It was a metal tiger that stood about ten foot tall. It was for the local high school whose mascot was a tiger. It was going on their front lawn.

She alternated silver with copper to create the effect of the tiger stripes. Once everything was put together, she took off the welding mask and put on a painter's mask. Putting a thin coat of color so it reflected off the metal, she loved how the colors reflected the light. Topping it with a glaze over all of it, she sealed the colors.

"Okay. All done," she said, satisfied. "That's going to bring in a pretty penny."

She locked the shed behind her and went into the house to call the school district to schedule a time for them to pick it up.

Afterward, she went out to the front porch and sat on her porch swing. Pulling out her phone, she started reading a book on her e-reader she started a few days before.

"Afternoon," the postman said when he walked up to her still on the swing. She just about fell off the swing. "Sorry to scare you!" he said with a chuckle.

"It's-it's okay. Whatcha got for me?" she asked, sitting up.

"Just a few letters. Here you go," he said, handing them to her. Her mailbox was attached to her home by the front door.

"Have a good day," she said as he left for the next house.

She flipped through the few bills. "Great. Need to pay these," she said, getting up. Noticing something out of the corner of her eye, she opened the mailbox to find a letter with her name on it. She looked around, heart racing. *Should I call Nate or his cop friend?*

She went ahead and pulled it out. Going into the kitchen, she grabbed a pair of scissors to open the envelope. There was a letter inside, which read:

Robin,

I hope this finds you well! I miss you and hope you know how much I love you. I cannot wait to take you out on a date. I think dinner at Barlow's would be ideal. I will send you a dress in a few days. See you on Friday night at 5 PM.

"What?" she asked aloud. She pulled her phone out and called Brett.

"Officer Carmichael," he said, answering his phone.

"Brett, this is Robin Flynn. You were at my house last night."

"Nate's friend. Yeah. What's up?"

"I got a creepy letter today. It's on my counter."

"I'm on patrol today. I'll call this in and head over to your house to bag it and write a report."

"It says he's planning on taking me out on Friday night. It says he's picking me up at five."

"Stepping it up. Hmm. Okay. I'll be right there. Don't answer the door unless you know the person or it's us. I'll call Kyle, too."

"Thank you," she said and hung up.

Brent and Kyle were both over in a matter of minutes.

"Thank you both for coming so quickly," Robin said, opening the door.

"We called Nate on our way over. He said he would stop by tomorrow morning when his shift ends. He wanted to know if your friend, Kent, could stay the night?" Brent asked.

"I'll give him a call. If not, I should be okay."

"Do you have an alarm system?" Kyle asked.

"No."

"You should get one," he said. "This guy sounds sketch at best."

"Will do. The letter is on the table in the kitchen," Robin said, gesturing toward the kitchen.

"Wow," Kyle said and then let out a low whistle. "Okay. We'll have patrol pick it up in this area for your safety. Please get an alarm system."

"I doubt they would come today," Robin said, scanning her phone for a security company.

"Do you have a certain budget for this?" Kyle asked.

"No."

"If you want, I can call a buddy of mine who runs an alarm/security company?"

"Please," Robin said.

He left to call his friend, while Brent wrote the report. He was back in a matter of a few minutes. "Okay," Kyle said, coming back into the room, "Are you going to be home today around five?"

"Yes."

"My buddy is coming to set one up at five for you. If an alarm goes off, they will immediately call your cell. They give you two codes. One is for everything is fine. The other is if you are in danger."

"I like that idea. Thank you for working that out."

Kyle shook her hand. "My pleasure. We would rather you were safe."

"Are you going to call your friend to come over?" Brent asked.

"I can."

"I think it's a safe idea. This guy probably won't do anything with another person with you," Brent said.

"Good point," Robin said. She went to the living room while the pair spoke quietly in the kitchen.

"Hey, darlin'!" Kent said, answering his phone.

"Kent, are you busy tonight?"

"I actually have a date. Why? What's up?"

"Nothing. Have fun on your date!"

"Thanks, doll!" he said and hung up.

"Hmm," Robin said, mulling things over in her mind as she walked back into the kitchen.

"Well?" Brett asked.

"He can't tonight. Well, he could if I pushed it, but the guy needs a night out. So, hopefully, your friend will be here at five, and then I'll be all set."

"Are you trying to convince us or yourself?" Kyle asked, cocking his head to the side.

"Both?" Robin offered.

"Nate gets off in the morning. I'm sure he'll stop by. In the meantime, this is my friend's phone number. His name is Scott. He and one of his guys will be here at five. If they aren't, call me. I'm not comfortable with you here by yourself after this note," Kyle said, handing her a card.

"Agreed." Brett stood. "It also says you'll be getting a dress before then. Don't open it. Just call us and we'll come get it. If push comes to shove, we'll put you in a hotel for Friday night. Do not tell anyone except your friend who spent the night here the other night, and Nate. No one else needs to know what is going on."

"Okay," she agreed.

"When do you work next?"

"Tomorrow from eleven to eight."

"Yuck!" Brett crinkled his nose. "How did you get that horrible shift? Your day is pretty much shot!"

"Low-man on the totem pole," she said with a shrug.

"We're on tomorrow, so we'll make sure to patrol both the restaurant and your house over the next few days," Kyle said.

"Thank you. I appreciate you guys coming so quickly."

"Do not open the door except for Scott, your friend, Nate, or us," Brett cautioned.

"Isolation. Got it," Robin said.

"More like protection," he corrected.

"I understand," she said, walking them to the door. Tucking a portion of her hair behind her ear, she asked, "So, how long will I have to be under protective detail?"

"Probably until we're comfortable. Right now, he's climbing the stalking ladder pretty quickly," Brett explained. "He seems to know a lot more about you than we're comfortable with. Just be smart."

"I will. Thank you," she said as they walked to their vehicles. She locked the door behind her after she went inside. "Well, this could be fun!" she said and sighed heavily.

CHAPTER 7

FEEL THE BURN

That evening, a few minutes before five, Robin got a knock on the door. It was Kyle's friend Scott with the security system. It took his assistant and him a good hour to install everything. When he finished, he handed her a piece of paper with four different codes.

"This phrase means you're safe," Scott said, pointing to the first phrase. "This phrase means you're in trouble," he said, pointing to the next phrase. "Don't say them aloud anywhere. Just memorize them."

"Will do."

"Here are the codes for the system to lock it and unlock it," he said, pointing to two different six-digit codes. "This one is for *help*, and this one is that you're good. Again, do not show them to anyone. These are for your safety."

"Thank you," she said and walked them to the door.

"Even when you're home, turn the system on. It's currently on."

Front door, open, the system announced.

"See?" Scott said. "These are also on all the windows and doors. It will tell you if something is open or if it is broken."

"Got it," Robin said with the paper still in hand. "Thank you for coming so quickly."

"My pleasure. Stay safe and make wise choices," Scott said as he and his assistant walked off the porch.

After they left, she locked the door behind them. Looking around the house, she felt uncomfortable. "I don't like this," she said aloud to herself. Rubbing her arms with her hands, she felt a chill go down her spine and shuddered.

"I'm going to need to paint tonight," she said aloud, heading into her room. She pulled her bag out from under her bed and stared at it for a few moments. "I felt bad, but the firefighters all said it was a good thing. I'm not going to burn it down. I'm going to go paint. It's safe."

Was she trying to convince herself? The fire was beautiful. She loved painting flames. She relished the way the candles she lit had the colors dance from blue to red and orange, to white at its hottest point.

She closed her eyes and took a deep breath as she remembered the fire from the night her family died. A fire, she found out later, was her fault. Her grandparents hid the police report for years until she found it one day, searching for some of her other records.

Her phone interrupted her thoughts. "Hey, Nate," she said, answering her phone.

"Are you okay? Did Scott come by yet?"

"Yes. I'm okay. And, yes. Scott came and went. Security system installed and armed."

"Good," he said, relieved. "Is Kent coming tonight?"

"No. He has a date. I didn't want to tell him about the letter because I knew he would break his date to come here."

"I wish these things would quit happening on my shift nights," Nate grumbled. "It's like this creep knows when I'm at work and decides to torture you on those days."

"Who knows," Robin said with a shrug. "Either way, it's me and the security system for the night."

"Did he install any cameras?"

"No."

"Do you work tomorrow?"

"I work from eleven to eight tomorrow."

"Would you mind if I grabbed a couple guys and we installed cameras that you can access with your phone while you're at work? That way you can see around your house. I don't want you being snuck up on."

"Actually, that sounds like a great idea. If you come by the restaurant, I'll give you my phone to hook it up, as well as the keys."

"Great!"

"Would about three hundred cover the cameras?"

"Robin, you don't need to pay me for them."

"You guys are doing the work for free. It's the least I can do."

"Nice hint. I'll bring them to the restaurant afterward to feed them. I'll call ahead and make sure we're at your table so you can get the tip."

"That sounds good."

"I'm not comfortable with you being home by yourself all night with this creep out there."

"I know. Unfortunately, there's nothing we can do."

Nate huffed. "Brett and Kyle said they have you on more frequent drive-bys. Hopefully, that will help deter creeper dude."

"Here's hoping."

"Are you okay?"

"Sort of. No. Not really," she admitted. "Unfortunately, there's nothing we can do."

"I'll be praying for you all night."

"I appreciate that. Maybe we can go out on my next day off."

"Are you working the day after tomorrow?"

"Nope."

"Great! It's a date!"

"Well, it's Friday, so definitely. I not only don't want to be here, but I also enjoy spending time with you."

"Thank you. I enjoy spending time with you, too."

"Then it's settled: Friday date night."

"Perfect!"

"Do you feel a little better now?" she asked.

"Not really, but I'll take what I can get."

"I appreciate your concern, but I'm a big girl. I used to work with rough necks. I know how to handle myself."

"I appreciate that, but I'm still going to worry."

"I know. Try to focus on your work, though. I don't want you worrying about me and getting hurt."

"I am always focused."

"Keep it that way."

"Is it okay to call around nine to wish you goodnight?" he asked.

"Of course!"

"Great! I'll talk to you then," he said and hung up.

Robin grabbed her keys and purse and then headed out the back door.

Back door, open.

"Oh. Right." She sighed and she rolled her eyes. She set the code for leaving and locked the door behind her as she headed toward the garage for her Jeep.

Strolling through the grocery store, she thought about what food she wanted to eat. She also grabbed a few meals to take to work. While she appreciated the good food, if she continued to eat there, she may start to gain too much weight for her comfort.

"What can I get ya?" the man behind the meat counter asked.

"May I please have a couple of these steaks," she said, pointing toward the T-bone steaks. "And four pounds of hamburger, please?"

"Easy enough. Coming right up," he said. He measured and wrapped the meat and handed each to her. "Anything else?"

"Nope. Thank you." She accepted the meat, and then headed into an aisle.

There were several people in the aisle with her, but she was paying more attention to the salad dressing options. That's when she saw it out of the corner of her eye. There was a note with her name on it tucked between the ranch dressing and the walnut vinaigrette.

She looked around to see if anyone was watching her as she slid it out from between the salad dressings. There were only a few people still in the aisle with her, but a couple had already moved on.

When she opened it, it read:

Robin,

I cannot wait for Friday. Are you going to cook for me? Are we having steak? I cannot wait to see the candlelight reflecting off your beautiful face. Be on the lookout tomorrow for your dress. I got your favorite colors of red and black.

Your true love.

Robin gulped as her heart skipped a beat. She pulled her phone out and took a screenshot. Then she went to the front and grabbed a grocery bag. She dropped the note in before tying it closed. She then put it in the lower basket where she could keep an eye on it while she finished.

As she headed into the next aisle, she called Kyle.

"Masters," he answered his phone.

"Kyle, this is Robin Flynn."

"Uh-oh. What happened?"

"What makes you think something happened?" she asked, trying to lighten the call. "Can't I just call our boys in blue to encourage them?"

"Robin?" he asked.

She sighed. "I was shopping. I got steaks and hamburger at the meat counter. When I went down the next aisle, there was a note in an envelope with my name on it tucked between two salad dressings."

"Okay," he said, uneasy.

"It mentioned the steaks I just got. He asked if I was going to cook for him. Then he said to look out for the dress tomorrow and that the colors are my favorite – black and red."

"*Are* those your favorite colors?"

"Yes."

"And he mentioned the steaks you just bought."

"That I literally just got from the meat counter," she corrected.

"Oh!"

"Yeah."

"I'm going to put a tracker on you. Which store are you in?"

Robin chuckled before she told him which store she was in.

"Do me a favor and wander around that store. I'll be there as soon as I can. Keep moving. Pay attention to those around you."

"I will. Thank you."

"I'll call you when I get there."

"Thank you," she said and hung up.

She looked at each face of those around her. Her chest felt heavy. She couldn't get a full breath of air. *Whoever this is, has reached a new level of creepy.*

About ten minutes after she hung up, Kyle called. "I'm here. What aisle are you on?"

"The baked goods aisle. I figured most men don't want to hang out in this aisle."

"Good thinking. Let me radio in, and I'll head your way."

"Thank you," she said and hung up.

She slowly looked at every item in that aisle before Kyle walked up to her. "Where is it?" he asked.

She held up the bag with the note in it. With gloved hands, he took out the evidence bag from his pocket and shook it open. Then he unknotted the bag in her hands and pulled out the note.

He let out a low whistle as he scanned the note. "Are you almost done shopping?"

"I can be. I just need to check out."

"Self-check?"

"I can do that," she agreed.

They went to the self-check, and she checked out. They got a few strange looks, but she ignored them.

As they headed out, Kyle asked, "Did you see anyone you recognized? This has to be someone you know...or knew."

"I didn't see anyone, but I may or may not recognize them now, to be honest."

"Just do your best. If you see someone you recognize, take a picture and let me know. I can run facial rec on them."

"Okay. Thank you."

"Let's get your car loaded. I don't want to leave you here still loading."

"I appreciate that."

As they walked up to her Jeep, Kyle groaned. "Don't move," he said and ran back to his car."

"What's wrong?" Robin asked, watching him.

"Just stay there," he said. He reached into his car and pulled out another evidence bag. Looking around the parking lot, he then reached for the envelope on the windshield wiper of her Jeep.

"Oh no." Robin groaned. "What does this one say?"

Kyle opened it with gloved hands. Robin read over his shoulder:

Robin,

I am looking forward to Friday night. I know how much you

love candles, so I will make sure there are plenty for you to enjoy. If you would like, I will even have a blank canvas for you to paint. I enjoy watching you get lost in your element.

Kyle looked over at her with a raised eyebrow. "You paint?"

"I do," she said, tucking a portion of her hair behind her ear. "It, um, seems that he's watching me?"

"Yeah. Really not comfortable with you being home by your-self," he said, sliding the envelope and note into the bag. "This has not been touched by you, so we should be able to get good prints off it...if there are any." He turned to her and asked, "So, question, what are we going to do with you tonight?"

"I'm going home," she said. "I have the alarm system."

"That's not enough. You won't sleep knowing he's been this close to you."

She shuddered. "You're right."

"Let's go drop off your groceries and get your refrigerated stuff put away. I have an idea. I'll call on the way to your house. I'll follow you. If there is a red light coming, stop before it changes. Don't lose me."

"Fair enough," she agreed.

They loaded the Jeep and then headed to her home.

After they unloaded the groceries. As she was putting her food into the refrigerator, Kyle went into the living room. When he returned, he said, "I have two ideas. Kind of more comfortable with one instead of the other."

"Okay. Do you want some coffee while we talk?"

"No. Just come and have a seat," he gestured toward her table as he took a seat.

When she sat down, she let out a slow breath of air. "Why do I feel like I won't like either of the choices."

"You are an intuitive one."

"Okay. Spill it. What are my options?"

"Well, technically there are three: One, call your friend Kent to come spend the night with you. Two, spend the night in at the firehouse – surrounded by firefighters, with police officers coming in and out throughout the shift. Or three, we get you a hotel room. With option three, you will still have to have someone in the room with you."

"Oh," was all she said.

"So, I need to know your choice in this matter."

"How many nights?"

"Right now...two – tonight and tomorrow night...at least."

"Hmm." She rubbed her chin in thought. What if...what if I stay here tonight and let you choose tomorrow?"

"Can I ask why?"

"I feel like he isn't going to do anything tonight. He keeps talking about tomorrow night. To me, in his notes, he's focused on Friday."

"He is. I'm just concerned. He's brazen. He left notes just after you got something. He was right there. He seems to know a lot about you as well."

"I understand. If I'm about to go into lockdown, I would prefer at least one night of freedom."

"I can't make you do anything. I would just rather keep you safe. I don't want Nate ticked off at me for failing to protect you."

"I have an alarm system. I have y'all on speed dial. I appreciate your concern. If I feel afraid one more time, I'll do whatever you guys want. Fair enough?"

"Fair enough," he agreed. "Call if you have *any* issues. Understand?"

"I will."

"Thank you. I would rather not report to Nate that you are in the hospital or dead."

"I would rather you did not have to do that either."

"Lock and alarm the house," he said, getting up. "While you

are not under house arrest, I would ask you to be very selective on where you go and who you go with."

"I will."

"If you leave, do you have protection?"

"I have a knife."

"What about mace?"

"I don't, but I can go get some?" she said.

"Tell you what," Kyle said, dialing his phone, "let me work on something." He left into the living room.

While he was gone, Robin got up and paced the room. Out of nervous energy, she pulled a couple eggs out of the fridge and made scrambled eggs.

When she was about halfway through making them, Kyle came back in. He handed her a piece of paper. "Go to this store. They have your mace ready and waiting for you. I pulled a few strings."

"Okay," she said, looking at the paper. "This is a half-hour away."

He shrugged. "As I said, I had to pull a few strings."

"Thank you," she said, accepting the paper.

"Be careful," he cautioned before he left.

As he walked down the walkway, Robin locked the door and set the alarm. She then looked up the address of the place on the GPS before grabbing her wallet and keys.

"I'll go get the mace so poor Kyle can sleep at night," she said, setting the alarm before she left.

CHAPTER 8

BURNING THE MIDNIGHT OIL

W hen she returned from going to get the mace, she flopped on the couch and looked around her living room. The anxiety ratcheted up several notches since even yesterday.

She went to her bedroom and got her paint bag. It was only around five in the evening. Normally she wouldn't go this early, but her anxiety was driving her crazy. She grabbed her bag and walked out of the house.

The peacefulness of her neighborhood never ceased to amaze her. There were kids playing in the front yard with the dog next door. There was an elderly couple on the front porch across the street, watching and talking as they held hands. To her, that was a life goal she never thought she would get the opportunity to fulfill.

As she continued to walk, she headed into town. "Hey, Shawn," she said to the cashier at the small general store. "Do you have anything fresh made?"

"Yeah. Actually. Jen just made some tuna salad."

"Great! I'll take a tuna salad sandwich with lettuce."

"Sure. Give me a few," Shawn said and went to work on her sandwich. "Do you want anything else with it?"

"No. I'm good. Thank you," she said, grabbing a small bag of chips. "I got these."

Shawn chuckled, shaking his head. "You're a junk food junkie."

"That's rich coming from a teen," she shot back with a smirk.

"Well, what can I say?" He shrugged. "My metabolism is at an all-time high."

"For now," she corrected.

"I'll enjoy it while I can. Here's your sandwich."

"Thank you, kind sir," she said and paid for her food. "Always a pleasure."

"Agreed. You are one of the few adults I actually like."

"And you are one of the few teens I actually like," she said and left.

She ate her sandwich as she walked. Once she reached the other end of the town, she took a quick look around before ducking into the woods.

It took her several minutes to reach the old warehouse district. As she walked by the burned-out footprint of the warehouse that burnt down the last time she was there, she felt a wave of guilt.

"No. No. It was an accident," she said aloud. "Remember, it was not on purpose. Get it together, Robin!" She looked around to see if anyone else was around or heard her.

When she was satisfied there wasn't anyone around, she ducked into an abandoned warehouse. Walking through the halls, it took her a few minutes to find the office.

"Ahh." She heaved a long sigh. "A clean canvas."

She sat on the floor, studying the wall. She cocked her head to the side as she saw what looked like a fire climbing the wall. The flames started at the bottom and slowly scaled the wall with stunning colors of red, orange, yellow, blue, and white.

She could see the design as she finished her sandwich. Draining the water bottle, she then got off the ground. She pulled out the various paints she would need. She did not want to use spray paint today. She wanted to use acrylics for this one.

She lit the candle and left it on the end table in the office. The decrepit stand had a few pieces broken through, and a couple others lay in their final resting place in front of it, deep in dirt and dust. She found a place where it balanced well enough to hold the candle.

Turning back to the paints, she got them ready. After pouring the paints she wanted, she picked up the palette and brush. "Okay."

Stroke after stroke, the picture in her mind was produced onto the wall. The colors blended beautifully. It was as if the projected design left her mind and planted itself onto the wall without her help.

Surrounded by her element, she lost track of time until she finally finished. Taking a step back, she admired the way the colors blended perfectly. It took on a life of its own.

Resuming her position on the floor, she leaned against the wall, lost in the mural. She glanced at her watch and realized she had been there for over seven hours. It was already midnight.

"Oh no." She groaned. "Nate was supposed to call at nine. He probably thinks I've been kidnapped or something."

Pulling her phone out of her pocket, she realized she had it on silent. "Ten missed calls?" She groaned again. "I gotta get home first. If I call him, he'll want to come here."

That's when she looked up and saw the mural on the wall. If anyone were to look at it, they would know in a heartbeat it was her work.

She looked around the room. "I need to get rid of this," she said, panic welling inside. Looking around again, she grabbed her paints and tools and tossed them into the bag.

Picking up the candle, she went to blow it out but stopped. Glancing at the mural again, she then looked back down at the candle. "I could..." her voice faded as an idea surfaced.

She picked up one of her spray cans. Aiming it at the mural, she put the candle in front of the mural and sprayed the spray can. It instantly lit up.

While Robin should have been terrified, she was more memorized. She blew out the candle. Placing the blown-out candle and the paints back into her back, she never took her eyes off the mural.

The fire climbed the wall, making her painting look three-dimensional. The hypnotic effect caught her in its snare. She stood there watching the fire eat more and more of the wall.

Once it reached the top, she turned to leave the office. That's when she realized that while the fire ate at the wall, it attacked the interior walls and blocked her in. Her heart sped up to an alarming rate as she looked for an escape.

Seeing no exit, she ran right into the fire. About ten feet in, it cleared. Unfortunately, her bag caught fire. She threw it on the ground to stamp it out, but it didn't work.

Throwing it into the fire, she ran the other way as cans started to explode. Covering her head, she ducked into an office to collect herself. With as dry and dilapidated as the building was, it lit up!

She ran to the window. It was locked. As a matter of fact, it was rusted shut. Grabbing a chair, she flung it toward the window, crashing through it.

She lunged through the window, cutting her hands with the glass on the sides. Once through, she ran as fast as she could.

Reaching the tree line she hid in before, she leaned against a tree, breathing hard. Blood dripped from her hands onto the ground.

Hearing the sirens wailing in the distance, she watched the warehouse light up. The flames danced along the roof before it caved, sending debris toward the night sky.

Once the fire engines pulled up, she slowly turned and walked back toward her house. She wanted to stay and watch, but she knew she needed to get back home. She also needed to call Nate back, even though she knew he was at the fire.

Finally arriving at home, she set the alarm and then went to the bathroom to clean her hands. Holding the hydrogen peroxide over her hand, she hesitated.

"Ohhh, this is going to hurt," she groaned. "I don't want to do this."

She hesitated again.

"The only way is to do it. Don't be a baby. Just do it already!"

She closed her eyes and then poured the hydrogen peroxide over her hand. She let out a scream. "It's on fire!" she howled. "Oh! Make it stop!" she yelled, tears streaming down her face.

Stomping her feet, she just about ran in place. "Oh! Noooooo!" She hissed as she sucked air through her teeth in pain.

When it finally calmed, she quickly grabbed the hydrogen peroxide and poured it over her other hand. The screech she let out even scared her.

She ran in place, seething in pain and agony for several minutes. Both hands pulsated in pain.

"Oh," she looked toward the ceiling in agony, "make it stop!"

She was in so much torment it finally calmed enough to rest her head on the side of the sink as she sunk to her knees. "Why?" she groaned. "Make it stop!"

She slowly sunk the rest of the way to the ground and curled up in a ball with her hands sticking out. Through her tear-blurred eyes, she looked at her hands. There were cuts and scrapes all over them.

"How am I going to cover this up?" she wondered aloud. "This just got complicated."

After twenty more minutes, she was finally able to breathe. She wrapped her hands in gauze, sealing them with medical tape.

When she finished, she pulled out her phone and texted Nate:

Sorry I missed your call. I burned my hands cooking dinner and passed out from the pain. I'm fine. They're wrapped. Hope you're having a good night. – Robin

She lied, but it was a good lie. It was one she could share and get away with. After she sent the text, she dropped her phone on the floor and closed her eyes.

It was a long night. One she wanted to forget. One she hoped would fade away like a bad dream.

The next morning, her phone chimed, waking her up. She was still on the bathroom floor. Her hands still pulsed as she picked up the phone. It was Nate.

"Hello?" she mumbled, answering the phone.

"Robin, are you okay?" Nate asked.

"No. It was a long night. Well, I mean, I'm fine. Just that my hands hurt."

"I just got off work. Want me to stop by?"

"What time is it?"

"Seven."

"Bring breakfast, and I'll welcome you with open arms."

"You got it. See you in a few."

After he hung up, she got herself off the floor. Going to the bedroom, she jumped in the shower. After a quick shower, she quickly got dressed and then ran a pick through her hair.

Just as she finished, she heard a knock on the door. "Nate!" she said, excited.

Running toward the door, she slowed when she got closer. She brushed her pants to calm her nerves.

Opening her door, she was stunned to find no one there. "Okay," she said, taking a step out onto the porch.

Out of the corner of her eye, she saw a note sticking out of her mailbox. She pulled it from the mailbox and opened it. It said:

I know what you did last night. I saw you. I cannot wait to talk to you about it tonight at dinner. See you at five o'clock. Your dress will arrive around three when you get off work.

She couldn't call the police regarding this note. This one would take some explaining, and she really did not want to do that. She folded it and stuck it in her back pocket.

Hearing a truck coming down the road, she looked up to see Nate's truck. "Good timing," she said under her breath.

As he pulled in, she looked up and down the street to see if she could see anyone walking. She shuddered when a chill ran down her spine. Rubbing her arms, she shuddered again.

"Hey, darlin'," Nate said, getting out of the truck. He pulled a bag, along with two drinks, from the seat before he kicked the door closed.

As he got closer, he got a good look at her. "What happened? You look like you've seen a ghost. You're pale." He set the food on the banister.

"It was a long night."

"I hear ya. We had another fire last night around midnight. Do you need a hug?"

"Yes. Please."

Wrapping his arms around her, he pulled her in for a hug. "Talk to me."

"They hurt," she said, holding her hands up.

"Want me to take a look at them?"

"No. They're fine. I'm fine. Everything's fine. I have to work later. I'll just take it easy with them."

"Kyle mentioned you have to make a choice regarding where you're going after work today."

"That's true. I'm not sure which option I want to do."

"If you want to do the hotel, I can stay there with you as well if it will make you more comfortable. Same for the firehouse."

"I appreciate that. I haven't figured out yet which direction I want to go. I told him he could choose. I'm just not sure what to do. I feel like we may be making a bigger deal than we need to regarding this situation."

"He's obviously following you. That's stalking. The note at the grocery store was super creepy."

You should see the one I got this morning, she thought, but said, "Yeah. Not very comfy with how close this guy seems to be."

"C'mon, let's eat breakfast before it gets cold," he said, wrapping his arm over her shoulder as they went inside.

After they ate, they moved to the couch in the living room. Once settled, Robin asked, "So, what are you going to do on your day off?"

"I feel almost like I need to spend it in your restaurant with you, but I know there are many others there who will look out for you. This guy doesn't make me comfortable at all."

"You could take me and pick me up if it will make you feel better?" she offered.

"Actually, it would."

"Done. Glad to make you feel comfy. This is kind of a little nerve-wracking."

"I can't imagine what it's like for you. It's scary for me, too, and the person isn't messaging me."

"It's not a great feeling. Stalkers are creepy. Never thought I would have a stalker, though. Kind of thought they were only for hotties and popular people."

"Don't sell yourself short."

"I'm not all that."

"You're more all that than you know. You're pretty, smart, super talented, and have your stuff together. Trust me. In this day and age, that's rare. That's blue-moon rare. And the fact that you're single? Like solar eclipse rare."

"Hmm. Sounds like someone else I know," she said and nudged him.

He smiled as his face flushed. Shrugging he said, "Thank you. I don't think of myself like that."

"You're hot. You're a firefighter. You have a brain. You are kind and considerate. You, yourself are solar eclipse rare, honey," she pointed out.

"I appreciate that. Thank you."

"So, what are you going to do while I'm at work?"

"Well..." He bent forward. "There was another fire last night. Dad and I are going to look at it today in the sunlight. We may be able to see more than we did last night."

"Oh," she said, heart racing. Nervously clearing her throat, she asked, "Another accident?"

"Possibly. We're not sure. We found remnants of some spray cans."

"They didn't melt?"

"Oh, they did. There are still little bits of them."

"Anything else?"

"Where we found the cans was pretty much gone. The fact that we even found those was questionable. We're not sure if they are connected or if they were just left in there."

"Did you find the source of the fire?"

"Not yet. That's why we're going back."

"Gotcha."

"Dad's starting to wonder if we have an arsonist," Nate admitted.

"You think?"

"We're not sure."

"Well, I'm sure you and your dad will figure it out."

"I hope so. This zero-dark-thirty fire thing is getting old."

"I'm sure."

"I honestly can't complain too much, though. It's not like I'm working tons. The shifts are twenty-four hours, but they are every few days. Generally, unless there is a conflag or I'm on the ambulance, I get a good night's sleep."

"Conflag?"

"Conflagration. Wild fire."

"Gotcha. Lord knows those kick up."

"They do. And when they do, we need to be gone a lot longer than those twenty-four-hour shifts."

"Yuck."

"I know. Well, what do you want to do for the next few hours?"

"Let's take a walk," she suggested.

"Sure."

They got up, set the alarm, and left the house. Walking the neighborhood in the morning was peaceful and calm. Walking it, holding Nate's hand, added a special element to it. His strength allowed her to relax. It was just what she needed.

CHAPTER 9

LIFE, LIKE A FIRE, BEGINS IN SMOKE AND ENDS IN ASHES

"Have a good day," Nate said as he opened her door of the truck at the restaurant.

"You too. Have fun trying to figure things out with your dad," she said, hopping out of the truck.

"Is it too soon to ask for a kiss?" Nate asked, holding her hands.

"I don't think so. I would like that. I think it would be a great way to start the day. Breakfast, and then a kiss? Yep. Sounds good."

He rested his hand on the side of her face and leaned forward. Once their lips touched, it sent tingles through Robin's body. She took a deep breath and joined him deeper in the kiss.

After a few moments, they separated.

"Wow," Nate said, taking a deep breath. "That was..."

"Amazing," Robin finished.

"Definitely. Okay. Um, have a great day at work."

"Thank you. Have fun with your dad."

"Always."

With that, she headed into the restaurant.

"Hey, Robin!" Kent called when she walked in.

"Hey, Kent!" She greeted him with a smile. Walking up to him, she asked, "How was your date?"

"Really good. Um?" He looked down at her hands. Picking them up, he asked, "What happened?"

"I burned them cooking last night."

"I told you cooking was bad for your health."

"Actually, cooking is better than continuously eating out regarding health. How was your night off?" she asked, trying to change the subject.

"Oh, girl! I had an amazing night! Let me tell you..." he went on, giving her details of the night as they set up for their shift.

"So, as you can imagine, only good things, sister. Only good things," Kent finished.

"Sounds it."

"And you? How are things regarding creepy dude? Heard anything else?"

"Well, funny you should mention him."

He crossed his arms and tapped his foot. "What happened?"

"Got a message from him yesterday afternoon, so the officers came over last –"

"You got to see the officer hotties again?" he asked with a smile.

Robin smirked. "Yes. They came over, and Kyle called –"

Kent grinned. "*Kyle* now, hunh?"

"Did you not see the kiss when Nate dropped me off?"

"Oh yeah! Steamy!" He fanned himself.

"Stop!" She playfully pushed him. "Nate's more than super-hot. He's sweet, kind, and way smart."

"Honey, he's all the things."

"He is. So, yeah, I'm not looking elsewhere."

Kent rolled his eyes. "Some girls just get all the luck."

"Oh, sure. Like having some stalker follow me in a grocery store is fun."

"Wait! What? What grocery store? What happened?"

"Creepy dude followed me to the grocery store. I got steaks.

Then, after I got the steaks, I went down an aisle to find a note to me regarding those steaks."

"Why didn't you call me?"

"Because you had a date. I didn't want to ruin that for you."

"Girl, you are more important to me."

"I know. I just wanted you to have a good night."

He rested his hands on her shoulders. "Robin, you are more valuable and important. When something like this happens, I don't care what is going on in my world. You call me. Understand?"

"I do," she agreed.

"Now," he dropped a bit to look right into her eyes, "what's the plan with the officer hotties?"

"Tonight, I am either staying at the firehouse or in a hotel room. Creepy guy is supposed to pick me up at five for a date."

"Do you want me to come with you?"

"Nate is, but you're welcome to as well if it will make you feel better?" she offered.

"It would. Besides, spending the night in a firehouse with a whole shift of hotties. Yeah. I'm there!"

Robin chuckled, shaking her head. "Okay. Nate's picking me up after work, and then we'll go whichever direction they tell us to. I told them they could pick."

"Okay. I'll go home and grab an overnight bag and meet you wherever you tell me to."

"They may have you meet us here and leave your car. They're kind of paranoid right now. Kyle had his buddy set up an alarm system on my house."

"Sounds like they're looking after you."

"They are."

"Okay, people, time to open the doors," Rick announced.

"Ready?" Kent asked.

"Ready," Robin said with a nod.

"Just be careful with your hands."

"I will. Thank you."

With that, they went to their stations. It didn't take long for the restaurant to fill. Robin happily enjoyed the business of work. It would get her back to Nate that much quicker.

"Seriously!" Sarah-Ann came over to where Robin was filling drinks.

"What's wrong?"

"That idiot who held my table for hours the other day is back," she said, rolling her eyes.

Robin looked around the restaurant. "Where?"

"Table six."

"The two-top?"

"Yep. I mean, he tips well, but still. Super creepy. He literally just hangs out doing work."

Robin searched for table six. She squinted to see better. He looked vaguely familiar. When he saw her looking over, he tossed a bill on the table and casually got up and left.

"He's gone," Robin said to Sarah-Ann.

"Thank the Lord!" Sarah-Ann said. "I need to go clear that." She sighed. "I'm just here living my best life."

Robin rolled her eyes. "Aren't we all,"

While she did her job, the man who left continued to play in the back of her mind. *Who was he? Why did he look familiar?*

After her final table left, Robin and Kent both clocked out. Kent was waiting for her to finish, since he finished about fifteen minutes prior.

"Okay, what's our plan?" Kent asked Nate when they walked up to Nate's truck together.

"Our?" Nate asked.

"After what happened yesterday, I'm not letting her out of my sight."

"Agreed."

Robin crossed her arms. "Are you two finished?"

"Yep," Nate said. He gave her a hug and a kiss on the cheek. "Talked to Kyle," he said as she hugged him back. "He suggested that the firehouse, surrounded by police officers and firefighters, was a safer bet."

"All right!" Kent cheered with a grin that went ear-to-ear. "I mean..." He nervously coughed. Putting his hands on his hips, he calmly said, "I mean, I'm good with that."

Nate and Robin burst out in laughter.

"It's all good, Kent." Nate waved him off. "Want to meet us back here and leave your vehicle for the night?"

"Not really. Why don't you pick me up at my apartment?" Kent asked.

"That sounds good. Robin, do you know where he lives?"

"Yep. We'll see you in about twenty minutes?" Robin asked.

"Sounds good," Kent said. He got in his car and left.

Nate opened her door for her, so she climbed in. "Our turn."

When they got home, there was a package on the porch. "Great!" Robin said, picking it up. She glanced at her watch. It said it was three-thirty. "At least he's prompt."

"What do you mean?" Nate asked.

She handed him the package so she could unlock the door. "He said it would be here around three o'clock."

"Got it. Do you want to open it?"

"Sure," she said, walking through the door. She set the alarm once they were inside.

Taking it to the kitchen, Nate set it on the table. "Do you want me to do it or do you?"

"I'll do it," she said, setting her mail on the table next to it.

Heart racing, she pulled the paper off the package. It was about three inches tall, by two-feet long, by a foot and a half wide. She picked out a pair of scissors from her utility jar to open the box.

Pulling the lid off, she was taken aback. She let out a low whistle as she held the dress up. "Wow. Okay. Dude's got style."

"That's not funny."

"I'm not laughing. He *does* have a great sense of style."

It was an asymmetrical satin dress, with an A-line silhouette. The black lace top had an illusion scoop neck and was sleeveless. There was a lace trim around the bottom that matched the top of the dress.

"Knows your colors, too. That would look gorgeous on you."

"Seems he thinks so, too," Robin said, picking up the note.

Nate read over her shoulder. The note said:

Robin,

I'm looking forward to taking you out tonight. I will pick you up at five. I cannot wait to see your latest creation in your shed. Maybe someday you can teach me to work the way you do. Your creativity amazes me. I especially love the way you paint.

"Great," Robin said on a sigh. "This will be fun."

"Not so much. Let's go. I'll come back later with Kyle and Brett to bag this."

"Are you planning on leaving me at the station?"

"Actually, I am. Since Kent's coming with you, I thought it may be okay for me to come back with Kyle and Brett to sit here at five to wait."

"That will work," Robin agreed. "Probably can't have much go on with police and firefighters all over the place."

"True. Want to go get Kent?"

"I do."

After she packed, Robin left the dress, box, and note on the table, and then they headed out the door, with Robin setting the alarm before they left.

After picking Kent up, they went to the firehouse.

"So, I understand her or me not driving, but why are we not concerned with you driving?" Kent asked Nate.

"Probably because this is where I work," Nate said, pulling into a parking spot. "Even with a tracker on, it wouldn't matter. I'm here a lot anyway."

"True."

"Okay. Let's get you two handed off to the officer on duty," Nate said, getting out of the truck. He ran around to Robin's side and opened her door. Offering her a hand, he said, "Milady."

"Thank you," she said, taking his hand.

Nate grabbed Robin's bag, while Kent grabbed his own, and together they headed into the police station side of the building.

"Hey, Nate," the young lady behind the counter said with a smile. "What brings you by today? I thought you worked yesterday. You wouldn't happen to be looking for me, maybe?"

"Uh, no, sorry, Gianna. I'm looking for Kyle Masters and Brett Carmichael. This is my girlfriend, Robin Flynn."

"Oh." Gianna sat up straighter in her seat before she called over the radio for Kyle and Brett to call into the station. As they called in one at a time, Gianna told them Nate and Robin were waiting for them. When she hung up, she looked to Nate and said, "They'll be here shortly. You can have a seat over there." Then she looked toward Kent and asked, "I don't suppose *you're* here for me?"

"Oh, no, honey," he said with a smile. "I'm with them." He pointed toward Nate and Robin. When she raised an eyebrow, he said, "I appreciate you checking on me, though."

The three of them snickered as they headed over to the couches.

"You mean, you don't want her?" Robin asked quietly.

"No, but some of the others around here would be sure to make my list," he said with a twinkle in his eyes.

"Enough," Nate said with a chuckle.

"Whatever is wrong?" Kent playfully asked.

"You're a mess."

"I am, and I own it."

"You are also loyal, and I appreciate that," Nate said.

"Thank you."

After Kyle and Brett got Robin and Kent settled, they, along with Nate, took off for Robin's house. Robin gave Nate the security code for the house before they left as well.

"Okay, so, how are you feeling?" Kent asked.

"A little nervous. Not sure what they're going to find. I'm still a little freaked out by the dude from Sarah-Ann's table today."

"What dude?"

"The same dude who was at her table for hours the other day was also at her table today. When he saw me looking at him, he got up and left."

"Do you know him?"

"He looked familiar. I was trying to place him when he left."

"Interesting. The plot thickens."

"I'm sure. Kind of getting a little messed up."

"That it is. However, not going to complain about where we landed tonight."

"Always looking for the best side of things," she said, shaking her head.

"I try."

"Let's hope tonight turns out on the best side of things."

"True," she said.

They picked out a game from the game shelf. Sitting at the table, they pulled it out and started to play while the firefighters trained outside.

"What time is it?" Nate asked as he sat in the back of the patrol car.

"Four-forty-five," Kyle said. "Fifteen minutes."

"Kind of torture," Brett said. "The glory side of being a police officer."

Kyle rolled his eyes. "That is an accurate statement."

They chatted for about twenty minutes when Nate asked, "What time is it?"

"Too long," Kyle said with a groan. "He's not showing."

"What if he already did?" Brett asked.

"What do you mean?" Kyle asked.

"What if he is inside?" Brett suggested. "What if he went inside and found she wasn't there?"

"Wouldn't the alarm go off?" Nate asked.

"Unless he knows the code," Brett suggested.

Both Kyle and Nate looked at Brett, eyes wide. All three scrambled out of the vehicle at the same time and ran toward Robin's front door.

Nate took out the key and unlocked the door. As soon as they got inside, he turned toward the code box to reset it. When he finished, he turned around. "What is...oh wow!" He gulped.

There were candles lit all through the room. On her coffee table, there were a dozen red roses in a vase. Her dress was laid out diagonally across the couch. On the dress was a note in an envelope with her name on it. Then, over on the wall was a poster.

"Don't think I want to know," Nate said, pushing his way

between the officers. "I don't even...wow." He ran his fingers through his hair and then rubbed the back of his neck.

The two officers went over to the wall. "We need to call CSI, and she needs to not come home for a bit. He obviously has the code, or we would have been notified," Kyle said.

Brett took a pair of gloves from his pocket. After slipping them on, he went over and picked up the note. "Wanna see?" he asked.

The other two went over and read over Brett's shoulder as he pulled it out of the envelope. It said:

Robin,

I regret that you were not here. I would have loved to have seen you in that dress. We will try again on another day. I understand things come up. I made you a poster, and I have the same one. That will allow us to be together even when we are apart. Until next time...

The guys turned back to the poster and looked closer at it. There were pictures of Robin at various places at various ages.

"He's been watching her for a long time. This is from high school," Kyle pointed out. "These are even her on the oil rigs. How is that possible?"

"Obsessed much?" Brett said, shaking his head. "This is a legit stalker. He's obviously been around a while. Why now?"

Kyle looked at Nate. "Because now she's taken."

"Which means *you* may be in trouble as well," Brett pointed out.

Nate waved them off. "I can handle myself."

"How many fires have y'all had since you two started dating?" Kyle asked.

"Two, but it –"

"What if they're set by him to lure you to a fire? What if it's a firefighter?" Kyle asked.

"If it is, she and Kent are currently at the firehouse," Nate said.

They all looked at each other wide-eyed before running out the door to the car.

"CSI," Kyle said.

"Robin," Nate pushed.

"I'll call it in and stay," Brett volunteered. "You two get to the firehouse. Leave Nate there," Brett suggested. "We need to get this figured out fast."

"Robin!" Nate yelled, running into the firehouse. "Robin! Kent!"

"Up here!" Robin called back. Seeing their flushed faces, she asked, "What's wrong? What happened?" She gulped. "Where's Brett?"

"Brett's at the house waiting for CSI," Kyle said. "Are you two okay?"

"Yeah. Why?" Kent asked. "The guys are right outside, and there are police officers all over this place. He would be a complete moron to try anything here."

Kyle and Nate looked at each other.

"What is that look between you two?" Robin narrowed her eyes. "What happened?"

"He got into your house," Nate admitted.

Her jaw momentarily dropped. "Even with the alarm?"

"Even with the alarm," Kyle said. "We need to not let you go home until the cameras are up."

"I'm not okay with cameras around my house. I already feel funny with the alarms...which apparently don't work," she said in a huff.

"We have to figure out how he's getting in," Nate said, hoping she would understand.

"I do not want people knowing when I'm coming and going in my own home. I hate that I have to enter a code as it is."

"Robin, if you saw it, you would understand. Please let us put up cameras?" Kyle pleaded.

"If I do, the cameras go to *my* phone and no one else's phone or system. I will put up with the code thing," she relented. "I *do not* want people tracking me. I want my own life. I don't want to live under a microscope."

"I can understand that," Kyle agreed. "When do you want us to set it up?"

Robin let out a long breath of air. "How long do I have to stay here?"

"At least tonight," Kyle said.

"Do I have to stay tomorrow night?"

"Up to you."

"If he's already been to the house, why can't I go home tonight?"

"Because he could come back."

"Do you think he'll be back, or do you just think I would be safer here? I almost feel like I'm the criminal."

"We're trying to keep you safe."

"I can't sleep in my own home."

"Here you go," Brett said, coming up the stairs with a rolled-up object in his gloved hand. "I figured she may need a little persuasion. No one can touch it, but this may convince her."

"How did you know?" Kyle asked.

"Because I've seen her stubbornness. My sisters are the same way," he said with a wink toward Robin, who sat there with her arms crossed, watching him. When she didn't respond, he cleared his throat before he said, "Here. This was on your wall when we walked in tonight."

He laid the poster on the table with his gloved hands. Both Robin and Kent stared at the pictures, eyes wide and jaws dropped.

"H-how is this possible? Why now? I-I mean he obviously has

been watching me for a long time," Robin said to Kyle. She looked back at the poster.

"We think it may be because you started things with Nate," Kyle explained. "That's the only thing that's changed recently."

"That makes no sense." Robin shook her head. "Why would my dating Nate trigger this?"

"You said before that you didn't date much over the years," Nate pointed out.

"I haven't. But we just started dating. Why would whoever this is panic over *you*? That doesn't make sense."

Nate crouched next to Robin and took her hand into his. "I don't understand this. Frankly, it's freaking me out. However, I need to keep you safe as best as I can."

"I don't understand this cretin's fascination with me, though."

"You have no idea of your true value. That was true in high school just as much as it's true today. Someday, it's my prayer that you will figure out what those of us who love you already know. You are a pearl of great price. One day, you will understand that, too. Until then, it will be my pleasure to prove it to you each day I get the honor of being with you."

"Oh! That's so sweet!" Kent gushed.

Snickers were heard around the room. "You have a way of lightening any situation," Robin said to Kent.

"Thank you. I'll take that as a compliment."

"As you should," she said with a wink. Turning back to Nate, she said, "Okay. You guys can install cameras, but they go to my phone. Now, what's the point of the security system if he can obviously bypass it?"

"Let me call my friend, Scott, and see what we can do," Kyle suggested.

"The security guy?"

"Yes."

Robin rolled her eyes. "Not sure how it will help if his company was the one who installed the system in the first place."

"Let me give it another shot, please?" Kyle asked.

She huffed. "Fine."

"We can get the cameras tonight and set them up. I'll need your phone to connect them to your phone if you're okay with that?" Nate asked.

"I'm off at six," Brett said. "I can help you. The place may still be crawling with CSI people anyway. There is also a detective on the case now."

"Do you know who it is?" Nate asked.

"Roger Simms."

"My dad likes him," Nate said. "He's worked with him before."

"He sure knows his stuff. This is beyond our pay grade, but we can still help where we can. Here's Roger's card." Brett rolled up the poster and set it aside before he pulled a card out of his pocket. "He will probably be in touch with you sometime in the next twenty-four hours to talk to you."

"Okay," she said, accepting the card. "Things are getting deep."

"That they are. Please be careful," Brett said, picking up the poster. "I need to get this to evidence."

"Wait. Can I see that again?" Robin asked.

"Sure." Brett unrolled it on the table in front of her.

She skimmed the photos, looking specifically at those where she was on the oil rigs, in welding class, and when she was in high school. Crouching down to get a closer look, she squinted to see better...to no avail. The photos with other people were tiny. Those where she was by herself were clearer, but she was alone in the picture. She was hoping to find the guy in the restaurant.

"Okay. If I need to look at this again, can I?" she asked.

"Of course. Just come down to the station and tell them to contact me or Kyle. If we're not available, tell them who you are and what you want to look at," Brett explained.

"Thank you."

"Okay," he picked up the poster and rolled it up. "Going to leave you all for the night if you're okay."

"We're good," Robin said, picking up her cards. "Texas Hold 'em?" she asked Kent.

"That sounds good," Kent agreed.

"Want help with the cameras when I get off shift?" Brett asked Nate.

"Please...and thank you," Nate said.

"Okay. Let me do shift change, take a quick shower, and I'll be with you as soon as I can."

"That will give me time to get Robin sorted. Thanks," Nate said. With that, Brett left. Once he was out of eyesight, Nate asked, "Are you going to trust me with your phone?"

"Of course," Robin agreed. "I have nothing to hide."

She gave him her phone, along with the phone password. "Now, what about the security code issue?" she asked.

"That will be a Kyle question. This will give you a head's up to any movement around your house."

"How much do I owe you for cameras?"

"I'll let you know when we're done."

"Sounds good."

"Want me to play a few rounds with you?" Nate offered.

"Sure!"

Nate played for about forty-five minutes before Kyle and Brett came upstairs.

"Here are the new codes," Kyle said, handing Robin a piece of paper. "Scott is the only one with this code in his business. You and I are the only other people with the code. He has locked the numbers to only him."

"Okay. Thank you," Robin said, stuffing the paper in her pocket.

"Okay. We're going shopping, and then to your house. Kent, if something happens, call her phone, please? I will have it on me," Nate explained.

"Sounds good. Still think he's a complete moron if he tries

something while we're here," Kent said. "The guys are even inside now. Highly doubt he'll get anywhere near her. He'll also have to get through me if he got through the others...and that's not happening."

"Thank you," Nate said. "I tend to relax a little more when I know she's around you. I appreciate you."

"Well, thank you kindly!" Kent beamed.

That night, after they installed the cameras, Nate brought Robin's phone back to her. He showed her how to use it, and explained that Kyle locked her house and set the alarm.

After Nate left, Robin and Kent turned in. She read a book until she fell asleep using the app on her phone to read. As she slept, she had a horrific dream...

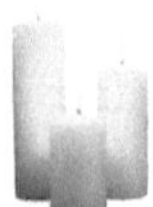

As she walked through the woods, her heart raced. The underbrush and trees cast shadows by the moonlight. The owl occasionally let her know she wasn't alone. He was joined by the chorus of cicadas throughout the path. Despite the earthy, musty scent of the woods combining with the pine and other tree scents, she still adored the woods. The peace that enveloped her was only surpassed by the rush of fire.

Looking around to ensure no one was near, she then tucked into one of the old warehouses. Two had already burned to the ground by her hand. This would be the third.

She headed to the office – her usual spot for art. Painting a phenomenal mural of fire on the wall, she stood back to admire its beauty. Using oil paints, she created a painting that looked almost three-dimensional. She then used layers to put a lift on the outline of the fire.

Once she finished, she pulled out her lighter and a can of spray paint. "I almost don't want to do it to this one." She lit the lighter and sprayed the paint, lighting up the wall in an instant.

She watched for only a moment before she tossed both the lighter and spray can into the bag and scooped them up. In the hallway, she turned for a moment and looked at the fully-engulfed room, before running the other way.

When she was almost to the stairs, she felt pain attack her head from every direction. Heading toward the ground, she barely got out any noise before blacking out completely.

Groaning, she moved her head side to side. The overpowering scent of burning flesh and sulfur assaulted her sense of smell. Covering her mouth, she used her hand to filter some of the scent.

Opening her eyes, she was lying on the shore of a massive body of water. She shook her head, not believing what she was seeing. The lake had fire dancing across the top of it, as if gasoline was on fire. What was more horrifying were the people actually in the lake. There were some with skin hanging off their bones, while others screamed and shouted in pain and agony.

"I-I don't –" her voice halted as a man walked out of the lake.

She really couldn't call him a man. He was human at one point. He was a walking corpse. Skin and parts of clothing hung off his body. He looked in the distance, only half there, mumbling to himself, "I need to tell them. They need to know. This is not what I want for them. They have to learn about this. Why didn't anyone tell me? I need to tell my family." He continued as he walked away.

Robin heard something else and looked to her right. There, in the distance, she could see people. There was a bright light. She sensed peace in the distance, so she got up to walk toward it.

"*Where* are you going?" A hideous creature stood in her way. Reddish-black scales coated its body. It had a set of reddish-black wings to match. Its yellow eyes with black slits searched deep into her soul. It drummed its talons on its chin as it stood before her. "Are you in the right place?"

"I-I don't...I don't know," she stammered. "I just woke up here."

"You sssssseem too good," it hissed. "But," it sniffed her, "you don't smell too good. I don't sense *Him* in you. You are not one of His, are you?"

"One of whose?"

"We are not allowed to say that name here. If you were, you would know. You *are* in the right place. If you are not one of His, you are ours."

"Wait! What?" Robin squeaked out.

"You have to make the choice to be one of His. If you have not, then you are one of oursssss. That meanssss you belong here."

"What choice? What do you mean? I was never given a choice," Robin objected.

"Do you know Who created the birds of the air and the fish of the sea? Do you know Who clothes the lilies of the valley? Do you know Who created your human race? Do you not know Who died on the cross to save you from your sins? Your people quote that verse all the time. Are you telling me you never heard it?"

"I have."

"Can you quote it? If *you* say it, I will not get into trouble with *him*."

"Who him?"

It crossed its arms in a huff. "Just quote it," it snapped.

"John 3:16, *'For God,'*" as she said *God*, the earth shuddered below their feet, "*so loved the world, that He,*" the earth shook below their feet a little harder, "*gave His only Son,*" the ground shook again, and there was a roar that rattled through her entire body, "*that whosoever believes in Him,*" the roar got louder, as the ground shook once again, "*should not perish but have eternal life.'* Are you saying if I don't believe in God and Jesus," when she said those words, she had to grab onto the creature before her to stay on her feet. The force of the roar shook the entire area. Several around them cowered in fear. "...That I am not going to have eternal life?"

"Oh! You will have eternal life, but not with *Him*," the creature clarified. "You will spend it with us...here...in eternal torment."

"Why are you telling me this?" she demanded. "You had me quote that, which obviously angered something very powerful."

"Oh! He is! It's the Prince of Darkness himself."

"You mean Satan?" The color drained from Robin's face as the creature nodded. "I don't want to! That man who walked by said he wanted someone to tell his family. How do we tell them if we are here?"

"Others need to tell them."

She gulped. "And if they don't?"

A smile slowly formed on its face as the earth below them finally calmed.

She shook her head. "No. No! Please! There has to be another way!"

It got in her face, less than an inch from her nose. "I will send you back. If you come back here and not there, it's on you! It's up to *you* who you choose. Be warned: if you do not choose Him, you are choosing to come back here."

"Why would you do this?"

"I made a mistake once. I followed the wrong one. I ended up here. I do not get this chance often, but you are the one we are sending back. Use this opportunity wisely. Do *not* wait."

"I-I won't," she promised.

"I have no more choice. You can choose. Know this opportunity does not happen often. It has only happened a few times that I know of. Do not waste it."

"I won't."

"Close your eyes."

She closed her eyes.

"Wait! Leave her alone!"

Robin opened her eyes to see several creatures running toward her. Feeling a talon on her arm, she squeezed her eyes shut and screamed as loud as she could.

"Robin!" Kent was shaking her to wake her. "Robin! Please wake up! Robin!"

Breathing heavily, with sweat dripping off her face, she stared into Kent's eyes. There were several firefighters standing around as well. One had her wrist and was watching his watch to figure out her pulse.

"Here," a firefighter ran in with a small brown paper bag. "Breathe into this. You're hyperventilating."

Robin used her free hand to put the bag to her mouth. The bag would not inflate.

"Deep breaths, Robin," the one holding her wrist coaxed. "In...and out. In...and out. C'mon, you can do it. In...and out." When she finally got the bag to fully open and close, he said, "Good job. Keep going. In...and out. Good job, Robin."

"Okay. Show's over. Ozzy's got her," the lieutenant said, shoving the guys out of their room.

"Ozzy?" Robin asked while still breathing into the bag.

"Ozzy Thomas," he said, sticking out his hand. "I'm a friend of Nate's. He's on the other shift, but we went through school together. You can take the bag down now since you're breathing better."

"Thank you."

"That seemed intense. Are you okay?" Kent asked.

"I-I think so. Is-is Nate still here?" Robin asked.

"No. He went home to get some sleep. He was planning on coming back in the morning around seven to take you two to breakfast," Ozzy explained. "He waited until he was sure you were sound asleep.

Robin nodded. "Thank you."

"My pleasure. If you need me, you know where to find me," he said, and then got up and left them in the room.

"What was the nightmare?" Kent asked, his brow furrowed as he studied her.

"It was horrific!" Her breathing started picking back up as panic shot through her system.

"Shh." He wrapped his arms around her in a hug. "Stay calm. I just wanted to know. You don't have to tell me if you don't want to."

She vigorously shook her head.

"Do you think you think you can go back to sleep?"

"I-I can probably read some to relax."

"Okay. Is it okay if I go back to sleep?"

"I-yeah. Go ahead."

"Do you want me to push the beds together?" Kent offered.

"No. I'm okay. Get some sleep."

"Okay."

It took her a few hours to calm down before she was able to relax enough to go to sleep. When she finally did, it was a restless sleep. She tossed and turned all night long.

CHAPTER 10

WHEN FIRE IS APPLIED TO STONE, IT CRACKS

The next morning, Nate came to pick up Kent and Robin from the firehouse. Kent asked to be dropped off at his apartment so he could get ready for work. This left Nate and Robin to go out to breakfast together.

At the restaurant, after they ordered and the waitress left, Nate asked Robin, "Ozzy said you had a nightmare last night. Want to share?"

Robin took a deep breath, slowly letting the air out. "It was scary."

"Ozzy said it took them a bit to calm you down."

Her eyes met his as she said, "It was literal Hell."

"As in...?"

"As in, I'm pretty sure it was a demon who was talking to me." She shuddered. "The lake looked like gasoline lit on fire. The people were..." She closed her eyes and shuddered again. "The smell was awful. It smelled like burnt flesh and sulfur mixed. The people had skin and clothes just hanging off them. The weird thing is once they got out of the lake, the skin grew back. It was as if they would never die. Then, there was this guy mumbling about telling his family because he didn't want them to experience it."

"Hell is scary."

"He...It...it said..."

Nate furrowed his brow. "What did who say?"

"This creature. It said if I did not choose God, I was choosing them." When Nate just nodded, she asked, "How fair is that?"

"Well," Nate took her hand into his, "whatever that creature said was correct. Jesus came into the world to save it. He died on a cross, giving His life for everyone so they have the chance to escape Hell."

"How does that work?"

"You have to understand who Jesus is. You have to understand that He is the Son of God. Do you know John 3:16?"

"Yes. My grandmother taught me that verse. That thing had me quote it, too."

"Do you know John 3:17?"

"No."

"It says, *'For God sent not His Son into the world to condemn the world; but that the world through Him might be saved.'* Jesus, being the Son of God, was the only One who could make the sacrifice because He was perfect. He was sinless. You see, back then, in order to make up for sin, people had to make a blood sacrifice. It had to be a perfect animal, without spots or blemishes. In order for the world to make up for their sin, there had to be bloodshed. It could only come from a perfect human. With Jesus being the Son of God in human form, He was the only one who was perfect and without sin."

"Did He do it willingly?"

"Yes."

"Why?"

"Because He loves us. He loves you."

"He doesn't know me."

"I'm probably doing this wrong."

"Just do your best. I need answers. That creature sent me back and told me not to waste time. I don't want to waste this chance. I *really* don't want to go back there again."

"I'm sure! Here, let me try it this way. I'm a firefighter, right?"

"Right."

"If there's a fire, and someone didn't or couldn't get out, it's my job to go in after them."

"Right."

"I don't have to do it. I choose to do it. Jesus chose to come to Earth. He did it, knowing He was going to have to die a gruesome death. He did it willingly and did it for the entire human race. Do I know every person I go in to save?"

"No."

"Well, with Him being God's Son, He does and did. If it were you, a friend of mine, or my family, don't think for a moment I wouldn't risk life and limb to get you out of the fire. Jesus did just that to save everyone from the literal fires of Hell. What you saw was just a glimpse. Imagine being there for all eternity."

"I did see another area off in the distance. It was an area where there was a bright light. There was a feeling of peace coming from there."

"That was probably Heaven," Nate said. "Was there singing?"

"I don't know. It was too loud with people yelling and screaming in agony where I was." She shuddered again. Looking up at him, she asked, "How do I get to that other place. Heaven?"

"In Romans 10:9 and 10, here," he talked as he looked it up on his phone, "I don't want to misquote it. It's right here. It says, *'If you declare with your mouth, "Jesus is Lord," and believe in your heart that God raised Him from the dead, you will be saved. For it is with your heart that you believe and are justified, and it is with your mouth that you profess your faith and are saved.'* Let me explain a few words. If you understand them, just let me know." He smiled. "I don't want to be accused of mansplaining something."

She smiled in response. "Go ahead. This is all new to me. Like, for example, the word 'justified.' Pretty sure I have an idea of what it means, but how does it pertain to what we're talking about here?"

"Basically, it means to be made right. By Jesus's sacrifice, we are made right in the eyes of God. You see, when Jesus died on the cross, He paid the penalty for every sin. It was so bad that God even turned His back on Jesus for a bit."

"Oh no!"

"It's true. He died on that day. We recognize it today in remembrance as Good Friday."

She furrowed her brow. "Why do we call it Good Friday if it's to remember someone dying? That doesn't make sense."

"That's because we know what's coming."

"What?"

"On that day, Good Friday, He died on the cross. He took the sin of the world and paid it with His own blood. In doing so, He made us right with God. Now, yes, He did die. They buried Him in a tomb. They placed a massive boulder in front and had guards around it to make sure no one stole His body. He was in there on Saturday. Then, on that Sunday, the women went to put herbs, oils, and spices on the body. Back then, that was what they used to help with the smell. When they got there, the guards were passed out, the stone was rolled away, and there was a literal angel sitting there. The angel told them not to be afraid because He had risen from the dead."

"How did people know it wasn't a hoax?"

"It would have been a pretty elaborate hoax. But, to answer your question, over five hundred people saw him in the days following."

"Wow!" She rubbed her chin in thought. "So, was He really dead, then?"

"Oh yes! When they arrested Him, they beat Him with a cat o' nine tails down to the bone. When they hung Him on the cross, they nailed his hands and feet. When He didn't die fast enough for them, they jammed a spear into His side. He was dead. That was confirmed. However, God wasn't done with Him yet. He raised Jesus from the dead. That is still His Son, after all."

"I see. So, according to that verse, I just have to believe what you told me?"

"That, and pray to Him to accept His sacrifice. Once that happens, you have a responsibility to tell others so they don't experience what you did in that nightmare."

"What do you mean to *accept His sacrifice*? What does that mean?"

"Let me see if I can explain it this way. Say, you are in jail for some crime. There is a lawyer who comes in. He says he won't charge, but you have to accept him as your lawyer."

"Free of charge?"

"Yes. All you have to do is say yes."

"Okay. So, I say yes. Then what happens?"

"He goes to the judge and says he will take the penalty for the crime."

"But he didn't do anything!" Robin objected.

"Doesn't matter. He's willing to take the penalty. All you had to do was say yes, and he took it from there. You are free."

"Okay."

"All he asks is that you tell others about him. That's what Jesus did. He's just waiting for you to say yes, so He can step up and take care of things."

"I see. You looked up those verses on your phone. Can I look up the things you said on mine?"

"Of course! There are many Bible apps, or you can literally just look it all up."

"Okay. Let me do some research."

"Go for it! In the meantime, I would be remiss if I didn't ask if you wanted to come to church with me. Not this Sunday, but the next one? I have to work this Sunday."

"I think I can do that," she agreed. "That will give me time to check this out."

"If you want to talk sooner, feel free to ask questions as you go."

"I appreciate that."

With that, they enjoyed the rest of their breakfast before he took her home. Since she had to work at ten to set up for the day, they agreed to meet for dinner that night.

After work, she rushed home and took a shower. Excited to go out with Nate, she worked as quickly as she could. When she was almost ready, her phone went off. "Hello?" she answered.

"Robin, I'm sorry. I can't make it tonight. Dad needs me to work with him at the warehouses. With there already being two warehouse fires in the same area, he doesn't want to miss anything. And, since I go back to work tomorrow, he wants to do it tonight. We would have done it during the day, but I needed to sleep a bit."

"I understand. I hate it, but hopefully you can get this sorted before someone gets hurt."

"Thank you for your understanding."

"Anytime."

"Can I call after we're done?"

"Of course!"

"Great! Talk to you then."

"Okay. Enjoy!"

With that, they hung up.

"All dressed up and nowhere to go." She sighed. "What's a girl to do?"

She grabbed her laptop and lay down on the couch. Doing research on her computer helped pass the time, as well as answer a lot of her questions from her conversation with Nate earlier.

Around nine, she and Nate chatted on the phone. When they hung up a couple hours later, she was tired but antsy. So, she made the conscious choice to go paint again.

She changed into all black before leaving the house with her gym bag.

She hurried through town, making sure not to be seen by anyone. Once she reached the warehouse district, she ducked further into the woods.

That's when it hit her. She had seen this before. The lighting was the same. The shadows were the same. Even the smells were the same. *Was she losing it, or did she originally have a premonition?*

When she stepped into the warehouse, she was taken aback. It was the same warehouse from her nightmare! The same boxes and old machines were there. The smell of old paper and oil mixed with dirt and musty, moldy scent.

She looked around to make sure she was alone. When she was convinced, she headed up the stairs to the office.

After about an hour of painting, she was finished. She pulled out the lighter and a spray can and then lit up the mural. The colors immediately blended, creating a stunningly beautiful and hypnotic mural.

As the colors danced, she was entranced. She watched them almost roll up the wall, changing from white to blue, to orange, then red, and finally yellow. Despite the acrid odor of the wiring, insulation, wood, and other electrical components in the wall catching fire, she still stood there, almost swaying.

That's when she heard it. Something fell out in the warehouse.

She threw all of her stuff together. Before she could grab her bag, she was hit in the side and landed against the wall.

"I-I don't –" was all she could get out. She struggled to get air back into her lungs, but it was difficult.

"I knew it was you!" he hissed. "I saw you light that other one on fire! You have always had a fascination with fire. It was only a matter of time."

When she opened her eyes, she was staring face-to-face with her ex-boyfriend Liam, from high school. He was considerably older, but it was definitely him!

Things started to line up in her mind. The man from the restaurant – it was him! She would place a bet and probably win that Liam was the one who was stalking her!

"What do you want from me?" she demanded.

He sneered as he leaned in closer to her face.

"No!" she shouted. Jamming her knee into his groin, he rolled over, grabbing himself in pain and agony. She wiggled out from under him. Leaving her bag, she ran out of the room with him yelling profanities at her.

When she was just about to the stairs, Liam lunged toward her, knocking both of them down the staircase, with him on top of her. After the fourth hit of her head on the wood, she surrendered to the black cloud that overtook her.

Liam took a moment to shake off the dizziness. Hearing a loud rumble, he looked toward the top of the stairs to see the office fully engulfed.

"Robin?" he asked. That's when he saw it. There was blood coming out from under her head. "Robin?" He swore again. He got up and ran out of the warehouse, making a beeline for the woods.

Just as he made the edge of the woods, he heard the fire trucks in the distance. By the look of the building, he wasn't sure if they would make it to Robin in time...if she was even still alive. He chose not to stick around to find out.

"Get those hoses hooked up!" the lieutenant shouted. "We need to get this place cleared so we can keep the rest of the buildings from catching fire! Move it!"

The firefighters scrambled from the apparatus and jumped to their job with intense focus despite the late hour. Adrenaline and training kicked in as they moved like a well-oiled machine. Some hooked the hoses, others grabbed tools, while another got the engine ready, all while the lieutenant shouted orders.

Once the hoses were hooked up and the lines were charged, eight firefighters split between two main hose lines and breached the entrance. What they ran into was a flaming inferno. There were few areas not touched by the fire in one way or another.

"The ceiling is going," one warned.

"What's that over there?" another asked.

"Where?"

"At the bottom of the stairs. Look!"

That group turned their hose toward the bottom of the stairs.

"It's a body! Can you guys turn your hose over here, too?" one of the guys asked. "Balfour and Salazar, go get the body and get out of here. We got this!"

"Yes, sir," two of the firefighters said in unison.

When they reached Robin, one of the guys cocked his head to the side. "Isn't this Mitchell's girl? I think I saw her this morning at the station."

"Doesn't matter. Let's get her out of here."

After a quick check to make sure neither her neck nor back was broken, one of the firemen placed his air mask on her, and then the other lifted her over his shoulder. The pair were followed by the shower from the hose as they ran to the entrance.

"Medic!" shouted the one who wasn't carrying Robin. "Need help!"

"Coming!" said another paramedic as he and his partner ran over with a medical bag.

"Let's get her to the rig," the female paramedic said. "We can work better there."

"Isn't that –"

"That's what I said," the one firefighter said, cutting off the male paramedic. "It's Mitchell's girl, right?"

"Right. Better give him a call," he said, as they loaded her into the ambulance.

"Hello?" a groggy Nate answered the phone.

"Nate?"

"Yeah. Who's this?"

"It's Baker from the station."

"What time is it?" Nate mumbled.

"It's 12:45. We're en route to the hospital with Robin. She was found unconscious in a warehouse fire. Salazar and Balfour pulled her out."

Nate sat upright in the bed, eyes wide. "I'm sorry. Can you please repeat that?"

"It's Baker. I'm driving the ambulance to Mercy. We found Robin unconscious in a warehouse fire tonight. She's hurt pretty bad."

"Um." He ran his hands through his hair. "Yeah. Thanks. I'm on my way."

"Okay. See you there," he said and hung up.

Nate jumped out of bed and got dressed. He snagged his keys out of the basket before running for his truck.

Once inside, he started the truck and took off out of the driveway. Turning onto the road, he dialed his dad's phone number. "What's going on, Nate?" Ian mumbled. "Is it an emergency?"

"You know I wouldn't call this late if it wasn't. Baker and Nelson are on the ambulance tonight, and they're on the way to Mercy with Robin. They found her unconscious in another warehouse fire tonight."

"Whoa! Okay. I heard the warehouse call. I had my alarm set to get up in about an hour to go to the scene. I'll get up now and grab Mom."

"What's going on?" Nate's mom asked.

"Robin's on the way to the hospital," Ian explained. "Nate said they found her in the warehouse fire that's going on right now."

"Seriously? What's she doing there?"

"Not sure. You coming?"

"Yes," she said, getting out of bed.

"We're on our way," Ian told Nate on the phone.

"Thank you," Nate said, relieved. "She doesn't have any family."

"We know. We're on our way."

"Thanks, Dad," Nate said and hung up.

CHAPTER 11

WHAT YOU LOSE IN THE FIRE,
YOU WILL FIND IN THE ASHES

Hearing the beeping of the monitor, she struggled to open her eyes. The heavy bleach and antiseptic scent were overpowering. She groaned, shaking her head side-to-side to shake herself awake.

"Robin?" she heard. The voice sounded hollow like it was coming from a deep hole. "Robin?"

She finally got her eyes opened and looked up to see a handsome man above her. He looked like he had some stubble growth where she was sure he could grow a full beard. He had stunningly piercing blue eyes, slightly shaggy black hair and a strong jawline.

"Robin? Are you in there?" he asked.

"Who?" She slightly shook her head. "Who is Robin?"

He frowned. Blowing out a frustrated breath of air, he said. "Just a second. Get your bearings while I go get the nurse."

"Nurse?" she asked.

"I...just a second," he said and left the room.

She looked around. It was a one-person hospital room. The IV pole automatically dispersed the chilly IV into her arm. The automatic blood pressure cuff was on her opposite arm, and the pulse oximeter that fed the information to the monitor was on the same arm as the IV.

That's when it hit her. The splitting head pain was almost too much to bear. She groaned as she reached up, grabbing both sides of her head. "Oh. Make it stop," she said with a moan.

"Miss Flynn?" the nurse asked, coming in with the handsome guy right on her heels. "Robin?"

"Who is –?" She stopped and groaned again. "Pulsating pain. Please make it stop."

"I can, but I have to check you out first. This is the first time in four days you've been awake."

"What?" she asked.

"You are Robin," the guy said. "Your name is Robin Flynn."

"No. It's not," she said, shaking her head. "Oh! I feel like I'm going to throw up."

The nurse yanked the drawer in the stand next to the bed open and pulled out a vomit bag. "If you do, throw up in here."

She opened it and put it to her mouth just in time. After throwing up five times, she lay back on her pillow. Her head hurt worse than she ever imagined. "The pain is going to make me throw up again."

"Not sure what you're throwing up. You don't have anything in your system, honey," the nurse said, turning on the blood pressure cuff to get a reading.

She handed the cute guy the bag, who promptly disposed of it in the hazardous materials trash can.

The nurse handed her another bag. When she raised an eyebrow, the nurse shrugged and said, "Just in case."

"You'll make the pain stop, though, right?" Robin asked.

"Not yet. I need to know what you know."

"What does that mean?" she asked.

The nurse took the chart off the footboard and wrote in it. As she wrote, she asked, "What's your name?"

"It's –" She stopped short. "I-I don't...I don't know." Her heart rate raced as panic set in. "I don't know. What's my name? Where am I? What happened?"

"Sweety, please calm down," the nurse said, sitting on the side of the bed.

"I don't know who I am! I can only guess that I'm in a hospital by what's around me. Otherwise, I don't know. I don't know who I am, where I am, or what's going on. And you're telling me to calm down?"

"If you don't, I'll have to give you a sedative, and I don't want to. You've been awake for less than ten minutes after being unconscious for four days. While it made my shift easier, I would really like to know what you *do* know, and we need him here to verify."

"Verify what? Who is he?" she asked. His face dropped as the color paled. "Whoa!" she said, wide-eyed. "Does *he* need a doctor?"

"Nate, please sit down in that chair," the nurse asked, continuing to speak in a smooth, serene tone. She then turned to the girl and explained, "Sweetheart, Nate is your boyfriend. I need him here to verify what you say so we know what's accurate."

"I-okay," she said, hoping to calm the cute guy down. "Your name is Nate?" she asked him.

Eyes wide, he slowly nodded his head.

"And you're my boyfriend?"

He nodded again, actually losing more color than he had previously lost.

"Hey, all!" Another guy walked into the room. "Oh! She's awake! Oh! Thank God! Robin, you had us scared to death!" He walked past Nate and gave her a hug. Robin froze. He looked down at her, cocked his head to the side, and asked, "What's wrong?"

"She doesn't know who she is," the nurse explained. "She doesn't know *where* she is either."

"I see," he said, studying her with his chocolate-brown eyes. Brushing his light brown hair out of his face, he asked, "Does she know Nate?"

"No," Nate said, visibly downcast.

He looked at her and asked, "Do you know who I am?"

With a blank look on her face, she shook her head.

"Well, I'm your BFF, Kent. Don't you worry, girl. I got you. We'll figure this out," he said, patting her leg.

She looked from his face to his hand and back again. Then, she looked at the cute guy, who looked like he got punched in the stomach. "I'm sorry."

"Oh, girl, it's okay. I'm sure it'll all come back to you –"

The nurse cleared her throat, cutting off Kent. "I'll go have a chat with the doctor about this. Can I leave these two with you?"

She looked at the two guys and then back to the nurse. "I-I don't know anyone. I don't know what to do."

"Well, why don't I take Kent with me? That way you can chat with Nate?" she suggested.

She nodded. So, Kent followed the nurse into the hall. They went straight to the nurse's station.

"I'm sorry," Robin said to Nate.

"I wish I could help you. I really wish you could tell me what happened in that fire."

"What do you mean?" she asked. "What fire?"

He gently picked up the end of the blanket to reveal her legs wrapped in gauze. "You have third-degree burns on your legs."

"Oh. Why don't I feel them?"

"They have a lidocaine cream on them. Also, with third-degree burns, the nerve endings are burnt. Thankfully, you've been out these first few days, or this would be a different story. That gave them time to clean these really good without you screaming in pain."

Robin's eyes bulged.

"No. No. I mean...oh! I'm so sorry! I forgot you don't know much. I-I'm sorry," Nate stammered.

"It-it's okay."

"Let me try this again. While you were out, they deep-cleaned the wounds for the first few days. With you being unconscious, it allowed them to do what they needed to do. Your legs are healing well. There should be minimal scarring."

"Okay."

"Do you mind?" he asked, gesturing toward the side of her bed.

"Go for it."

He sat on the side of her bed and explained, "There's a lot to clear up for you. Where do you want to start?"

"Where are my parents?"

"Starting with the big one first, eh?"

"Where are they?"

"Well, um," he cleared his throat, "they're gone."

"Gone? Gone where?"

"They died when you were eight...in a house fire."

"Oh!"

"Your little brother died with them. After that, you lived with your dad's parents. They died in a car accident a week or so ago."

"Oh. Um, okay." The tone of her heart rate sped up as her breaths became short.

"Breathe slowly. It's okay."

"Do I-do I have *any* family?"

"Not in America."

"What do you mean by that?"

"Your mom's family lives in Mexico."

"So, no other family?"

"No, but you have some very good friends. You have me and Kent."

"You and Kent?"

"Kent is the guy at the nurse's station. He's sweet. He's a good guy. He's like a brother to you."

She nodded.

"You and I have been going out for about a week or so. We actually knew each other in high school. However, we lost touch after I graduated until we reconnected about a week or so ago. In the meantime, you are an incredible artist. You are also a welder. And you do amazing metal artwork."

"That's a lot."

"It is. You used to work on the oil rigs as a welder. That's where a lot of your savings came from."

"Okay. Do I work now?"

"Yes. You are a waitress at Rousseau's. It's a local restaurant. You work with Kent."

"I see."

"Wow." He took a deep breath. "You're going to have to start over. Oh! One more thing. There seems to be some cretin who is obsessed with you."

"What does that mean?"

"He's been stalking you. You spent the night at the firehouse a couple nights ago because he was supposed to come to your house."

"Why?"

"No idea. I guess because he doesn't like that we got together."

"That seems –"

"Wild. I know."

"A lot."

"It is. Just know I'll be with you until we figure this out."

"Thank you. It's kind of weird for me."

"My parents will be coming by later. Dad was actually at the fire where you lost your family. He's a fire marshal."

"Okay. I'm not really sure where to go from here."

"When you get out, we'll give you a few days, and then we'll go see where they found you."

"Why?"

"To see if it'll trigger any memories."

"Okay," she said quietly.

"Look, we'll take it one step at a time. Don't worry. I'll be with you as little or as much as you want."

"Thank you. I'm sorry. I wish I could remember. I feel something toward you, but I don't really know you. It's weird."

"I'm sure it *is* weird. We'll figure it out."

"Thank you."

"Okay. You seem a little more relaxed," the nurse said, coming back into the room with Kent. "I'm going to let you stay non-sedated. I'm also going to change this morphine drip to you pushing the button as needed. Know the soonest in between is twenty minutes. Try not to get behind. It will make the pain worse."

"Okay," she said and pressed the button.

"Do you remember anything else?"

"No. I only know what Nate told me."

"If you remember anything, write it down in this notebook," she said, setting the notebook and a pen on the table beside her.

"I will."

"Can you write your name on it?" Nate asked, handing the pen and paper to her.

"How will I if I don't know –"

"Please just try? Don't underestimate muscle memory."

She took the pen and paper. Positioning the pen in her hand, she put it to the paper. She shook her head. "I don't –"

"Give it a try, Robin."

She shakily wrote: *R-o-b-i-n*, and then stopped briefly before she wrote, *F-l-y-n-n*.

"Good job!" Nate said with a smile.

His dimples stood out on his handsome face. She couldn't help but smile. As she sat there, a wave washed over her. "Oh, um."

"What's wrong?" Kent asked.

"Morphine," the nurse said as she finished writing in Robin's chart.

"Let's go to the cafeteria," Nate suggested to Kent. "She's about to conk out on us."

Robin lay further down on her pillow.

"Get some sleep," Nate said, standing. "Maybe it will look better after a nap."

Her eyes felt heavy as the guys and the nurse left her room.

While she slept, in her dream, she was walking through the forest. It was dark as the moon cast shadows with the trees onto the ground around her. The heady wooded scents blended with the pine and earthy scents as she inhaled.

She rested her hand on a tree while she looked around. To her, things were moving all around her. An owl hooted as it sat on its perch high up in the tree. A squirrel scurried up to its spot on a higher branch, chittering as it went.

In the distance, a structure sat bathing in the moonlight. Her heart raced when she wandered closer. The windows glowed orange and red. The overpowering scent of burning wood mixed with chemicals while fire wafted from the building in waves.

When she opened the door, a whoosh of hot air almost blew her over. What she walked into was not what she expected. There was a massive lake of fire with an endless beach around it. There were caves to the left that contained catacombs. The smell of sulfur, burnt flesh and hair, and death suffocated her. The screaming, wailing, and yelling were almost deafening.

"You are back," a creature hissed, suddenly in front of her. Its reddish-black wings fanned out behind it. Its yellow eyes studied her for a moment. "You do not remember me."

She shook her head, unable to form any words. She was frozen in place, unable to breathe as she trembled in fear.

It leaned in closer. "What happened to you?"

"I-I don't –" She shook her head.

"Oh! Preciousssss. Thissss is rich."

She stared at him, dumbstruck.

"You do not remember coming here." It threw its head back in laughter. "Oh, precioussss! Do you like it here?"

She vigorously shook her head.

"Then," it said in a low voice, "you need to talk to your friend. He can sssstop you from coming back. Are you paying attention?" It used its talon to lift her chin so she was looking right at it.

Eyes wide, she nodded.

"Do *not* come back here. Sssspeak to Nate. If you come back, I will not be able to help you."

"W-why are y-you helping n-now?"

It leaned in so it was within inches of her face and said, "No one should come here. I made my choice a long time ago. Thissss issss your only chance. Do you hear me?"

She nodded again.

"Good. Close your eyessss like a good girl," it instructed.

She closed her eyes and took a deep breath. When she opened them again, she was in the hospital room. Her heart monitor was racing. She couldn't speak. She could barely form a thought.

Robin looked toward the monitor. There was a man standing there. He seemed familiar. Her heart raced faster as she froze, unable to breathe.

He leaned down closer to her face. Tilting his head, he asked, "Do you know who I am?"

She just stared at him. Her mouth opened to form words, but none came.

"You don't, do you? They said you lost your memory." He brushed his fingers on her cheek.

Color drained from her face as she did her best to memorize the man's face.

"Oh, sweetheart. One day you will remember. Until then, I will dream of us," he said and then kissed her cheek before he left the room.

She gulped. *Was that real or still a part of the nightmare? Who was he? What did he mean about one day remembering?* The hair on her arms stood on end. She shuddered.

She reached over to the call button. Unsure if she pressed it if he would come back, she moved her hand away from the button. Looking toward the ceiling, she struggled to focus.

Seeing the cell phone on the table, she picked it up. She pressed the contacts list. *Nate. The creature said to talk to Nate.* She pressed Nate's number.

"Robin? Are you okay?" a sleepy Nate answered the phone.

"I-no. A-a t-terrible nightmare."

"I'm at work. They won't let me in because it's not visiting hours. I can go there after I get off work at seven in the morning."

"Please? It said to talk to you?"

"What? Who?"

"Th-the c-creature."

"Can you tell me what it looked like?" he asked quietly as he got out of his bed and left the bunk room for the hallway.

"It was black, with a bit of red in color. It was, um, c-covered in scales and had creepy yellow eyes. They were soft, though. It was trying to save me from going back. It said not to come back again, or it-it wouldn't be able to help me."

"Got it. Sounds like a dream you had a few days ago."

"It said I was there before."

"Where did you go?"

"It was some old warehouse, but inside, it was a completely different place. There was a huge lake. Fire danced along the top of it. People were screaming and yelling in pain and agony. It was..." She shuddered. "I-I don't want to go back."

"You don't have to," he said. He took the time to explain everything he did the other day. About an hour later, he finished with, "I told this all to you a few days ago, but you said you wanted to do more research."

"I'll have to take your word for it. I-I don't know what to do." She then lowered her voice as she looked toward the hall, "There was some guy here when I woke up. He scared me, too."

Nate stood up straight. "What do you mean by that? What guy?"

"I-I don't know who he was, but he looked familiar. He

touched the side of my face and told me that he would dream of us until I remembered him."

"Robin," he said cautiously, "when did he leave?"

"Just before I called you."

"Why didn't you start with that?" He ran his hands through his hair and then sprinted down the hall, over to the police station side of the building.

"What's going on?" she asked.

"Just a second. I'm going to put you on mute. Do not hang up. Okay?"

"I won't."

"Good. Just a minute," he said, and then put his phone on mute as he ran up to the dispatch desk. "Who's on tonight?"

"Here." The dispatcher handed him a list of names.

"Can you call Simms? Robin had a guy in her room when she woke up tonight."

"You don't think...do you think it was *him*?" she asked.

"Wouldn't surprise me."

"I would imagine only a situation like this would bring you running to this side of the station looking like that," she pointed out as she picked up her phone and dialed Detective Simms's phone number.

Nate's face flushed as he looked at his t-shirt and shorts. "Sorry."

"Oh! No apologies are needed. Made *my* night," she said with a smirk. Then she looked down as she answered the phone, "Detective Simms, this is Melody in dispatch. Nate's here. There was a guy in Robin's room when she woke a little bit ago." She nodded to his response and then handed the phone to Nate.

"Hello?" Nate answered.

"Nate? Is she okay?" Simms asked.

"She's creeped out. I'm on shift, so I can't leave."

"My badge will get me in. I'm on my way. Can you talk to her on the phone until I get there?"

"Yes."

"Good. Tell her I'm on the way."

"Thank you," Nate said and then handed the phone back to Melody. "Thank you," he said to her before turning back to his phone. Taking it off mute, he said, "Robin? Are you still there?"

"Yes."

"Detective Simms is on the way. Make him show you his badge and ID when he gets there. We can talk until he arrives."

"Thank you," she said, relieved.

They talked as he made his way back to his side of the station. He sat in the common area and talked to her until Detective Simms walked into her room.

CHAPTER 12

OUT OF THE FRYING PAN INTO THE FIRE

An older man, who looked to be a little taller than six-foot, walked in. His silver hair was cut short, which made his green eyes stand out on his kind face. He was carrying a little weight around his middle but looked like he could hold his own in a fight.

"Hello, Ms. Flynn, I'm Detective Simms," he said, coming into the room. He showed her his badge.

"Nate, Detective Simms is here," she said into the phone.

"Are you sure it's him?" Nate asked.

"Yes. He showed me the badge and ID," Robin explained.

"Okay. You can trust him. I will be there right after I get off work in the morning. Sleep well," Nate said and hung up. He couldn't go to sleep even though he wanted to. He paced the common room as he prayed for Robin's safety. He would have the next forty-eight hours off, and he would use his pull to stay with Robin until he couldn't anymore. Whoever this guy was found her in her room. Who's to say he wouldn't do it again?

obin hung up the phone. Setting it on the table beside her, she asked, "Did Nate tell you about the guy?"

"Yes. What can *you* tell me about him?"

"May I have that notebook and pen on the table?" she asked. It was slightly out of her reach.

He handed both to her. "Did you recognize him?" he asked as she opened the notebook and started drawing.

"I did, but I can't tell you where from. It seems that my memories are there but just slightly out of reach."

"Do you know your name now?"

"Yes. Only because they told me. However, when I wrote it down, I was able to write my whole name. Our best guess is muscle memory."

"Is that it, or are you faking?"

Her head snapped up toward him. "Excuse me?"

"Well, you were found in a burning warehouse. It wouldn't be a stretch to say that you started it. Who knows? You may have started the others. Whoever broke into your house and set that lovely scene up had your code. Who's to say you aren't doing this for attention?"

Robin narrowed her eyes. "How *dare* you!"

He put his hands up in surrender. "Okay. Okay. I was just doing my job. If I didn't ask, I would be doing a disservice to the community."

"Get out," Robin said in a low, menacing voice.

"It's fine. It's all good. I had to ask."

"No. You didn't. Leave now."

"Now, Robin, I'm your friend in this. I'm just doing my job in making sure you aren't faking all of this," he said, waving his hand through the air.

"Leave now, or I'm calling the nurse."

"What is she going to do? I'm a police officer...detective, actually. She can't kick me out."

"You are wrong about that," the nurse said, coming in. "Her

heart rate has been elevated for a little bit, mostly since you came in. A few moments ago it shot up. You need to leave. When it comes to medical, we overrule police."

"I don't think so," he said, producing his badge.

"It is past visiting hours. You are obviously upsetting her. You need to leave," the nurse insisted.

"I'm not going anywhere until I talk to Ms. Flynn."

The nurse picked up her phone and called security. When she hung up, she informed him, "You have until security comes up here. At which point, they will remove you from the property."

"They can try," he said with a shrug. "Real cop outweighs rent-a-cop."

The nurse picked up her phone and dialed another number. She explained what was going on to the person on the other end of the phone. Then she held it out to the detective and said, "It's for you."

"Who is it?"

"Your chief. He's my brother," she said, handing him the phone. "Pretty sure Chief outweighs cop."

"Well played," he said, accepting the phone.

When he went into the hallway to talk to his chief, the nurse asked, "Are you okay?"

"No. He accused me of orchestrating this whole thing. He said I was the one who set the fires and who is making up all of the stalker stuff for attention." As she talked, her bottom lip trembled. She fought the urge to cry. "First off, I have no idea what he's talking about. And secondly, to accuse me of that stuff is insulting at best."

"Reprehensible and shotty investigating at worst." She clicked her tongue. "Accusing the victim. Where did he learn his skills?"

He walked back in and handed the nurse the phone. "Adam says to say hi."

"That's *Chief* to you," she snapped. "He's Adam to *me*."

"Yes, Ms. Armstrong," he said and left, just as the security officer arrived.

"He's leaving. Thank you," the nurse said to the security officer. Turning back to Robin, she asked, "Are you okay?"

"I'm going to draw a bit before I try to get some more sleep."

"Sounds good," she said and left Robin's room.

As she drew, Robin debated in her head whether to call Nate again and tell him what happened. When she finished the drawing, she closed the notebook and laid it next to the phone on the table. Still on edge from her discussion with Detective Simms, she chose to watch television for the rest of the night.

The next morning, Nate came in after work. He brought a vase of flowers with him. "They're not roses, but –"

"They will more than do. Thank you!" she said, as he placed them on the tiny dresser next to her bed. "They smell heavenly."

He sat in the chair next to the bed. "So, got a call from Adam this morning, apologizing for Roger's behavior."

"The nurse said her brother's name was Adam."

"Right. He's the police chief."

"She said that, or he did. I can't remember. I didn't get back to sleep."

He reached over and took her hand into his. "May I?"

"Yes."

"Thank you. Look, what Roger said last night was uncalled for. I'm sorry."

"He thinks I'm making this all up. The stupid part is that I can't remember what he's talking about or asking me about? All I know is what you told me, and I can infer from what he said regarding what is going on."

"I mentioned there was a creepy stalker."

"According to Simms, it's all me. According to him, I set the fires, too."

"I highly doubt that. You have a tender heart. As for you faking the stalker – who does that? Besides, you were with me or Kent that night. There is no way you set all that up in your house."

"I'm going to have to trust you on that."

"This is weird. I know you better than you know yourself right now."

"Considering I don't know much, that's not saying much. Oh! Here," she said, grabbing the notebook. She flipped it open to the picture she drew earlier and handed it to Nate.

"Um, I know him. You drew this?"

"Yes. It's of the guy who was in my room last night when I woke up."

"Oh. Okay." He tore the page out of his notebook. "I'll get this to someone who will actually do something about it."

"I would appreciate that. They did an MRI and CT on me yesterday. I don't know what came of it."

"I'm sure the doctor will tell you when he comes in this morning."

"I don't know what to do here. I feel like I know you, but I don't have any memory of you."

"I know. It will come in time. We'll take this one day at a time. You have more than enough going on."

"I appreciate your patience. Thank you for walking through this with me. I feel helpless."

"Seriously, don't worry about anything. Adam posted an officer to watch your door last night. They'll be on shifts. There shouldn't be any more visitors you don't know."

"I appreciate that. It was honestly terrifying. I couldn't talk, move, or even breathe."

"I'm sure. Waking up to him after your nightmare could not have helped at all."

"It didn't."

"Do you want to walk with me to stretch your legs? The sooner we get you moving, the better off you will be."

"Sure," she said, sitting up.

Nate went over to her closet and opened it. "No robe. There is a pair of pants if you want to put them on to take a walk?"

"That'll work."

He brought the pants over to her. She slipped them on under her blankets before sitting up.

"Do I have to tell anyone I want a walk?"

"No. I'm with you. They know me in this hospital and know I won't put you in danger," Nate explained.

"I would appreciate that."

With that, they walked the halls until the doctor appeared on the floor.

"I think we should get back to your room before we miss your doctor," Nate suggested. "Catching him can be tricky."

"Good call, I –" Robin stopped, staring at the guy from the night before as he ducked into the stairwell.

"What's wrong? Are you tired? You're losing color."

"I-he...it was him."

"Who him?" Nate asked, looking around the floor.

"The guy...last night...stairs," she stammered.

"Sit in that chair. I'll go see if I can find him," Nate said as he ran toward the door for the stairs.

Robin sat down on the chair in the hallway. Her heart raced. She dropped her head into her hands.

"Can I help you get somewhere?" a male nurse asked.

"I just need to get back to my room," she said and then looked up to see the guy from the night before standing in front of her. "I-I...no. That's okay. I'll stay here."

"I can help you." He put his arm out. "Come on."

Robin furrowed her brow. "Do you remember me from yesterday?" she asked.

"I was off yesterday," he explained.

Robin looked at his nametag. It said, *Logan Rogers.* "No. I saw you last night. You weren't in scrubs, though."

"It wasn't me. I was at a concert in Dallas last night. Made for a long day today, but totally worth it."

"I feel like I'm going crazy."

"You're really pale. Can I get you back to your room, please?"

"I can't find –" Nate stopped short as he stared at the nurse.

"Hi." Logan put his hand out to shake Nate's. "I'm a nurse on this floor."

Nate cocked his head to the side. "Liam?"

"No. I'm Logan. I have a brother named Liam. He's several years older than me."

"You're Liam's brother?" Nate asked, shaking his hand.

"Yes. Why?" Logan crossed his arms. "What's he done now?"

"You look *a lot* like him," Nate said.

"Yeah. That's gotten me in trouble a time or two."

"Where is he now?" Nate asked. "Does he live around here?"

"Not really sure. Haven't heard from him in at least a year. Last I knew, he was in Georgia, not Texas."

"Do you have his cell phone number?"

"Yeah. Why?"

"Detective Simms may want to talk to you."

Robin growled at hearing his name.

"Don't worry. You don't need to talk to that man unless you want to," Nate said to Robin.

"Here is Liam's cell number," Logan said, writing it down on a piece of paper. "Not a fan of Detective Simms either. He's not the nicest of the officers I've met."

"Agreed," Nate said, tucking the paper Logan handed him into his front pocket.

"I would rather not talk to him. However, I *would* like to get this one back to her room. She's looking a little too pale for my comfort. I'll let Ariel know once she's settled."

"Thank you," Robin said, slowly standing. "How long do I

have to be here?" she asked as they made their way toward her room.

"That depends on your doctor," Logan said. "If I remember the board correctly, your doc is Dr. Fitzpatrick. He's a good doctor. We'll go with what he says."

After getting her settled, Logan went to find the doctor.

"Wild," Nate said, watching him leave.

"For sure. Are you going to verify that?"

"Definitely."

The doctor said they would keep her another day for observation, but the swelling was going down in her head to his satisfaction. He said her memory may return soon. If she still felt good enough the next morning, she would be able to be released.

With the appearance of Liam twice in the last twenty-four hours, the doctor gave Nate permission to stay the night in the room. The police officer standing outside the room was also put on high alert.

"I need to go get something to eat. Are you good while I'm gone?" Nate asked later that night.

"Yes. I can't get into too much trouble with a cop right outside my door, right?"

"I would think that's accurate. However, I'm not really sure. We'll have to see afterward. Do you want me to bring something back for you?"

"Sure. I know you know more about me than I know about myself, so I will leave it up to you as to what to bring back."

"Sounds good," he said and left the room.

About twenty minutes later, Logan came in, pushing a wheelchair. "Doctor wants another MRI."

"Okay," Robin said, getting out of bed. When she stood, he jammed a needle into her neck and emptied the syringe. "What is –"

"My brother has been off shift for about an hour," he whispered into her ear as she sunk into the wheelchair. "I have been waiting for *him* to leave. Now, it's our time."

She could not control the wave of nausea and blackness that overtook her as she slumped into the chair and closed her eyes.

He took the blanket off the bed and wrapped it over her legs before draping it onto her shoulders. "Don't want you to catch a chill."

When he got to the door, the police officer stopped him. "Where are you taking her?"

"I'm Nurse Logan. Dr. Fitzpatrick has requested another MRI for her. That way, he can figure out if she can go home tomorrow morning."

"All right. See you in a few. She's looking pretty tired."

"I know. I hate to wake her, but doctor's orders," he said, and then headed for the elevator. He stopped at the room nearest the elevators, out of the view of the police officer. It was an empty room.

"Here we go," he said, picking her up and setting her in the bed. "Let's get you covered with some oxygen. That way, no one will ask questions." He placed the mask on her face. Then, he reached down and turned on the oxygen tank. "That should help."

He then unlocked the bed and moved it toward the door. He quickly shut the door, though, as the elevator doors opened.

Seeing Nate get off the elevator, he moved just out of sight until Nate turned the corner.

Liam then threw the door open and hit the elevator for the floor. Afterward, he ran back and grabbed the bed with Robin asleep in it and pushed the bed toward the doors just as they opened for their floor.

"Here," a doctor said, getting off the elevator. He reached behind him and held the door open until Liam was in with Robin in her bed.

When the doors shut, Liam hit the button for the garage floor. "Hopefully, I can get you out of here before alarms sound," he mumbled while the elevator began its descent.

Once on the bottom floor, he tied the surgical mask around his face. Then, he pushed Robin out, bed and all. He shoved the bed against the wall before picking up Robin off the bed, wrapped in her blanket.

Hitting the button on his key fob, the side door of the van opened. Liam gently rested her on the floor of the van and then closed the door. He ran around to the driver's side and got into the van.

He glanced down at Robin and saw her still asleep. He then ripped the mask off, as well as his scrub shirt. He put on his T-shirt, and then quickly changed his pants before driving out of the garage.

Turning right onto the street, he saw several people looking around anxiously. Driving away from the hospital, he happily whistled a tune.

CHAPTER 13

FIGHT FIRE WITH FIRE

Robin woke the next morning to find her hands tied to the headboard above her. "Oh. This looks like fun."

"Robin. You're awake."

"And you are not Logan," Robin said, getting a better look at him. "You look like an older version of him."

"Do you not remember Logan?"

"I don't remember anything...including Logan or Liam...or whoever you are."

"I'm Liam, and I'm hurt. Did you remember *Nate*?" he asked snidely, as he crossed his arms.

"No. I don't remember anything. That's why I was in the hospital. I should go back."

"According to your medical record, you were getting released this morning anyway. I just sprung you a little early. I would think a word of thanks would be appropriate."

"Where am I?" she asked, looking around the windowless room. "Seriously. Where is this place?"

"Oh. This is somewhere no one will ever look. Don't worry. You're safe here," he said, bringing a tray of food over. "I prepared you something to eat. You used to love these."

Robin glanced up at the tray as her stomach growled. "What is that?"

"Your favorite: toasted cheese sandwich, macaroni and cheese, and warm apple pie with vanilla ice cream."

"That actually sounds good, but –"

"No buts. Here. I'll help you eat."

Feeling her stomach growl again, she let him feed her. "That's actually pretty good."

"I know. I made it. You love this type of comfort food."

"How do you know?" she asked after she finished her bite.

"Because I *know* you. We dated for years in school. You were my world."

"I don't understand."

"Open up," he said and then fed her another bite of macaroni and cheese. "There you go. Now, enjoy your meal while I tell you a story."

She nodded as she finished her bite.

"As I said, you were my world. You lit up my life. I knew everything about you. You supported me in all of my sports, and I encouraged you and loved to support you in your art. You were... are...an incredible artist. You took that talent and transformed it into a career as a welder. Oh," he sighed, looking up in remembrance, "I *loved* watching you build with welding." He gave her another bite of food. "What you do with metal is phenomenal! It's unmatched! I actually bought quite a few pieces of your artwork. I could bring them here to show you if you'd like. Or... wait! Here," he pulled out his cell phone. He showed her the lock screen. "See? This was us when we were younger."

He opened his phone and scrolled through his pictures. "Here's one." He showed her. He gave her another bite of food and said, "There's another one I want to show you." He scrolled a little more. "This one is my favorite. I love how you used the color of the metal to create the different shading on this piece. Incredible."

"Thank you?" she said as a question.

"You are seriously good! Here's the thing, though. While I wanted you to notice me, I didn't." He dropped his head. "I know you cheated on me, which hurt more than you will ever know. You chose *him* over me. That hurt a lot. I didn't want to face that rejection again. You broke my heart. I tried to get you to see reason. I was willing to still take you back afterward, but you wanted to stay with him. I wish you could see things from my perspective. I feel you would understand more if you did. I have so much love for you."

"I don't know you. I don't know anything about you. I'm also not sure who *him* is either."

"*Nate*," Liam said with disdain. He took a deep breath and slowly let it out. "You chose Nate over me. He doesn't love you. He just likes how you look."

"I know you said Nate, but how do you know how he feels?"

"Locker-room talk." He shrugged. "We went to the same high school and were both in sports. What was said in the locker room, to me, holds more water than what they said to the girls they liked." He put the last spoonful of macaroni and cheese into her mouth. "Once you finish that, we can dive into the apple pie and ice cream. I remember it's your second favorite, but I couldn't find the chocolate éclair cake."

"What can you tell me about me?" she asked.

"You are tenderhearted. You love art. You are fascinated with fire, which is why welding was such a great option for you. You have a creative heart. What you do, ordinary people only dream about." He looked down for a moment and then said, "Your family died in a fire when you were young. It shattered you. After all the dust cleared from the fire, you lived with your grandparents. Around graduation, they moved into a retirement home, and you pushed forward. You got your certification to be a welder. From there, you worked on oil rigs and did other odd welding and construction-type jobs, while you also sold your metal art. I assume when you figured you had enough, you decided to leave welding and you started working at Rousseau's as a server. I have

been able to see you a few times at the restaurant. I feel like...
here," he said, feeding her the apple pie and ice cream. "I feel like
we could be really good friends and maybe lovers after a while if
you so choose. I know we get along."

"Not if you are tying me to a headboard. Apparently, we're
not *that* good of friends," she said between bites.

"Aww, don't be like that. I'll release you soon. Then you'll see.
I have all of your favorites ready to cook. I know you will love
them!"

She swallowed the bite she had and said, "Trust is thin right
now. You're going to have to earn it."

"Here," he said, giving her another bite. "Look, I know it will
take time. I also know that, in time, you will forgive me for taking
you this way. I know it was the only way you would come
with me."

"I didn't have a choice!" she snapped.

Feeding her the last bite, he said, "Things will turn around. I
have faith in us. I have faith in you."

As she finished the pie and ice cream, she felt a wave of dizziness. "What...whoa."

"Just a little something in the ice cream to help you sleep," he
said with a satisfied grin. "You rest. When you wake, things will
look better."

She shook her head, hoping to fight the medicine. Lesson
learned. Don't eat the food. That she can sustain. Drinking is
another story.

Robin opened her eyes to find herself alone in the room. She
took stock of what was in the room with her. The first
thing she noticed was that her hands were no longer
tied to the headboard. Sitting up, she saw a dresser, along with a

television mounted on the wall. Other than that, and the bed, the room was sparse regarding furniture. There was also a toilet against another wall, with no barrier to stop anyone from seeing her if she needed to go.

She got out of bed, slowly standing. The room still spun a bit. She went over to the dresser and opened the drawers. She recognized the clothes. Well, they seemed familiar anyway. She took out a shirt and a pair of shorts. She then pulled out underclothes and got changed into clean ones. After she got changed, she threw the gown in a ball next to the door.

She took another look at the door. "Hmm," she said quietly. She lightly rested her hand on the doorknob, heart racing. Tightening her fingers around the knob, she tried to turn in to find it locked. "Of course," she said under her breath.

She lightly patted the walls, trying to find some sort of exit. When that didn't work, she pulled the dresser away from the wall and tried that wall. "Nope."

She looked up to see a vent. She pulled the bed over just below the vent and stood on it to look in. "Oh!" she said, her jaw dropped. There was a camera in the vent.

She looked from the camera out toward her room. Her face flushed when she figured out the camera was on her when she changed. "Well! I hope he enjoyed the show."

She got down and moved the bed back to its place. That's when she noticed the pictures on the wall. Getting a closer look, she saw they were pictures of her and Liam. As she looked at the pictures, she had a few flashes of memories pierce her mind, bringing on a wicked headache.

She lay down on the bed. Holding her head, she closed her eyes, praying to sleep and hopefully get rid of the headache. She needed to think clearly if she was going to get out of this mess.

"What do you mean you can't hold him?" Nate snapped at Detective Simms.

"We can only hold him for so long without charging him. There is no evidence Logan did anything. As a matter of fact, he has an alibi," Simms explained. "I need to let him go. He hasn't done anything."

"But his brother –"

"Is the one we actually *do* have a warrant for," Simms cut Nate off. "That's the one we're looking for. Now, if you have any evidence regarding him, I'm all ears!"

"Isn't that *your* job?"

"It is. Are you going to let me do it, or are you going to keep pushing me to detain an innocent man?" Simms challenged.

Nate crossed his arms as he stood there, fuming. "It has been over forty-eight hours. How could you not have a single idea where he took her?" Nate demanded. "This guy has been stalking her this whole time. What leads have you followed up on?"

Simms crossed his arms, took a step forward so he was nose-to-nose, and explained, "We followed up with the alarm company. Seems Liam worked for them for a bit. He quit last week."

"Convenient."

"Precisely. We followed up with the address he used, but there was nothing there."

"So, what's the next step?"

Simms quietly said, "We are going to tap Logan's phone. We have to release him first. Do I have your permission to proceed?"

Nate huffed. "Just find her."

Simms half-bowed. "Thank you for your permission."

"Simms!" the police chief shouted from his office. "Get in here."

"Great!" Simms said. "I gotta go."

Nate stomped off into the firehouse side of the building. He dropped into one of the chairs at the table and then dropped his head into his hands.

"Mitchell, are you okay, man?" Wright asked, coming in with a towel around his neck. "I was just working out," he said, sitting down. "If you don't mind the smell, I would be happy to listen."

"I'm afraid for her," he admitted. "This guy abused her in high school and has tracked her since."

"Seriously? Wow," Wright said, sitting back in his chair. He blew out a slow breath of air. "Any idea where he took her?"

"Not really. His brother said last he knew, Liam was in Georgia. Apparently, that is incorrect. He's been here since at least the point we started dating. I'm afraid for her," he admitted. He shook his head. "The way he set up her living room was creepy at best."

"What do you want to do?"

"Find her. Find *him*! Get him arrested and out of our lives."

"Is she worth this?"

"What?"

"Is she worth the stress you are obviously under? Seems like she comes with a lot of baggage. Is she worth it?"

Nate looked up at him. Considering his words for a moment, he answered, "Yes. She is. She's worth every sleepless night. She's worth every daydream. She's worth every...smile. Every laugh. Every thought of her. She's worth it all."

"Wow, dude! You have it bad!"

"I know. I'm in love with her."

"The big, bad Nate Mitchell actually has a soft spot for this girl. Never thought I would see this day."

"She's the only thing that can derail me from fire marshal."

Raising an eyebrow, Wright asked, "How would she do that?"

"If I stop my training or leave the company to find her, that would derail everything I ever wanted."

"And, she's worth it?"

Looking him dead in the eyes, Nate firmly responded, "She is."

"Then, let's find her." Wright stood up. "Let me get a shower, and then we'll gather the troops."

"What? What do you mean?"

"We have three shifts of men and women in this fire department. This department is family. If one of us is hurting, then we are all hurting. No stone unturned. We'll find her."

"Really?"

Wright rested his hand on Nate's shoulder. "You're family."

"I know some servers at Rousseau's who would probably help as well."

"Then, you call the troops. I'll take a shower. When I get out, we can call the others."

"Agreed. Thank you."

"We'll find her," Wright said confidently as he walked down the hall.

"I hope so," Nate said, picking up his cell phone.

After Nate explained everything that was going on, he let it process in everyone's minds. Finally, he asked, "What do you think?"

"I *think* you should have told us a lot sooner," Bennet said. "That would have been some good information."

"What are we going to do about it?" Kent asked, sitting among the servers in the corner while the rest of the room was filled with firefighters.

"We're going to find her," Patterson said. "What you have on the board is good information on her. We need to write what we know about Liam. Also, we need to keep it from the cops, especially Simms."

"Agreed," Nate said. "Sooner than later, and yes, I agree. We need to keep the police out of it. I have a feeling they will try to stop us."

"And, when we *do* find him?" Robin's manager, Ricky, asked.

"We call the police and get him arrested."

"If he resists?" Ricky pushed.

"We sit on him until they get there," Nate said. "The main point is to make sure Robin is safe."

"Let's fan out through the town and see who knows what," Ozzie suggested. "If this guy has been anywhere near this town, *someone* knows *something*."

"Agreed. Let's go in teams," Nate said.

They divided into teams. Some had servers, some had firefighters. As soon as they got any information, they were to text Nate's phone. Nate would be the central figure in this.

"Where are we going?" Kent asked Nate.

"What do you mean?" Nate asked.

"I *mean,* we're partners, partner. Where are we starting?"

"You mean a trio," Patterson came back into the room with a soda in his hand. "We're the leftovers."

"Technically, I'm home base," Nate pointed out.

Kent rolled his eyes. "Like *you* would sit on the bench."

"Not my top choice, no."

"Then, what are we doing? Where are we going?"

"I say we have a strong conversation with brother Logan first."

"Agreed," Patterson said. "Let's go."

"Logan, buddy," Nate said, walking up to him as he walked toward the entrance of the hospital. Nate rested his arm over his shoulder. "We need to talk."

"No. We don't." Logan rolled his eyes. "Look, I have been held in jail for no apparent reason except that my brother looks just like me. This is not something that I'm not used to, but it is the first time I landed in jail for it."

"Here's the deal," Nate said, as Patterson and Kent flanked

the pair, "he has my girlfriend. Wherever he is, he will not be hidden for long."

Logan stopped walking. "What does *that* mean?"

"It means that the entire police station, fire station, and the staff of Rousseau's is looking for her. Right now, you are our only lead. However, wherever he is, *someone* knows *something*. We *will* find her. The choice is whether you will help or not."

"If I could, I would. I really don't know anything. I would tell you if I did."

"So, are you volunteering to help?" Kent asked.

"I can check around with the hospital people if it will help."

"I feel like it will," Kent said. "I could walk with you?"

"I'm good. I have an in with them. If someone else is there, they may not offer any information," Logan explained. "Give me your phone number and I'll text if I find anything."

"That'll work," Nate agreed. He handed Logan a card with his number on it. When Kent raised an eyebrow, Nate explained, "I wrote them out in order to give them to people who could get me information."

"Fair enough," Kent said, hands in the air in surrender.

"I'll see what I can find out. If nothing else, to clear my name," Logan said. "I don't want any other visitors either."

"I can text people not to come to you, but I can't guarantee they won't ask," Nate said.

"I'll take it. I'll do what I can. I just ask you to do what you can."

"Done," Nate said to Logan.

"Okay. Let me go to work. I'll text if and when I have something."

"Thank you."

"It's what I would want someone to do for me if something happened to the one I love," Logan said and went into the hospital.

"Okay," Patterson rested his arms over both Kent and Nate's shoulders, "let's go shake some other trees and see what falls."

CHAPTER 14

FIRE STORM

Robin lay in the bed in the room facing the opposite wall from the door. Hearing the door open, she did not roll over.

"Robin? Honey. Why didn't you eat?"

Robin did not move.

Liam went around to the side she was facing, so Robin rolled in the opposite direction. When he went to walk around the bed again, and she went to roll over again, he jumped onto the bed on top of her. Holding her down by her wrists, he straddled her.

"What are you thinking?" he asked, studying her face.

"That I don't know who you are. That I don't know why you are holding me hostage. That I don't trust you. You drugged my food before. What's to stop you from doing it again and then taking advantage of me being unconscious?"

"Oh, honey. I don't need you to be unconscious."

Her eyes widened in horror as her heart raced.

"I'm not really worried about you trusting me or even liking me. I just want you to eat."

"No."

"You need to eat and drink."

"Why?"

"If you don't, you could die. I can't have that. I just got you back. This is a good thing. We should be celebrating."

"You and I have two very different definitions of good."

He leaned closer to her face, and she froze.

"He abuses you. Why are you so loyal to him?"

She rolled her eyes. "He does not."

"He's controlling. That's abuse."

"And *this* isn't?"

"I'm trying to save you. It's tough love. I'm trying to show you how you should be treated."

"By locking me up? No phone. No windows. Drugging my food. Yeah. That all sounds perfectly sane."

"I *am not* crazy!" he snapped. Getting off her, he stormed out of the room.

"Obviously, a trigger," she said before rolling back toward the wall again.

Just as she was settling, he came back in. Shaking his finger at her, he said, "You *will* eat and drink. If you don't, I will have to punish you."

"Seems you already are."

"Why are you so insubordinate?" he demanded.

She rolled over and sat up, looking at him. "You drugged me and kidnapped me. You shove me into this room with only a vent for any air, and there is even a camera in the vent. So much for trust."

"I need to make sure you don't hurt yourself."

She got out of bed. He watched every move she made.

"The only one hurting me here is *you!*" she said, getting loud.

"I know you better than you know yourself. You love me."

"I don't know you!"

"You did. Before the fire."

"What fire? I know there are burns on my legs, but I have no idea what fire you're talking about."

He furrowed his brow. "You really don't know?"

She crossed her arms in a huff. "No. I don't. I don't know

about the fire. I don't know who you are. I don't know why you kidnapped me. I don't know what I'm doing here! I *want* to go home!"

"I can't do that. I love you too much to put you back into that position again."

Dropping her fists to her sides, she took a few more brave steps forward until she was toe-to-toe with him. "Let me go!" she shouted.

"No."

"This is illegal. Let me go home!"

"No."

She used the one tool she had against him. "You *are* crazy! Insane! You need to go into a facility!"

He grabbed her arms and, in one fluid motion, swung her around, slamming her into the wall. Getting in her face, he swore before he said, "Don't you *ever* say that again! I am *not* crazy! I love you!"

"I don't love you! I don't know you! You *are* crazy! No one in their right mind would kidnap someone and stick them in a room like this! You planned this!"

Quietly, near her ear, he said in a low tone, "Yes. I did. I planned it for you. I just had to wait for my chance to show you what kind of a man I am."

"A crazy one!" she snapped.

He spun her around and let go, sending her across the room, tumbling onto the bed. When she stopped, she looked up at him, but he was gone and the door was being locked.

"No!" she shouted. "You *are* crazy! You need serious help!" She slumped on the bed. "*I* need serious help."

The silence was almost deafening. The lack of any street noise was discouraging. No television or radio playing. No train. No vehicle. No kids. Nothing.

Then there was the camera, watching her every move. She didn't know if he could hear as well, so she remained quiet as she got out of bed. The vent was above the door. Going up to the door, she felt it. It was not hot, nor was it cold. She rested her hand on the doorknob and tried to twist it. It didn't budge.

She looked toward the dresser to see two small trays resting on top of the dresser. The one had food. She searched it and found nothing she could use. The other tray had toiletries of sorts. There was a brush, deodorant, toothbrush, toothpaste, a couple hair ties, a headband, and two Bobbi pins.

"Jackpot!" she said quietly.

She brushed her hair and put it up into a ponytail. Then, she used both Bobbi pins to clip down stray hair.

Afterward, she lay down on the bed. Since getting him angry did not work, she would have to try something else. She needed him calm. She needed him to feel 'safe' with her. She would do what she had to do in order for him to relax. Without knowing what time it was, she would just have to let the minutes creep by. She would have to eat, but she would do it sparingly. She would eat just enough to get him to relax.

"Okay. What do we know?" Nate asked the several groups sitting in the room at the fire station.

"We know Logan is his brother and that he used that connection to get her from the hospital," one guy said.

"And we know Logan was able to talk to multiple people," Kent said. "They said Liam would talk to them like he was Logan. So, they did not get any information that Logan did not already know."

"He said he would keep asking around," Patterson added. "Hopefully, he slipped somewhere."

"We are not going to focus on the hope that he could have slipped somewhere. We're going to stay focused on what we *know*," Nate said.

"We know he's been doing this a while," another guy said.

"What if he has her somewhere he already set up?" Jett, one of the servers, asked.

"What do you mean?" Kent asked.

"Well, in looking at this from his perspective, you said he was stalking her for a long time."

"Right," Nate said.

"While he thought he had time, for some reason he felt threatened by you," she said to Nate. "And has been since you two started dating a few weeks ago."

Nate nodded. "Right."

"He was supposed to have a quote 'date'," she made quotes with her fingers, "last Friday. What if he was planning on taking her on Friday? Would it be safe to assume he had a plan in place?"

"I'm following you," Kent said. "So, since Friday didn't happen, and then the fire, he had to go to plan B."

"Which was to figure out a way to take her," Nate said, finishing his thought. "Why wait? She was in the hospital."

"She wasn't cleared to leave yet," Patterson said. "Wasn't she supposed to be released the next morning?"

"Yes. How did he know?" Nate asked.

"You said he was there the other night. Was he impersonating Logan? If so, that would give him access to the charts. If people thought he was supposed to be back there, it wouldn't look different to them. He was just another nurse."

"Good line of thinking," Nate said. "I like where you're going with this."

"So, if he planned on taking her," Jett continued, "then he would have somewhere set up to take her."

"*That's* what we need to find," Nate said. "Let's make a list of possible places. There are enough of us in this room that know this town like the back of our hand."

"Most of us have grown up here," Wright said. "We should know all the hiding places."

They took the next two hours and made lists of places he

could have taken Robin. Afterward, they were sent off in teams of four. They did not want anyone to be caught off-guard if they found him.

"Breakfast," Liam said, walking into the room. When Robin didn't move, he said, "Come on. You need to eat. You need to keep nutrition flowing through your system."

"Why?" Robin asked, still not looking at him.

He came and sat on the side of her bed. Stroking her hair, he said, "I want you to be able to relax, and maybe we can go out on a hike or something."

"Did you drug it again?"

"No. I did the first day because I still needed to set a few things up. The food since then has been drug-free."

She rolled her eyes and sighed. "Like I believe you."

"You should. You can only go three days without water. You are two days in. Here," he got up and got the bottle of water, "you can see. It hasn't been opened." He gave the bottle a squeeze. "No water came out. That means no needle holes. This is a safe bottle to drink."

"And if I need to go to the bathroom?"

"There's a toilet over there."

"With a camera on it. That's not right. You want me to trust you, but you won't even let me go to the bathroom in private."

"Would you feel better if I hung a curtain?"

"Only if you hung it so I could not be seen by that blasted camera. I feel like an animal at the zoo. It's creepy. I can't get changed. I can't go to the bathroom. Do not even tell me when my last shower was."

"Would a shower help you feel better?"

"Actually, it would." She looked over at him. "Is that possible?"

"I think I can make it happen."

Her face brightened. "Really?"

"Wow! You *do* smile. Didn't think a shower would make you that happy."

"My legs should get cleaned as well. They haven't since the hospital."

"That's true. You could take a shower, and then I could clean them for you?"

"That would be great!"

"Okay. I'll be right back," he said, getting off the bed.

"Where are you going?"

"To get a couple buckets of clean water so you could clean yourself."

She just nodded her head and then laid back down. If she overreacted, he might get suspicious. If she continued to play it laid back, then eventually, he may actually let her take a real shower, which would leave her in a bathroom with a window... and freedom!

"Okay. We're almost to the bottom of our list," Kent said, crossing off the last one they just checked on the list. "Only a couple more. I wonder how the other groups are doing?"

"So far, they have nothing," Nate said, checking his phone again. "There are only so many places to hide in this town."

"What if they're not here?" Kent asked.

Nate, Patterson, and Wright all three looked at him, dumbfounded.

"No. Hear me out," Kent said. "What if he figured everyone

would look around here and took her somewhere outside the town limits?"

"I mean, that is logical," Wright said. "How far do we look?"

"Has anyone checked her house?" Patterson asked. "I don't remember putting that on the list."

"What do you mean? That's the first place they checked," Nate said.

"We know he had access to her house. What if he got in there and made some sort of shelter? What if he's right here in town...in her own house?"

"That's a wild idea."

"So is stealing someone from a hospital from a room being guarded by the police. Talk about a wild idea!" Patterson said.

"It can't hurt. Kent, please add that to the list," Nate said.

Kent wrote it down. "Done. Let's go here next," he said, showing them the list.

After checking the next three places, they went to her house. The living room looked normal, but they looked under all of the furniture to be sure there were no trap doors.

Then, they headed to the bedroom. Clothes were strewn about the room.

"Stop. Don't touch anything," Nate said.

"Why? We know there will be Liam and Robin's prints everywhere," Kent said. "That's obvious. We need to find what's *not* obvious. If we call the police, this will be a crime scene for at least forty-eight more hours. Is that what you really want?"

"No," Nate said, dropping his head. "I just want to find her."

"Then, leave the police out of this for now. Finding her... alive...is the most important thing."

Nate nodded, so they looked under all of the furniture. A couple moved the dresser, while a third looked under the rug that was resting on top of the hardwood floors. Afterward, they followed suit with the nightstands and bed.

"Hmm...I wonder," Kent said, going to the closet.

He opened it. Stomping on the floor, it did not sound hollow. He started knocking on the wall in the closet, to no avail.

"Well, this is depressing. I was hoping for an 'a-ha!' moment," Kent said, closing the door.

"Let's check the other two bedrooms," Nate said, discouragement evident in his voice.

They thoroughly scoured the guest rooms. Then, they checked the kitchen and pantry. Nothing.

"What about her shed out back?" Wright asked. "Not many would think to look there."

"Could he do something like that and her not know?" Patterson asked.

"Who knows. I mean, he stalked her for literally years and no one knew," Kent pointed out.

They headed out to the shed and looked around. They stomped on the floor and heard nothing.

Patterson swore. "Where is she?"

"Honestly!" Nate crossed his arms. "I wish I knew."

Nate's phone rang. He looked at the screen and saw it was his dad. "Hello?" he answered.

"Nate, we need to get to the warehouses and figure out who —"

"Dad, I'm busy."

"You need to make time for this if this is what you want to do."

"I *want* to find Robin. That's where my time is staying right now."

"While I understand that, you have —"

"If this were Mom, what would *you* do?" Nate challenged.

"Your mom and I are in love and have been for years. You two just started –"

"Stop!" Nate cut his dad off. "Do *not* finish that sentence. I love Robin. I have been in love with her since high school. You may not have known that, but I do...or did, once I saw her again that first day in Rousseau's. That's the reason why nothing has ever stuck when it came to other girls. It's Robin, Dad. It always has been. I *need* to find her!"

"Okay. I'll handle this part myself. Just do your best, son. I'll keep you all in prayer."

"Thank you. Thank you also for your understanding."

"I do, but know I cannot cover you for too much longer. I know you're taking off work to look, too."

"I am. I have vacation time. I'm using it right now."

"I'll do my best to continue to cover with Simms as well."

"Thank you. I appreciate that. Speaking of Simms...?"

"Nothing. He's trying. He's checked with CI's from all over Texas. Do you know if Liam's family has a home in the country or a cabin somewhere?"

"Dad! That's brilliant! I'll check with Logan."

"I've been doing investigative stuff for a while now. I have a few cards up my sleeve."

"I don't doubt that. Thank you."

"Love you, son."

"Love you, too," Nate said and hung up. "We need to go find Logan."

Liam hung a curtain from the ceiling using a sheet and a nail gun. It surrounded the toilet. When he finished, he turned to Robin and asked, "Well?"

"Good. Thank you." She glanced at the vent. "Removing *that* would be better."

"I love you," he said, kneeling in front of her as she sat on the bed. "I don't want anyone to harm you. This allows me to keep an eye on you...for your safety."

"How long do I have to stay in here? I miss the sunlight. I miss fresh air."

"How can you miss what you cannot remember?"

"It's a feeling."

"Well, there are some buckets of water for you to wash up. Here is some soap and towels," he said, going over to the dresser and opening the bottom drawer. He pulled them out and then handed them to her. "You can feel free to bathe in the curtained-off area to make you feel more comfortable."

"It would make me more comfortable to take a real shower and to clean in a room without a camera at all," Robin said, her pulse quickening as her face flushed red.

"Don't get mad. I'll let you take one in a few days if you behave."

"If I...*what*? If I...*what*?" She stood, fists clenched to her sides. "*Behave*? Like some good little doggie?"

"Robin? What has gotten into you?"

Robin took one glance at the nail gun before she snatched it off the dresser. Aiming it at him, she said, "Don't move!"

Hands in front of him, he slowly backed away. "Robin, let's talk about this."

"No!" she shouted and shot the gun toward his thigh.

The nail impaled his thigh, and he went to the ground. When he dropped to the floor, she used the nail gun and smacked his forehead, producing blood. He swore as he grabbed his head.

She grabbed one hand, slammed it on the ground, and shot a four-inch nail through it. Before he could do anything else, she grabbed his other hand and nailed his other hand to the ground as well. Amidst his screams and howls, she yanked his legs straight and shot six nails quickly into each leg of the jeans, effectively nailing him to the floor.

Reaching into his pocket, she pulled out the keys.

"I *will* kill you when I get ahold of you!" he growled.

She took one last look at him before she fumbled with the keys, trying each one until the door finally gave way. She locked it behind her, locking him inside. If he were able to get out of the situation she put him in, he would not be able to get out. That she knew for sure.

Standing in the blackness, she felt around until she found a banister. Following it up the stairs, she found a door.

Heart racing, she reached for the handle. The door gave way to a brightly lit room. She slightly shaded her eyes until they adjusted.

She ran to the door leading outside. What she ran out to was pure woods. Everywhere she looked, she saw trees...for miles. She glanced back at the cabin before taking off into the woods. She decided she had a better chance in the woods than with Liam.

As she ran, lightning shot across the sky, followed by a clap of thunder that shook the ground under her feet. They were in for a wicked storm, but she kept running.

CHAPTER 15

WHAT MATTERS MOST IS HOW WELL YOU WALK THROUGH THE FIRE

"There's a cabin in an area where they used to go deer hunting," Nate said, hanging up his phone. "We're going to pick him up, gather the others, and head out to the cabin."

As Nate sent a group text to the head of each group to meet at the firehouse and why, Kent said, "I hate to make this part about us, *but* we're under a tornado watch. Is it safe to go out to the wilderness in this type of weather? It's coming."

"And she could be out in it. What happens if she's locked in that cabin and it gets hit by a tornado?" Nate challenged.

"Is there a way to do it safely?"

"Doubt it," Nate said, "Let's go."

They regrouped at the fire station. Once everyone was in the room, along with Logan, Logan explained where the cabin was amidst the one-hundred acres his family owned.

"If you are concerned regarding the tornado watch, I can understand that," Nate announced. "If you don't want to go, no one will think less of you. I'm going. Whoever wants to go can. You can meet me in the parking lot. We'll stay out there for five minutes before loading. If you don't want to go, stay in here for fifteen minutes, and then you are free to go. I appreciate your help in finding Robin. Lord willing, she's out there."

"Lord willing she's not," Samuels retorted. "There's a blasted tornado coming, and we're heading out into the wilderness? How is that safe?"

"We're going," Nate said firmly. "Whether you choose to go or not is up to you. If you want to come, come on out with me now," he said and left the room.

He could hear the strong discussion within the room as he left. He would go himself if he needed to, but he hoped that would not be the case.

As he leaned against his truck, people started filing out of the fire station. About eighty percent walked over to Nate. Of those who stayed, over half stayed at the station if needed. The storms were brewing. Nasty weather was on the way. How bad was unknown. What Nate did know was that he needed to find Robin.

As Robin ran through the woods, the branches seemed to reach out at her, slashing her arms, legs, and face. She fell multiple times over tree roots or underbrush. One time, she ended up rolling down a hill. More than once, she ran into a web. She really didn't want to know what was crawling in her hair. She just wanted to find somewhere safe.

That's when it started to rain. "Great!" she shouted to the sky. "Just what I need!"

It wasn't a drizzle or a mist. It wasn't even a steady stream. It was a torrential downpour accompanied by strong gusts of wind.

She looked around to find a shelter of some kind. She saw a wide pine tree in the distance. There were other trees taller than that pine, so she ran under it. As she did, lightning struck the ground about a hundred yards from where she hid. She covered her ears as the thunderous boom reverberated around her, shaking the ground around her. She screamed, "Get me out of here!"

As she sat there, a gust of wind that had to be around eighty miles per hour shot through, quickly followed by hail. She picked up a hailstone. It was about the size of a golf ball. She tucked further into the tree for protection.

That's when she saw it in the distance. There was a monster she would never forget. It came down from the clouds and started splitting the trees, throwing them all over.

Eyes wide, Robin stared, frozen in place.

The tornado danced with the trees. It went up and then down again. Some areas looked like a weedwhacker took the tops of them off. Other large trees looked like someone played a game of pick-up sticks with them. She screamed as a tree with a six-foot base dropped right in front of her.

Tears streaked her face and her body shook. "I need to get out of here!" She ran out from under the tree in the same direction she was going after leaving the cabin. She knew she was going away from the cabin...away from him. What she was running toward was a mystery.

"She's here somewhere. We could fan out with five to ten feet between us and then just comb the area?" Kent suggested.

"I don't think –"

Wright was cut off by a sight he hoped to never see again.

"Tornado," Nate said, not taking his eyes off it. "Everyone find somewhere to hide until it passes!"

"Where?" Jett asked. "Where are we going to hide? That monster will find us wherever we are!"

Hail started to drop around them.

"Get under the trucks!" someone shouted.

"Trees! Hide in the trees!" another shouted.

Various people shouted all around them.

"They are flying projectiles!"

"Like vehicles aren't!"

"What do we do?"

"There!" another shouted as they pointed toward a ditch surrounded by trees.

All twenty or so people ran to the ditch. They grouped together in an attempt to protect each other. Nate and a few others started to pray.

As the tornado neared, it lifted above them and their vehicles and then dropped about a quarter of a mile away from them.

"That was close," Patterson said.

"If she's here, that has passed her, too," Nate pointed out. "Fan out and stay within visual range of the person to your right and left. Do not go out of sight. If you cannot see them, they cannot see you."

Robin ran. She wasn't sure where she was running, but she kept going. She wasn't sure how much longer she *could* run.

She ran hard. She gripped the nail gun she still had in her hands. She was not letting go of her only weapon of defense. There was no telling what she would run into out here.

As they walked, they called out her name. If Robin was there, there was no way she would not hear them. At least, that was Nate's hope.

Robin ran. Every once and a while, she would glance behind to make sure Liam wasn't behind her. That's when she heard it. In the distance, she heard people yelling.

"I don't know if that's a good thing, but either way, it gets me away from Liam," she said and ran toward the sound.

"Help me!" Robin ran up to a pair of campers.

"Did that tornado hit you? Are you hurt?" one of the campers got up and asked as the other got her something to eat. Resting her on the log, he asked, "What happened?"

Robin sat there shaking.

"I'm sorry if our yelling –" the woman stopped when Robin looked up at her. "I'm sorry. What happened to you?"

"Kidnapped. Need police," Robin said. "Please call?"

"Out here?" The guy shook his head. "No. There's no service."

"Help me. Please?" Robin begged. "He's going to kill me. Please?"

"Gary, we have to get her back to town," the woman said. "This woman needs help."

"Do you want to take the tent down while I gather everything else?" Gary asked her.

"Yep."

As they set to work, there was more shouting in the distance.

"What's that?" the woman asked.

"Hello!" Gary shouted out into the wilderness.

After a few moments of them shouting at each other, Liam walked into the campsite and shot the man and woman without giving them a chance.

"Told you I would find you and kill you," Liam said, staring at Robin, who had blood and other matter splattered on her. The woman was right next to her when Liam shot her in the head.

Trembling, Robin stood. She straightened her body and lifted her head high. "If you are going to kill me, you will look me in the eyes when you do so."

"You think that's going to stop me?" Liam asked. He slowly walked toward where she stood in her spot, gun aimed at her, almost daring her to move. "I have been watching you for years... waiting for you to notice me. We were in love in high school. Then, that ingrate, Nate, steps in, and BOOM!" he shouted. "You're in love! He is *not* who you should be with! I am!"

Robin just watched him. The blood from the woman pooled at her feet.

Liam walked up to her. Tucking a portion of her hair behind her ear, he said, "What did they do to you? Did they hurt you? You look like someone whipped you."

"The only one who hurt me here is *you*."

"I took care of you! I made sure you had clothes, a bed, food, clean toilet. I can take care of you. That is something I *can* do. I need *you* to cooperate with me."

"You're bleeding. You need a doctor," Robin pointed out.

He roughly grabbed her face. The blood from his hands made a handprint on her chin. "I need *you*."

"You're obsessed."

"You took my teen years. Then, you jerked me around by

cheating on me with *him*. Of all people, it's *him*. That does not fly with me. It's you and me. It's always been you and me. Who do you think looked out for you all of those years you were on the oil rigs? You worked with roughnecks. You don't think any of them wanted you? What about living by yourself? I watched over you at night."

"No one asked you to. I didn't want you to!"

"If I didn't, you would have been attacked a long time ago."

"The only one attacking me is *you*!" Robin snapped.

He took another step closer, closing the distance between the pair. "I love you," he said softly. "And I feel you could love me if you would give me half the chance. We used to have something beautiful. We could have it again. Come home with me."

"Come home with you? You just shot two innocent people! I am going *nowhere* with you!"

He grabbed her arm. With her free hand, she tightened her hand around the handle and lifted the nail gun to his temple...and shot.

He stood stunned for only a moment before he released her arm and dropped to his knees. She watched as the blood ran down his face. She ran behind and shot the nail gun into the nape of his neck. He dropped backward onto the ground with a faraway look on his face.

Robin stared at him, waiting for him to move. When he didn't, she looked around at the devastation surrounding her. All of this because some guy was obsessed with her.

She shook her head. Dropping to her knees in the pooled blood, tears streaked her face. She rested the nail gun on her lap. She had no idea where she was, but she knew she needed help.

She took a couple deep, cleansing breaths. Then she felt around the woman's waist to find her cell phone in her pocket. She took it out and turned it on. It required a thumbprint, so Robin picked up the woman's hand and used it to unlock the phone.

"I'm sorry," Robin said as she opened the settings. She made sure the phone would never turn off automatically. Then she clicked on the navigational app on the woman's phone. Robin let out a low whistle as she zoomed out from their current location. It took her a few minutes before she finally found Hemlock. She clicked on Hemlock and sent the navigational app there from her current position. "An hour?" She looked up at the sky. "An hour from town driving?"

She stood. Grabbing the nail gun, she followed the app's directions. After about twenty minutes of walking, she heard more yelling. She froze. Straining, she listened.

"Robin!" Nate called out again.

"I'm sure I heard gunshots," Patterson insisted.

"We're in the woods."

"In the middle of a tornado," Kent added to Nate's statement. "We shouldn't be hearing gunshots in the middle of a tornado."

"Who's to say it's not a car backfiring or a transformer blowing?" Nate asked. Then he shouted out again, "Robin!"

"What's that?" someone down the line shouted.

Nate looked up as another person shone a light on her. What he saw made his heart skip a few beats. It was Robin. Her hair was matted yet full of twigs. There was blood, along other matter splattered all over her clothes. She had a phone in one hand and a nail gun in the other.

"Robin?" Nate asked, slowly jogging up to her.

She lifted the nail gun and pointed it at him.

He threw his hands in the air. "Robin? It's me, Nate. We're here looking for you. You're safe with us. Put that down."

"H-he shot them," she stammered.

"Who shot who?" Nate asked as others slowly surrounded her.

She turned and looked in the opposite direction before looking back to Nate. "Liam. He killed those two...there were two people trying to...he killed them."

"Can you show me on the phone where they are?" Nate asked.

Robin held the phone up and pointed to an area on the phone. Nate snapped a picture of it and then took the nail gun from her, handing it to Kent. Afterward, he took the phone from her and handed it to Patterson. Finally, he just wrapped his arms around her and held her while she broke down and cried.

CHAPTER 16

BURNING ISSUES

"I feel we should keep her for a few days," Dr. Fitzpatrick said to Nate and his parents. "I would like psych to talk to her. I have a friend who is a psychologist. She's really sweet. I think she should talk to her to find out where her mind is. The amnesia, on top of getting kidnapped and held hostage? That combination could take the strongest of us down.

"She's not crazy," Nate said, running his hands through his hair. "I really don't like her being in here. This is where he got to her. The hospital dropped the ball on that one."

The doctor put his hands up in surrender. "I get it. Security didn't do their job. The police officers at the door didn't do their job either. There were a lot of factors in play that created this mess. We could go back and forth for days about it. What we need to focus on is now. Her cuts and scrapes were cleaned. Her legs have been cleaned and bandaged regarding the burns. Thankfully, no further damage was done there. Now we need to focus on her mental stability. The amnesia coupled with the kidnapping, watching two people murdered in front of her, and her having to actually kill the guy?" Dr. Fitzpatrick shook his head. "That's *a lot*. She needs help. Alyssa can help her. Dr. Morrison is a good doctor. She knows her stuff. With as much as she's gone through, I wouldn't recommend anyone but her."

"Okay. Thank you," Ian said, shaking the doctor's hand. "Please have her contact us, and we'll get things moving."

"I can have her come in and talk with her?" Dr. Fitzpatrick offered.

"I think that sounds like a great plan," Ian agreed.

"Should someone give her a head's up?" Erin, Nate's mom, asked. "I don't think it's a good idea to blindside her. She won't take that well."

"Agreed. I think that's fair." Dr. Fitzpatrick nodded. "Do you want me to, or do you guys want to talk with her?"

"I will." Nate raised his hand. "She's got enough going on. I'm still using my vacation time. Can I still have permission to stay in her room?"

"Definitely. I'll mark it in her chart," the doctor said, making a note as they stood there. "I would actually prefer someone be with her, for her sake. I think it would make her more comfortable."

"We appreciate your help," Nate said.

"Now, she's currently sedated. Just be aware of that. I know the police have been chomping at the bit to talk with her. I really don't want them to until Alyssa has talked with her. I'll call her when we're done here and get her as soon as possible."

"That would be good. Thank you," Ian said.

With that, the doctor walked away, dialing his phone.

"I think we need to talk with her sooner than later," Erin suggested.

"Agreed," Ian said. "Let's go."

As they walked in, Robin looked up at them. To Nate, she looked broken. There was no light in her eyes. She looked like she hadn't slept in weeks. There were tiny cuts and scrapes all over her arms and face. He wanted to hold her and keep everyone away from her.

"Hi," Nate said awkwardly.

"Hi." She sat up in her bed. "You guys look worse than I feel."

"I don't know about that," Erin said with a smile. "Seems we've all had a few rough days. Some of us are worse off than others."

"I think hers has been decidedly worse than all of ours," Ian said. "As a matter of fact, Dr. Fitzpatrick is setting up to have a young lady come and talk to you. You know, just to see where you're at."

Robin furrowed her brow. "See where I'm at?"

"Between the amnesia and now this, the doctor's friend is going to come and chat with you."

"Oh. Okay." She nodded. "I guess that's okay."

"Good. Now, the doctor said you are under sedation. I also know the police really want to talk to you," Nate said. "Are you up for that?"

"Not really. My head's a little fuzzy."

"Fair enough. Get some rest. I'll stay in the room so you won't be disturbed," Nate offered.

"I would like that. There are a few things I wanted to talk to you about in private."

"That's our cue," Ian said, wrapping his arm around Erin's waist. "Ready?"

"Yes. Here." She leaned down and gave Robin a kiss on the head. "Take care of yourself. We will be back tomorrow. If you need anything before then, have Nate call us."

"Thank you."

"Get some rest," Ian said, and squeezed her hand before the pair left.

When the door closed, Nate sat on the side of the bed. "Just us. What's up?"

"Liam said something. I want to know what you think?"

"About?"

"He said you and he talked in the locker room. He said you only liked me for the way I look."

"Wow." He shook his head. "That guy's a piece of work. *He's* the one who said that. I just about punched him right there in the locker room for that one. He added a lot more detail. It took a couple guys to hold me back that day. No. I did not say anything along those lines. I would *never* say anything like that about anyone."

"I can see that in your face. He was a manipulator, for sure."

"Do you remember anything else?"

"I remember a lot of violence. I remember him shooting two people who were trying to help me. I also remember the nail gun."

"Do you remember what you did with that?"

"I do."

"You're going to have to tell the police what happened. We can only put them off for so long."

"I don't want to do that alone. Can you be here for that?"

"Yes. Do you want a nap first?"

"I think that would be good."

"Well, enjoy your rest. I'll be over there doing work on my computer. You don't need to worry about me. You won't be alone."

"Thank you. That's helpful.

After she took a nap, the police officer came. He took her statement and also asked a few questions. Once they finished, Robin was exhausted.

"I'm sorry you had to do that. I can only imagine how horrific it was to live through, let alone have to restate it," Nate said, moving her meal tray so it was on the stand over her lap.

"Yeah. Now I have to eat this," she gestured toward the chicken, broccoli, and salad on her tray. "You would think limiting trauma to once per week would be mandatory."

Nate chuckled as the door opened.

"Knock. Knock," a lady of about thirty years old walked in. She stuck her hand out to Robin, "I'm Alyssa Morrison, a friend of Dr. Fitzpatrick."

"Right," Robin said, shaking her hand. "He told us you were coming. Seems I have a little bit going on."

"I'll say!" She sat in the chair next to the bed. "Do you want him to stay?"

"*Him* has a name. Dr. Morrison, this is Nate," Robin introduced them. "He stays."

Nate sat there with a grin on his face.

"All righty then," Dr. Morrison said, writing something on her tablet. "Well, you can call me Alyssa."

"Okay."

"So, what can you tell me?"

"Pretty sure you can check with the cop if you want the story," Robin said, and then took a bite of the chicken. She cringed as she slowly chewed the bite. "Rubber," she added.

"Feisty one, aren't ya?" Alyssa commented.

Robin shrugged. "I guess."

"What happened?"

"Which time?"

"What do you mean?"

"Apparently, I'm a fun one to be around this week. Somehow found myself in a fire and lost my memory. Then, I was kidnapped, forced to watch my kidnapper kill two people who were trying to help me after I escaped, only to have to kill him anyway. I didn't want to."

"Why did you then?"

"I had no choice! I tried just nailing him to the ground, but he somehow got out and got out of the locked room where I left him. He shot the two people who were helping me and then tried to kill me. I used the nail gun to kill him."

"I see. You seem pretty clear on the events during the kidnapping, but what about the fire?"

"Howdy! Hi, y'all!" Kent said, walking into the room. He

stopped. "Whoa! There's a pretty hefty vibe in here. Do I need to go?"

"No. You can stay, too," Robin said.

"Okay." He glanced at Nate, who shrugged. Then he sat down on the chair next to the window. "Do I need popcorn? This looks intense."

"Basically, she wants to know what happened," Robin explained. "Not sure how restating what I just told the police is going to help me in the long run. I also can't tell her anything before the fire, so there's that."

"Hostile," Alyssa remarked.

"Irritated," Robin corrected. "I don't remember anything. I can't tell you anything."

"How do you feel about that?"

"Frustrated. How would *you* feel if you couldn't remember anything before a week ago?"

"Probably irritated as well," she said.

"Now, add getting kidnapped, watching people get killed, and then being forced to kill someone."

"I would probably be feisty too."

"Welcome to my world."

"What do you know about fire?" Alyssa asked.

"That it's hot."

Both Nate and Kent did their best to stifle their laughter, especially after Alyssa shot them both a look.

"What else?" Alyssa pushed.

"No idea."

"What do you mean?"

"I mean, I have no idea what you're looking for here. Fire is fire."

"What about the warehouse fire?"

Robin narrowed her eyes. "What about it?"

"What can you tell me about it?"

"Only from when I woke up. I can't tell you how or why I was there. I can't tell you how it started. I really can't even tell you where the warehouse is...or was. When I say I don't remember, I *mean* I don't remember."

"You don't remember *anything*?"

"Nothing."

"I would like to try something when you're ready."

"Like what?"

"I want to try hypnosis. I feel like you may be able to remember something under this form of treatment."

Robin shook her head. "I don't know."

"Get to know me. When you feel you can trust me, we'll talk about it again. Until then, I would like to see you in my office every week for a bit."

"And, who pays for that?" Robin asked.

"Insurance usually covers that."

"I am a waitress. I don't have insurance."

"We can work something out."

"I don't know if I want to see you."

"I'll tell you what. You give me thirty days, twice a week. That's eight sessions. If you want to continue, we'll work something out. This first month will be the most critical. That's why I want to see you twice. I'll leave an extra hour after yours in case we break through somewhere."

"I don't know."

"What do you have to lose? I'm the one losing money. What do you say?"

"Um." She looked at Nate, who shrugged.

Then she looked at Kent, who shrugged and shook his head. "Whatever you want, girl. It's up to you. I'll support you either way."

"Same," Nate agreed.

"Can I think about it?" she asked Alyssa.

"Definitely! Here's my card," she said, handing it to Robin. "I look forward to speaking with you again."

"Thank you."

With that, she left the room.

"Well, that was fun," Kent said with a smile. "Is it always this exciting?"

"Oh no. There were cops in here earlier. She's had the trifecta today," Nate said. "Doctor, cops, *and* a psychiatrist. Fun times."

"Was the cop at least hot?" Kent asked.

Both Robin and Nate burst out in laughter.

"Was he?" Kent asked.

"That depends on your definition of hot?" Nate asked.

"Patterson," he said with a smirk, as his face flushed bright red.

"I don't think I've ever seen you blush," Nate said, watching him. "And, quite possibly. He's Patterson's cousin."

"Oh!" Kent grinned. "So, quite possibly. I think I need to hang out with y'all more often."

"It's definitely not boring," Robin said. "Personally, I'd like to get out of here. Seems my house is safe once again, according to Simcox, the cop who was in here earlier."

Kent's eyes twinkled. "Simcox, huh?"

"Yes. Shawn Simcox," Nate clarified.

"Okay." Kent couldn't help the grin immediately plastered on his face. "We may need to change the subject before I get into trouble."

"Oh no. I'm enjoying watching you squirm instead of me," Robin said. "It's kind of refreshing after what's happened to me."

"Speaking of..." Kent moved to the chair Dr. Morrison just vacated. "I know you told her and probably the police, but I'm you BFF, so talk to me, sister. What happened?"

Robin spent the next few hours filling in Kent on what happened over the last few days. When she was finished, Kent slumped back in his chair. "Girl! I'm exhausted just listening to this. I give you major props! I don't know if I could have done what you did."

"I had to figure out how to get out of there. As for actually killing him, I really didn't have a choice."

"Simcox agrees with you," Nate said. "He going to talk to the

D.A., so hopefully, things will just fade away. In your case, it was a clear case of self-defense. With Liam dead, they really can't charge anyone for the deaths of the two campers. I feel horrible for their families, but you've honestly been through more than enough."

"I agree. I hope you're right," Robin said. "The thought of having to say all of this in a court terrifies me to no end."

"You may still have to make a formal deposition for the record," Nate said.

"I'm okay with that."

"Does anyone know anything about the warehouse fire they found you in yet?" Kent asked.

"No," Robin said, discouraged.

"Well, maybe a little something," Nate said. "Dad's been working it. He doesn't want it repeated. If the arsonist follows his pattern, there should be another fire soon."

"You're calling it arson?" Kent asked.

"Do you guys know who it is?" Robin asked. "You said *he*."

"Statistically speaking, the ratio of males to females who are arsonists is five males to one female. So, there is a one in six percent chance it may be a woman, but it's more than likely a man."

"Interesting," Robin said. "I didn't know that."

"Yeah, and their reasons vary. It's kind of fascinating. Pretty sure your friend, Alyssa, can tell you more," Nate said.

"I'm kind of curious to know why someone would purposely set something on fire," Robin said. "Liam told me I liked welding. I'm kind of curious to know if I can still do it with that....what did you call it? Oh yeah. Muscle memory."

"That's a good question. I wonder if you can do your art."

"I wonder too!" Robin said. "Is there a pen and paper around?"

"I can go get one. Maybe that cute nurse is still at the desk," Kent said, getting up.

"Logan? He's here?" Robin asked.

"Nope. There's a new guy in town," Kent said, wiggling his

eyebrows. "I'll be back. My senses are tingling. Pretty sure he's my pace."

Nate chuckled. "Just see if they have a pen and a couple pieces of paper, please."

"I can do that."

It took Kent only a few minutes to return with a pen and a couple pieces of paper.

"Well?" Nate asked.

"Mission accomplished. Unfortunately, nurse hottie is taken. So, that ship has sailed." He set the pen and paper on the table. "Story of my life."

"Assuming your date didn't go well earlier in the week?" Nate asked.

"No. One of these days, I'll find the right one. Until then, I'll have fun trying."

"Always looking for the good," Nate said. "I appreciate that about you."

"I try."

"Okay, give it a try," Nate said, handing Robin the pen and papers.

"Can you two both sit at the end of my bed together?" Robin asked.

Kent moved to the bed while Nate moved back.

"Okay. Hold that. Don't move," she said and then started drawing.

After about an hour, Nate asked, "Are you almost done yet? This is really starting to hurt."

"Baby!" Kent shot. "I can do this all day."

"I'm too antsy. I'm used to continuously moving."

"Me too. That's why I enjoy the stop when I get it," Kent said.

"Okay. Give me about five more minutes, please?" Robin asked.

"I can do that," Nate agreed.

When she finished, she turned the paper around to show them.

"Dang, girl! You can draw! Totally jelly!" Kent said, looking at the drawing.

"Amazing," Nate agreed. "It looks like a picture. Well done! I'm curious to see if you can still weld."

"I am, too," she said.

Kent moved back to the chair and cracked his back before sitting back in his seat. "I'm curious to see if your house brings back any memories."

"If so, we may want to venture to the warehouse remains and the cabin to see if you remember anything from those two places," Nate suggested.

"What about her childhood house?" Kent asked. "Is it still standing?"

"I don't think so. That fire was horrific," Nate said. "However, the one she lived in with her grandparents is still standing. So is my house. We could take a *this is your life* tour once you're set free."

"I think a few of those a day would work," Robin agreed. "Too many at once will overload me."

"I hate to say it, but I think you should take Alyssa up on her offer," Kent said. "She seems like she sincerely wants to help you."

"I agree with Kent. She's not going to charge you for eight sessions. It may be good to have her in between the various stops. It may help you sort things out," Nate said.

"All right. I'll call her and set it up. I just need to know when I'm getting out of here," she said, picking up the call button.

"Can I help you?" Came over the speaker in the room.

"Is there someone I can talk to in order to ask questions?" Robin asked.

"I'll send your nurse in there when she's available if it's not an emergency."

"It's not."

"Okay. Thank you," she said and disconnected the line.

"Okay." Robin shrugged. "Well, looks like I'm stuck here for a bit. Not sure what I'm going to do with all of this time."

"I wouldn't watch tv," Kent said. "The story's plastered all over the news. That's not the kind of thing I would want shoved back in my face."

"Same," Robin said. "What if we take a walk?"

"Are you sure you're good for that?" Nate asked. "Not sure what shape your legs are in."

"One way to find out. Would you please...oh!" Robin covered her face.

"What?" Kent asked.

"My clothes are covered in blood," she reminded them.

"They're actually in police custody. The only thing you have to wear right now is what you have on."

"Oh, honey! That won't do." Kent stood up. "Let me go to the store for you."

"No need. You can just go to my house," Robin suggested.

"No. Trust me. I got this. *This* is something I'm good at."

"Do you need money or my sizes?"

Kent burst out in laughter. "Girl, I told you I was good at this. I know your sizes by looking at you. Let me do this for you. It won't take long."

Robin put her hands up in surrender. "Okay. Do your thing."

"Would you mind bringing real food back with you?" Nate asked. He pulled out a fifty from his wallet. "This food here is questionable. She won't get healthy eating it, and neither will I."

"I got it."

"No. It's okay. Here," Nate tried to hand him the money again.

"I got you, boo," Kent said. "We are all in this together. I'll go to Rousseau's. Rick's working. He loves all three of us. Pretty sure he'll comp it."

"All right. Thank you. I appreciate it," Nate said.

"Me too," Robin said, putting her arms up for a hug.

As Kent hugged her, he said, "We always look out for family."

"Agreed," she said, and he left.

"I like him," Nate said after the door closed. "He's a really good guy."

"He is one in a million. I only wish he could find someone to love him the way he deserves it."

"Someday," Nate said. "Until then, he's got family in us."

Robin took his hand and gave it a squeeze. "There are so many memories I wish I had. You both seem super sweet. Everyone I seem to have around me seems sweet. I feel like I'm waiting for the other shoe to drop."

"Robin, you've been through a lot in your life. You have been selective in your friends and those friends you call family. I don't mind that you forgot some of that. There are some painful memories in there. I *really* wish you could forget what happened with Liam. Unfortunately, that's not possible. While you were sedated, I did have a couple conversations with friends of mine on the force. They gave me a little more information on Liam."

"Like?"

"Like his dad was a cretin and abused his mother."

"Oh!"

"Basically, what he did to you was a learned behavior. When his mom left his dad, the dad fought for custody of the sons. The mom got full custody of Liam and his brother, *but* his dad fought back. He stalked her until she literally went crazy, and committed suicide. Then the boys had to go back to the dad."

Robin gasped, slightly covering her mouth. "Poor Logan! How did he end up such a good guy?"

"Abused kids usually go one extreme or the other. They are the collateral damage many don't take into consideration. Many times, the abused parent stays in hopes of the focus being on them and not on the children. However, in this case, their mom had reached her max. It was because the dad turned on both boys. That's how she originally got custody. The dad did a bunch of stuff to make her paranoid. She couldn't prove it was him. She actually couldn't prove what was going on at all. That's what sent her over the edge...literally. When they divorced, she moved to Oregon. She jumped off one of the cliffs. Their dad brought them back here to finish raising them. You know the final product."

"How did Logan turn out so good, though?"

"When he went to college, he got counseling. He refused to talk to his dad after he graduated high school. He was eighteen and walked away. Liam, it seems, stayed with his dad, who died about a year ago of cancer."

"Good grief! Um, have you seen Logan today?"

"He's supposed to be on shift tomorrow. I asked," Nate said. "He's been on my mind. I've been praying for him since I found all of that out. Also, I'm sure he's catching flack regarding his brother kidnapping and torturing you. I can't imagine it went over well that Liam stole Logan's badge to get in here, either."

"I can't imagine! Is there a way you can call him to come see me today?"

"I can try. I'll go into the hall. I'll still be able to see the door. I'll be right back. Do not answer the phone or turn the television on, please."

"I won't. I promise." She crossed her heart with her fingers.

He leaned down and kissed her head before heading into the hallway.

She let out a heavy sigh as the door closed behind Nate. Everything was such a mess! She wasn't sure how she would clean it all up. So many loose ends!

Logan came to Robin's room about an hour later, just as Kent arrived with several bags. They came in at the same time.

"Did you buy out the store?" Robin asked, wide-eyed.

"Well, I was finally given the chance to add to your wardrobe. I took it and ran with it. Your style is super cas, but I feel you have a body under there. Now," he set the bags on the bed near her so she could look through them.

"Thank you for coming in, too, Logan," Robin said to him.

He awkwardly sat in the chair.

"Which do you want to do first?" Nate asked.

"Did you bring food?" Robin asked Kent.

"Of course! I told you Ricky likes us," he said, holding up three bags. "I brought plenty, so if you want some, we got you, too," he offered to Logan.

"Um, sure," he said, shifting in his chair.

"Thinking you need to let the poor guy off the hook first." Nate nodded toward Logan.

"Okay. So, going deep first," Robin said. She put her hand out, and he took it. "Nate filled me in on everything. Do you remember me from when you were younger?"

"I do. You dated Liam for a few years. That was just after we moved back...after our mom died."

"I know. I'm sorry for all you went through."

"You're apologizing to *me*?" he asked, stunned. "I would think you would be livid with me."

"Did you do it?"

"No."

"Then, why would I be mad at you?"

"I-I don't...I don't know what to say."

"Look, the way I look at it, we've both had a horrific start. Neither of us has a family."

"That's true."

"If you want, we could combine and be like brother and sister," she offered.

"Are you serious?"

"Yep!"

"Could I be a part of that family?" Kent asked. "When I came out, my family disowned me."

"You already are," Robin said. When he gave her a hug, she said, "And you always will be."

"Thank you!" Kent sat back in his place at the end of the bed.

"Here's the deal. I feel like we all need to stick together and look out for each other. None of us have that," Robin explained.

Kent grinned. "We do now!"

"Agreed!" Logan smiled. "Thank you!"

"Can we eat now?" Nate asked. "Kind of hungry."

"Then we'll look at the clothes?" Kent asked. "I want to see how you look in this stuff."

"Will it fit my style?"

"Oh, honey, I'm good. Just trust your brother."

"All right," Robin said. "Let's eat first, before Nate gets feisty."

CHAPTER 17

A HIDDEN FIRE IS DISCOVERED BY SMOKE

A couple of days later, Robin was released from the hospital. Nate stayed in the hospital, showering in the room, with his parents bringing him clean clothes. When she was released, he was more than ready to leave as well.

"So," he said, sitting in the car, "where do you want to go? The restaurant? Home?"

"Actually, the fire scene," she suggested. "I want to know if it triggers anything."

"That's a brave first step. Are you sure you want to start with the big one?"

"I go to see Alyssa tomorrow. I think if I'm going to do it, I should do it today."

"Do you have Kent coming to stay with you tonight?"

"Yes. You need to go home before your roommate thinks you abandoned him."

Nate chuckled. "I've received a few text messages like that, but Patterson's a cool guy. He usually just rolls with the punches. As long as I pay my half of the rent, it's all good."

"Well, Kent's working until eight. He doesn't have to close tonight."

"That'll work. That should give me plenty of time to get some sleep."

"That's what I was thinking."

"Okay then. Fire scene it is. Let me call Dad so he can meet us there. He'll want to be there with us."

"Okay," she agreed. "Ya know, I gotta hand it to Kent. He's got style. I love these clothes. I think we're going to have to go shopping some more."

"Agreed," Nate said, dialing his phone.

Ian agreed to meet them at the warehouse fire scene. So, they headed directly over there.

As they drove up, Robin looked at everything. She didn't miss a single detail. If this is where she would start to recover her memories, she would pay close attention.

Ian pulled up right next to them as they stood outside Nate's truck. "Hey, guys!"

"Hey, Dad," Nate said. He glanced at the skeletal remains of the warehouse. "With this much gone, were you able to find anything?"

"Actually, yes." Ian started walking toward the remains with a clipboard in one hand and a pen in the other. "Let's start over here."

They followed him carefully past the caution tape. "This looks horrible. Y'all found me in here?" Robin shuddered.

"Yes. Thank God, they actually found you. You wouldn't be here if they didn't," Ian said. He walked over to an area with partial walls, anywhere from six inches to two feet in height. "Okay, here is the origination point. This is where it burned the hottest the longest. It looks like it went into the walls. The entire warehouse was basically tinder."

"What's that smell?" Robin asked, covering her mouth.

"Decaying rats is my best guess," Ian said. "Along with the lovely burnt insulation and any other chemicals or materials left behind."

"That's nasty! I wouldn't think it would still smell six days later."

"Give it a few more, and it will go away. This is tame compared to a normal day," Ian explained. "It takes a few days to dissipate. Despite what it looks like in the movies, the stench is something that takes a bit of getting used to."

"I see," she said, looking around, making sure to watch where she stepped.

"Do you know what accelerant was used?" Nate asked, looking closer at what was left of the walls.

"Not really sure. It's not gasoline. As you can see by the pattern, it wasn't a flash, but it was." Ian pointed to an area, which both Robin and Nate went over to get a closer look.

"Spray paint, and matches or a lighter," Robin said, looking at the wall.

"What?" Ian asked. "What do you mean?"

"Most of this is pretty cooked, but as you said, the entire place was basically tinder, so it moved through here quickly. Look down here. Spray paint," Robin pointed to where two pieces of wood met at the corner of what was left of the room. "Looks black and red."

Nate and Ian both looked at each other before Ian asked, "How do you know matches or a lighter was used to ignite it?"

"Um," she tucked her hair behind her ear, "I feel it. It's like when you know how to do something like a difficult math problem, but you're not sure how to explain it to someone else."

"Muscle memory," Nate said in understanding.

"What?" Ian asked.

"We found out she can draw via muscle memory. That's also how she wrote her last name before she remembered it. If you recall, she painted with multiple mediums in high school. If we assume she's still doing it, it would be like second nature."

"That makes sense. But painting and burning buildings are two entirely different things," Ian pointed out.

Nate pulled his cell phone out and typed something into his search engine. He then clicked on the images. "Not necessarily."

"What do you mean?" Ian asked.

Nate typed into his YouTube app. Then he handed his phone to his dad. "Watch this."

Ian saw an artist create an amazing mural. After he finished, he set the painting on fire.

"That looks like a real fire," Ian said, amazed. "With the painting behind it, it looks wild! Look at that!"

"She's a welder and an artist. It's not a stretch to think she may have done that a time or two," Nate explained.

"I see what you mean," Ian said as he continued to watch the video. "That's a really cool effect."

"He's an artist. He gets paid a ton of money for that," Nate explained. "I've seen a couple of his YouTube videos."

Ian continued to watch as the artist put the fire out. "It's black. What's the point?"

"Keep watching," Nate said.

Ian watched as the artist used the soot from the blackness and repainted other colors with his fingers, creating an entirely different effect. "Holy cow! That's super cool!" he exclaimed when it was finished.

"The artist can only light it once," Nate said, "unless he wants to destroy it."

"That's wild!" Ian handed the phone back to his son. "Do you know if you ever did that?"

She shrugged. "I mean, if I know what it looks like, I would think I would have. I'm kind of along for the ride here."

"I wonder if we can use her to look at the other sites and see if she sees something we missed," Ian wondered aloud.

"Couldn't hurt," Nate said with a shrug.

"What else do you see?" Ian asked Robin.

"Did you find metal? If there were spray cans involved, the cans would have exploded."

"Yep. Those have already been entered into evidence," Ian confirmed.

Robin looked around some more. "Nothing else stands out to me here."

"Come on over here," Ian said, lightly tugging on her arm.

Together, they walked over to an area in the center of the burnt-out remains. Robin had a flash of memory shoot through her head. She fought to bring it back to the front.

"What is it?" Nate asked.

She looked up as if she could see the staircase. "Up there."

"What's up there?" Ian asked.

"Stairs. He-he rammed into me, and we fell down the stairs." She shook her head as she continued to pull the memory forward. She placed her hand on the back of her head. "I was on the bottom. Hit my head. Then, black."

"That would make sense," Ian said, wrapping his arm around the clipboard as he held it to his chest. "It's consistent with your injuries."

"Do you remember what he looked like?" Nate asked.

Robin shook her head. "The memory is too fast. He just looks like a shadow. I-I'm sorry. I wish I could remember."

Ian rested his hand on her shoulder. "It's okay. You may still remember. If you do, write it down as fast as you can. The memories may come back in time."

Robin stood there, rubbing her arms. "It's weird. It's like I remember it, but I don't."

"Do you want to go look at the others?" Nate asked. "Or will that be too much?"

"It may be too much for today. If you two go back to her home or anywhere in town for that matter, she could have flashbacks and migraine by the end of the day," Ian explained. "She has to take things slowly."

"She said she wanted them to come because she meets with Alyssa tomorrow."

"I don't know what to do," Robin said. "If it's this strong here, what's going to happen the further we walk into this?" She shook her head. "I don't know if I want to do this. Why was I here?"

"I don't know, but apparently you weren't alone," Ian said. "Just remember that."

"What if we just go to your house? Hopefully you have food there," Nate suggested. "I don't want to overwhelm you on your first day."

"Probably a good idea," Robin agreed.

With that, Ian went to work while Robin and Nate headed to her house.

When they drove up to the house, Robin got a few memories that flashed into her mind. "Alarm? Welding in a shed? Do these make sense?" she asked Nate.

"Yep. These are all real things," Nate confirmed, pulling into the driveway.

As soon as she saw the shed, she said, "Metal tiger."

"That could be the project you're working on. Let's go get your keys and find out." He got out and helped her out of the truck. He grabbed the bag with the clothes Kent got her.

When they went to the front of the house, there were flowers next to the door. Robin stared at them, heart racing.

"What? What's wrong?" Nate asked. He helped her over to the porch swing. Then he pulled off the card from the flowers. Opening it, he explained, "They're from Logan, welcoming you home."

"Oh. Okay. Why do I feel like I'm going to have a panic attack? It happened when I saw the flowers."

"Probably because Liam did that to you. Do you want me to go in first and take a look around? I can make sure nothing else should throw you too badly."

She nodded. "Please."

He handed her the vase before going into the house. When he walked in and turned the lights on, he was relieved to find it the way she left it that night. Everything was in its place. He looked in the kitchen and the bedroom before going out to bring her inside.

"It's safe," he said, taking the flowers from her. Then he picked up the bag and followed her inside.

She saw the votive candles on the coffee table. She remembered resting her head on the coffee table, looking at the red candles. She picked one up and inhaled the scent of the apple pie. "Mmm," she said. "Smells good."

"Do you want to go to the shed or rest in here for a bit?" Nate asked.

"Let me look around here first."

She went room to room, looking around. She had tiny flashes all through the walk. When she finished, she sat down on the couch. "Whew! This is exhausting."

"Any more memories?" Nate asked, sitting beside her. He handed her a soda from the refrigerator. Then he opened his and took a long drink. "Pretty sure this is going to be an ongoing thing until all the memories come back. What were the ones you just had?"

"I remember lighting those candles and that I love to look at them."

"Do you want me to light them?"

"Sure."

As he lit each candle, a new memory came.

"Oh! When will this slow down?" she asked, grabbing her head. "These literally hurt. They are small flashes. Nothing of significance yet."

"Gotcha." He sat back down beside her. "What if we start with us? Do you remember anything about me?"

"Any of the memories I've had sitting here have you in them, if that helps."

"What do you want to know? Do you want to know more about us in general?"

"I think that's a good place to start."

"Well, we met at my house. We had a bonfire after a football game. I played football. You were friends with my sister, Jenny."

"Blond hair? Blue eyes?" Robin asked.

"Yep. I'm one of her older brothers. She's a year younger than me. I also have two older brothers, Brad and Scott."

"Okay. So, I was friends with Jenny?"

"Yep. There was a bonfire. You were looking at it and talking to Dad when I walked up. Liam was your boyfriend at the time. He was controlling."

"Doesn't surprise me."

"Well, we kicked him out. Jenny had a sleepover that night. A couple girls spent the night, including you. Seems Liam came back that night. I didn't know it until I found you in the kitchen soaked by the rainstorm that night. You and I talked for a bit before you went back downstairs. One of the things we talked about was you and me going out the next day instead of you going with Liam to Homecoming."

"He punched you that night," Robin said, remembering.

"Yep. Well, he tried anyway. We ended up going mini-golfing. We had a great time."

"We did! I remember that night. It was the first time I was able to relax going on a date in a long time."

"Good. Do you remember what happened the following Monday at school?"

"The locker."

"Yes. He got suspended for that. We talked to your grandparents and you filed a restraining order against him. He had to change schools. I graduated that year, but I had the football team looking out for you after I left."

"Thank you," she said, taking his hand. "Seems you are always rescuing me."

"Not necessarily. Let's keep going. After graduation, your grandparents moved into a retirement home and sold their house. You got an apartment and went to welding school. A lot of this part I don't remember as my own memories, but what you filled me in on."

"Okay."

"So, you went to welding school and continued to do your art. You like to paint, which you won multiple awards for in high school – that I *do* remember. I guess when you became a welder, it gave you another medium to play with. My parents said they went to a couple of your art shows. They met up with your grandparents for a couple of them."

"That's cool."

"You did well. Once you had enough money saved up, you got off the oil rigs and came back here. You bought this house and have been working as a server at Rousseau's, which is where we reconnected."

"Your fire crew came with you, and you guys were at my table," she said as a memory flashed through. "Kent was all about you guys. When you asked me out, he told me he would disown me if I didn't go."

Nate chuckled. "Yeah. He's a character. I'm glad he is such a good friend, slash brother, to you."

"Same. I have a few flashbacks of us laughing."

"He definitely knows how to lighten a mood."

"That he does. So, I'm a server at Rousseau's?"

"Yes."

"What kind of restaurant is it?"

"A little bit of everything. The original owner was from Louisiana. He cooked a lot of Cajun food to start. Then, people asked for other things, so he slowly added to the menu."

"He changed his menu because people asked?"

"Rousseau's is one of the few decent restaurants in town. He added to his menu and made a ton of money. When he retired, he sold it to the Bakers. Their son, Ricky, is one of the managers."

"Wasn't that the one Kent said loved us?"

"Yep. Well, there's nothing wrong with your short-term memory. You always were smart. I can't imagine how frustrating this is for you."

"Very," Robin said. "It's like I know there are memories there. I just can't access them. The stuff you are telling me is familiar, but it's not. It's weird and frustrating at the same time."

"I can't imagine, nor do I want to."

"Good news is I feel comfortable with you. I also feel comfortable with Kent. We'll get to know Logan. Until then, he has a family."

"Which he seems to be taking seriously. The flowers were a sweet gesture."

"You work tomorrow, right?"

"Yep."

"Do you want to do a family meal with Logan and Kent the next day? That way, we can get to know each other better," Robin suggested.

"If Logan doesn't work, sure. Have to check with Kent as well."

"He's off tomorrow, so he can be with me while you're at work. He said something about getting off work at three the next day."

"Great! Check with Logan. If he's off, then definitely!"

"Awesome. Not sure if I remember how to cook or not."

"Well, to be honest, you weren't the best cook to begin with. You're pretty good, but I actually cook better. Would you be offended if I cooked?"

"Not at all...as long as I can help you."

"It's your kitchen." He shrugged. "Probably a good idea to explore it so you know where everything is."

"Good point. So, am I caught up regarding us?"

"Yep. Do you want to ask me questions, or do you want to go check out your shed?"

"Let's go to the shed," Robin said. "The memories are hitting a little less hard from us talking through them. Let's see what's in there."

"You have keys hanging by the back door," he said, getting off the couch. She followed behind. "Going to assume the shed key is among them."

"We'll soon find out."

"Good attitude," Nate said, picking up both sets of keys from the key ring holder.

As they headed toward the shed, Robin stopped in her tracks. "That's mine," she said, looking at her Jeep, "but I remember something else. A silver Nissan?"

"That was probably Liam's. He was following you for a bit. Correction: he has been following you since high school. We just didn't know it."

"That's creepy."

"Agreed. He made a poster of all the pictures over the years and left it the night he was going to take you out on a date."

"Why would I agree to that?" Robin asked. "According to what you told me, I wouldn't think that would be a smart move."

"He was stalking you. Moreso over the last few weeks. He was very aggressive. We think it's because you started dating me. Kind of the *last person he wanted you to be with* situation."

"Gotcha."

"Here we go," Nate said, unlocking the lock.

The storage shed was twenty feet by twenty feet. There were all sorts of tools, tables, and tanks scattered around in an organized fashion. There was a metal tiger in the back by one of the tables.

"Going to assume that's my current project?" Robin gestured toward the tiger. Nate nodded. "And this?" she asked, picking up the small welding helmet that looked like it was for a child. "Do I have a child? If so, why would I name her after me?"

"That's yours. Your dad was a welder too. He airbrushed the helmet for you to watch as he worked."

"Hood."

"What?"

"It's called a hood," she corrected him. "I have a few memories pass my mind of me and my dad at a table where he was working on welding projects. This is mine now." She picked up a bigger helmet. It was painted with a base color of purple. Her name was airbrushed, along with blue and white flames.

"This is cool! I haven't seen this one yet. Looks like you inherited your dad's talents for art."

"Thank you," she said, and then walked around the shed, commenting as memories surfaced.

"Seems like you're remembering quite a lot," Nate said, attaching lock to secure the door before they headed back to the house.

"They're small, short flashes. Not much substance. Even when you're telling me the memories, it's like they're there, but they're not. It's honestly giving me a headache."

"Okay. Why don't you take a nap?" Nate asked. They walked into the kitchen, where he hung up the keys in their place. He quickly looked around the kitchen for food. "I need to run to the grocery store. I can cook for you while you're sleeping."

"Sounds like a plan," she said and headed to bed.

In the bedroom, she found several photos. She picked up one of two adults and two kids. The kids were very young. "Possibly my family," she said, setting it back in its place.

She picked up the next picture. It was of her on an oil rig, along with several guys. They looked like a tough bunch.

She set it down and picked up another one. This was of her and who she was certain were her grandparents. She ran her fingers over the picture as a couple memories surfaced. One of them was in the art studio during one of her showings. Her grandparents and Nate's parents stood beside her, alongside one of her sculptures. The sculpture had a sold sticker on it.

She then picked up the last photo. It was her at her high school graduation. She was in the picture with other people. One of them she recognized as Jenny.

She set the picture back down and then sat on the bed. It took her a few minutes to calm her head from spinning from the memories. When she finally did, she lay down and graciously allowed sleep to take over.

When she finally woke several hours later, she heard Kent and Nate talking in the living room.

"She doing okay?" Kent asked.

"She's getting some memories back. We need to take it slow with her. They are giving her a headache."

"I couldn't imagine waking up and not remembering anything about myself."

"She's doing amazingly well."

"How long has she been asleep?"

"About five hours."

"Until now," she said, walking into the living room. "My head still hurts, but it's tolerable."

"Come and sit," Nate said, tapping the couch next to him. Kent was sitting in the chair. There was a movie playing in the background.

Robin sat down next to Nate, who put his arm over her shoulder. "How did you sleep?" he asked.

"Hard," she said.

"Good. Dinner is in the oven."

"Smells good. What is it?" she asked.

"Lasagna is in the oven. I just added garlic French bread a few minutes before you came out here. It's just about done. I also have a salad in the fridge."

"Can we keep him?" Kent asked. "He knows how to cook."

Nate laughed. "I'm not planning on going anywhere unless she drops me."

"Not planning on it," Robin said, tapping his leg. "You seem like a keeper."

Kent rolled his eyes. "Now, if y'all could just hook me up with some of those hotties he works with."

"Yeah, you don't want any of them, even if they were your type. Most of them, I wouldn't even trust with my sister. With our lives, yes. To date? No."

"No?" Kent asked. "Do tell. Why not?"

"They know they're wanted men. Some of them are good, but most of them really aren't mature enough for a relationship. Those who are, are married or dating someone."

"I see."

"Now, they may have some friends," Nate said. "I can check around for you."

Kent perked up. "Are you serious?"

"If you're looking for a serious relationship, then yes, I'm serious."

"Done!" Kent said. "I seriously just want someone to love me for me. I want someone to grow old with."

"That's pretty much what everyone wants," Nate said. "You seem to have a good heart. You deserve it."

"Thank you."

"Okay. I need to get our dinner out before I burn it," Nate said, getting off the couch.

When he was in the kitchen, Kent looked over his shoulder to ensure Nate couldn't hear him. He moved next to Robin. In a low voice, he said, "I like him."

"I'm starting to. He's really sweet and caring. He also knows me pretty well. He helped me by filling in a lot of blanks. As he did, I got brief flashes of memories."

"That's cool. So, when are you two going out on another official date?"

"Not sure."

"We need to go shopping first," Kent said. "I like shopping. And you have a great figure!"

"Why do I feel like a dress-up doll?" Robin asked with a smirk.

Kent chuckled. "Well, you have this great body, yet you hide it under these baggy clothes. That outfit looks amazing on you, by the way."

Robin had a pair of bootcut jeans and a belt. She has a spaghetti strap tank top with a vest over it. She originally had boots on before slipping them off when they walked into the house.

"Thank you. Seems my brother is a great stylist."

"I got style. That's for sure. One of these days, you'll let me tackle that mane of yours. All one length is pretty, but I'll bet layers would look fantastic."

"Do you know someone who would cut it how you want it?"

"Actually, I do. Tony is a good friend of mine. He and his husband have a great salon about an hour from here."

"Do you want to see if they can squeeze me in tomorrow?"

"Are you serious?"

"Yep."

"Yes!" he said. He jumped off the couch and went into her bedroom to call.

"Dinner," Nate called from the kitchen.

Robin got up and went into the kitchen. "Kent's on the phone with his friend trying to get me a salon appointment."

"For what?" Nate asked.

"He wants to put layers in my hair."

"I'll bet that would look good with your hair."

"I think it will."

"Oh! It will!" Kent said, coming into the kitchen. "Your appointment is at ten tomorrow morning."

"Great!" Robin smiled. "I'm actually looking forward to it."

"Also, thinking you two need some time away from this place together," Kent suggested, looking at Nate.

"What?" Nate asked.

"Well, as much as I'm all for it, Robin, didn't you want to have dinner together with Logan and Kent tomorrow night?"

"Yes, but you *do* have another day off the next day," Kent pointed out. "I have a brilliant idea if you're up for it."

Nate set the lasagna on the set table, which already had the salad and bread on it. "What are you thinking?"

"Well, I know of a place that has racing on small go-carts. It also has an old-fashioned arcade and a mini-golf area. Sound like something up y'all's alley?"

"Actually, it does. What do you think, Robin?" Nate asked her.

"Sounds like fun?" Robin offered. "I don't know any of that. I do remember you saying we went mini-golfing the first time we went out."

"Yep. Do you want to go out with me?" Nate asked.

Robin looked at him as he sat down next to her. "Yes. I would love to."

"Y'all are too sweet," Kent said. "See? That's what I want."

"Let me do some checking around," Nate said.

"I'd appreciate it."

"I am off on Sunday," Nate said, scooping some lasagna on everyone's plates, "do you want to go with me to church?"

"I don't know if I've ever been to church," Robin said. "I'm not sure about that."

"Just try it, honey," Kent encouraged. "Not that I want you to turn into a Bible thumper, but he's not one, so going to assume his church isn't that way." He raised an eyebrow as he looked at Nate.

"Not really," Nate said. "We're one of those *take you as you are* type churches. We're independent."

Robin bopped her head side-to-side before she agreed, "Yeah. I'll go."

"Awesome!" Nate said, pleased.

"Oh! What time is your appointment with Alyssa tomorrow?" Kent asked. "I forgot about that."

"It's in the afternoon, at two, I think."

"Okay. We'll be back in plenty of time," Kent said, satisfied.

CHAPTER 18

PLAYING WITH FIRE

Nate left around nine, so Robin and Kent watched a movie before going to bed. She had a busy day ahead of her. She had an insane schedule for the next few days. Logan had the next day off, so he decided to join them in their day's events.

"Hey," Logan said when she opened the door the next morning at eight-forty-five. "Am I on time?"

"Yep. We were just finishing getting ready," Robin said. She sat on the couch to put her shoes on.

"Have to say, Kent, you *do* have great style! The outfits I've seen you get for her look great. I have a horrid sense of style. I could use some help if you could spare the time? There's this sweet girl at work I asked out. We're supposed to go out on Saturday. The only thing she's seen me in is scrubs."

"Oh, I got you, brother. Let's do it. Name the day and time."

"Nate's working on Saturday. If you want some company, along with a woman's opinion, I'd be happy to accompany you?" Robin offered.

"Perfect!" Kent said. "It's a date!"

"Sounds like a plan," Logan agreed.

"Let's get moving with Robin's make-over, and then we'll get you taken care of," Kent said. He walked around Logan, looking him up and down. "I think Tony needs to do something with your hair, too, if you're up for it?"

"Does he have time?" Logan asked. "I've never been to a salon."

"Apparently," Kent said and clicked his tongue. "I think we can get you sorted. You have a great body as well."

"Why do I feel like I'm on one of those make-over shows?" Logan asked, as his face flushed.

"Honey, you were raised by a man and not a good one," Kent said. Logan's face blushed again. "It's all good. We'll get you sorted. You got a great body, too. Where did y'all come from? You got great genes."

"You do too," Robin pointed out. "You're a hottie in your own right."

"Just have to find someone who appreciates me for more than my looks." Kent crossed his arms and huffed.

Logan and Robin laughed. "You will. Give Nate time," Robin said. "In the meantime, we need to head out."

Tony fit Robin, Logan, *and* Kent for hair appointments. "I'm only about five minutes behind," Tony said when Kent apologized.

"I got you," Kent said, handing him a fifty-dollar bill as a tip.

"You don't need to do *that* much!" Tony exclaimed. "But I appreciate you for it."

"Honey, you fit us all in last minute. This is to let you know how much I appreciate you...and your hubby."

"Thank you. I'll pass that along to him." He sighed as he looked at the trio. "I feel like a proud daddy. You guys look amazing!"

"They look like models," a customer commented. "Where are you three from?" she asked as she walked up to the counter.

"We're from Hemlock," Kent said.

She handed him a card. "Email me with your contact information when you get back to Hemlock. I have a fashion show in two weeks in Dallas. I would absolutely love to have all three of you there as models."

"I-I don't model," Logan said, his face was just as red as Robin's.

Robin shook her head. "Me neither."

"What do you three do?" she asked.

"Robin and I are servers in a restaurant," Kent explained, "and Logan is a nurse."

"Seriously?" she asked, wide-eyed. "No. Absolutely not! You three need to get ahold of me. You're being wasted."

"Ms.," Kent looked at the card, "Ms. Walker, we appreciate your –"

"Don't finish that sentence. Email me first. And you can call me Kendra."

"Kendra's a long-time client," Tony said. "She knows her stuff. In the thirteen years she's been coming here, she's hasn't offered anyone what she just offered you."

"Look, I know talent when I see it. You three have it in spades. You are the hidden gems of Hemlock."

"Oh! You should see this one's boyfriend," Kent said. "He's a hot firefighter."

"Okay. Apparently, I need to take a trip to Hemlock," Kendra said. "Sounds like there may be quite a few I need to talk to. I've been looking for something different for a few months. You guys have all-American written all over you."

"I'm *definitely* interested," Kent said. "I'll email you. We'll talk more about it on our way home."

"I would appreciate it," Kendra said. "I'm serious about this. Look me up."

"We will. Thank you," Kent said, and they left the salon. "Well, *that* was productive!" He grinned.

"I'm not too sure about this whole modeling thing," Robin said. "That doesn't sound like it would fit me."

"It does me," Kent said. "That's right up my alley."

"Then," Logan rested his hand on Kent's shoulder, "we can say *that's our brother* when we see you walk the stage."

"Yeah. We can say we knew you when..." Robin added.

"Oh no! You're not getting rid of me quite that easily," Kent said. "I'll go this time. We'll see what happens from there."

"Are you sure?" Robin asked as they got into her Jeep.

"Girl, if opportunity knocks, you gotta grab it," Kent explained. "This is not one that comes along like ever. You, too, Logan. Obviously, Tony did an amazing job if she stopped us. I'm going to look her up."

Robin and Logan talked about his work until Kent abruptly sat up in his seat. "Dang!" he exclaimed.

"What?" Robin asked.

"She's out of New York. She's got a fantastic reputation in the fashion world."

"So, she *was* serious?" Logan asked.

"Serious as a heart attack," Kent said. "She's a trendsetter in the fashion world. She's done shows in Milan, Paris, London, Rome, Tokyo, New York Fashion Week, and more! She's crazy popular. Oh! Please do this with me?" Kent asked. "I will never ask you for another thing...like ever. Please?"

"I'll tell you what," Logan said, leaning forward from his spot in the back seat, "I'll do it with you. Robin's probably not ready for that yet, since she doesn't even know who she is."

"Good point. And, yes!" Kent said, clapping his hands. "I am so excited! We got this!" He gave Logan a high-five.

"Not sure what we're getting into, but the extra money couldn't hurt," Logan said.

"Agreed," Kent said.

They talked about it all the way back to the house.

That afternoon, Robin's appointment went well with Alyssa. Alyssa was thrilled to learn some of her memories came back when Robin saw familiar places and talked to Nate. She was fascinated and excited to find out how Robin progressed over the next few weeks.

That afternoon, when Kent and Logan were still there, Ian came to the door. "Hi, Robin," he said, walking in after she opened the door.

"Hi. Nate's at work."

"I know. I already talked to him. I know you've had a busy day. Would you mind making it a bit longer and go look at a couple of the fire scenes with me?"

"We could go shopping for Logan while you're gone," Kent suggested.

"That'll work," Robin agreed. "I'll call you guys when we're on the way back here."

"Perfect," Kent said. "Let's go shopping for you. I hope you brought your credit card."

"Why do I feel like I may regret this?" Logan said.

"Oh, honey, you know you're enjoying this," Kent said. "Us guys like it when we're fussed over. We just don't always like to admit it."

"You do," Robin pointed out.

"Babe, I'm not your average guy, in case you hadn't noticed."

"Wouldn't take you any other way, though. I love you for you," she said, and gave him a hug.

"I like our little family," Logan said. "It's nice to have people in it who actually like you."

Robin gave him a hug as well. "We do. We're still getting used to each other, but I think it's a good family."

"I'll take y'all over my birth family any day," Kent said. "Now," he put his arm over Logan's shoulder, "let's get you dressed for success."

"That means you're in my custody," Ian said to Robin.

"Let's go."

On the way to the warehouses, Robin asked, "How come you didn't want Nate with us for this?"

"I want you to feel comfortable telling me whatever you want to tell me without him asking questions. You have an unusually good grasp of fire. I want to find out how and why."

"Gotcha. I really wish I had my memories back. It would help fill in a lot of blanks."

"Can't imagine how frustrating it is for you going through all of this."

"It is. I can't tell you how or why I was in that warehouse. I can't tell you how or why I know the things I know, either. There's a lot I can't tell you."

"I know. We'll get there. In the meantime, I'm going to pick your brain. You have a talent when it comes to fire. I'm curious to see how much. This is a test. We're going to this scene. I want you to tell me what happened."

Robin shrugged. "Okay."

They pulled into the first warehouse parking lot. It was flattened like the other one she saw the other day.

As they got out of the truck, she looked around and shuddered.

"Are you okay?" Ian asked.

"Yeah. Just a bit creepy."

"C'mon. Let's go see what you know," he said, handing her a pair of gloves while he put a pair on.

Robin carefully stepped into the charred remains. There were only a few lingering smells left. It was a lot more tolerable than the first fire scene.

She wandered around, looking at the ground. Occasionally, she would bend down and move a piece of wood to see what was under it or pick up something to get a closer look.

She finally crouched down in what was the office area. "There looks like there may have been stairs, which would have put this area on the second floor."

"Very good."

"I think this is where it started. There's some wax here. Did it start with a candle?"

"Okay. I'm impressed. How do you know that?"

"I think I'm a bit of a pyro," she admitted. "This whole thing is fascinating to me. Don't ask me how I know things. I just do."

"I'm sure it will come with time. What else can you tell me about this?"

"What's this? It looks metal," she asked, picking up a piece about three inches by two inches.

"That's part of a can."

"A spray can?" she asked.

"Yes."

"Did you find more?"

"I did," he admitted.

"Weren't there spray cans at the other one?"

"There were."

"Is there another fire scene similar to this one?" she asked, standing up.

"There is."

"Where?"

"Right over there," he said, pointing down the street.

"Want to walk?"

"If you're up for it."

They walked down the road. When she walked up to the area, she shook her head. "I feel like I've been here."

"Did you have the same feeling with the other ones?"

"Not sure. I had a dream about the first one. That was also the one y'all found me in. This one feels different."

"How?" Ian asked.

"I'm not sure. It's like I was here before. It's almost like seeing shadows of a memory."

"What can you tell me about this scene?"

She scanned the grounds, zeroing in on one area. "Was that where the office was?" she asked, pointing toward an area.

"It was," Ian said hesitantly. Her extensive knowledge of the scenes concerned him.

She walked over to the area and looked through the remains. She shook her head. "No candle. This is like the first one you took me to. The one where we talked about lighting the mural on fire."

"Agreed. Okay. I'm going to take you to one more scene," he said.

She stood. "Fair enough. Let's go."

They arrived at a house fire scene. "This one happened about a week or so ago," Ian explained as they got out. "I still have it as a crime scene, so it hasn't been touched by anyone except me and Nate."

"Okay," she said, getting out of the truck.

She walked up to the remains of the house. While it was a total loss, there was a lot more of it still intact than with the warehouse fires.

She walked through, closely examining the area before each

step. In an area of the hall, she stopped and looked at Ian, "Someone died here, right?"

"They did."

"At least one, right here."

"Yes."

She wandered into what was one of the bedrooms. The remains of a crib was in the corner next to the wall. She shut her eyes tightly. "Please don't say a child died."

"No. They got out with the mother."

She grabbed her head as flashes flew through her mind. She groaned, crouching down.

He rushed to her side. "Are you okay? What's wrong?"

She groaned again. "Fire. Mom helping me to the door. I remember...I remember...you." She looked over her shoulder up at him. "You were there."

He knelt beside her. "I was."

"M-my family." She looked around the room, tears in her eyes. "My little brother, my dad, and my mom all died." She groaned as another hard memory shot through her mind. "My grandparents. They died in a car accident. Ohh!" She moaned, grabbing her head tightly. "Make it stop."

"Do you want to stop, or do you want to figure out what happened here?"

"Give me...give me a minute." She took deep, cleansing breaths in order to control the flashes of memory trying to push themselves to the surface. "Please stop," she whispered to herself.

"We can go."

"No. Just...give me a minute."

They sat where they were for about five minutes until she got the memories under control. She took a few more breaths to clear her mind before she stood.

"You're shaking," Ian said, holding her up by her arm.

"It's a lot."

"We can leave."

"No. The test. Give me a few."

"Okay."

She took a few more minutes before she continued. She was still a little dizzy, so she stepped cautiously.

Walking into another room, she took a deep breath. She zeroed in on one area in the room. "It started in here," she said, walking over to where the wall was partially standing. "The outlet."

"Good job!" he said, pleasantly surprised. "Your grasp of fire scenes is uncanny."

"I wish I knew why."

"I'm sure. I would wonder if I were in your position. What else can you tell me?"

She surveyed the area. "There," she pointed toward another burn area. "Someone died there."

"Correct. There were two losses at this scene."

She looked around again. "I-I can't anymore."

"It's okay. Let's go home. You had a wall of memories come crashing down and still seemed to be able to identify the scene and what happened. However, you're done. Let's get you home."

He held her arm as he escorted her back to the truck. It was quiet the entire ride home. She texted Logan and Kent before they left the house fire scene, so by the time they got back to her house, the guys were there.

They were sitting on her porch swing, waiting for her. When she got out of the truck, both stood.

"Robin?" Kent said, getting a good look at her. "What happened? You look pale."

"She had some heavy memories hit her at one of the scenes," Ian explained, helping her out of his truck.

"What memories?" Kent asked.

"When her parents and brother died in the fire when she was young. Also, when she lost her grandparents."

"Ouch!" Logan cringed. "Okay. We got her," he said, as Kent took one arm and Logan took the other. Together, they ushered her into the living room and rested her on the couch.

"Can I get you something to drink?" Kent asked.

"No. I-I just need to rest."

"Thank you for coming," Ian said. "It was enlightening."

"Do you know what's going on?" Kent asked. "She looks terrified."

"They were some heavy memories. She may need you two tonight," Ian said.

Kent brushed a portion of Robin's hair to the side. With his hands on each side of her face, he declared, "I'm not leaving."

Logan had his fingers on her wrist, checking her pulse. "I'm not either. She looks like she's in shock."

"She is," Ian confirmed. "And in her current state of shock, she still identified the cause of the fire and the fact that someone passed away during the fire in that house. I'm curious to know how she knows so much about fire."

"What are you thinking?" Kent asked.

Ian crossed his arms. "I don't want to say yet. Let me work on a few things."

"Fair enough," Kent said. "We have it."

"Thank you. I'll call in a couple hours to check on her."

"That will work," Kent said, and Ian left. When the door closed behind Ian, Kent said, "Okay, just relax. We got you."

"Thank you," Robin said with a faraway look in her eyes.

"Let's watch a movie," Logan suggested. "Comedy?"

Kent nodded. "Agreed."

They wrapped her in a blanket, and all three cuddled on the couch while they watched a movie. They actually ended up watching movies all night. When Ian checked in later, she was at least smiling.

CHAPTER 19

BURNING THE CANDLE AT
BOTH ENDS

As the days passed, Robin's memories stabilized. There was still a lot missing. Together, over the next several weeks, she and Alyssa walked through what they could. Robin's sleep habits were drastically changed. Every time she closed her eyes, those heavy memories of the fire scene with her family flashed through her mind. Seeing her mother on fire on the living room floor trapped by a bookshelf, was seared into her memory. She could still feel her father kiss her head before he sent them out into the hallway with her wrapped in a blanket. She could still smell the rancid scents of that horrific night. It was as if she were living it every time she closed her eyes.

On those brutal nights, she would get up and go into the shed. One night in particular, she went in and picked up the welder mask her dad made for her. She ran her fingers over the words and picture as the tears crawled down her cheeks.

She set it aside and picked up her hood. Placing it on her head, with shaking hands, she picked up her tools and started working on her current project. It was a metal wall of fire. Through those long nights, she cut individual slices of flame. There were hundreds in varying colors. She also created a ten-by-ten-foot square with metal wires in a crisscross pattern to attach the pieces she created.

After she cut each piece, she buffered the edges. Then, she cleaned them to a shine and added colors of red, orange, white, and royal blue. The colors were more stark than actual fire, but she wanted it that way.

That night, she started the tedious work of attaching each one to the frame...one after another.

"You have got to get some sleep," Nate pleaded with her one afternoon, as he and Ian arrived. "You have been struggling for weeks."

"I know. I can't."

"You have to talk to Alyssa and see if she can prescribe anything."

"I've stalled regarding the memories," she admitted.

"Speaking of the memories, we need to talk," Ian said as they sat in her living room. "I asked Alyssa to come. She should be here any minute."

Nate sat on the couch with his arm around Robin. Raising an eyebrow, he asked, "Why is she coming here?"

"She, along with a friend of mine are on their way."

"Who?"

"It's Sandra McClintock."

"Sandra?" Nate asked. "As in, lawyer Sandra?"

"Yes."

"What's going on, Dad?" Nate asked.

"Just wait until they...one of them is here," he said, getting up as they heard a car door close.

He went to the door and opened it. "It's both of them. Looks like they drove together."

When they came in, Alyssa took one look at Robin and shook her head. "I don't think this is a good idea. Look at her."

"That may be her saving grace," Sandra said as they walked in and sat on the chairs in the living room. Ian pulled a chair from the kitchen table and sat down.

"What may be her saving grace?" Nate asked, his tone sharp. "What's going on?"

"I've put the pieces together," Ian admitted.

"What pieces?" Nate asked. "Spill it, Dad!"

"She was the one who set the warehouse fires."

"How do you know?" Nate asked.

"The evidence."

"Please tell me this is some sick joke!" Nate snapped. "She's been through enough."

"I'll talk to you about the evidence later, but for now, Sandra, Alyssa, and Robin need to talk."

"Talk *now*!"

"No. This is between them. Come on, son," Ian said, standing. "They have some work to do before she turns herself in."

"Before she *what*? What is wrong with you? She didn't set those warehouses on fire!"

"According to the evidence, she did."

"How can you say that? Robin, say something."

"I-I don't know," Robin stammered. "I don't know what's going on." She looked at Alyssa with tears in her eyes as her heart raced. "What's going on?"

Alyssa got up from her chair and knelt next to the couch. Holding Robin's hand, she promised, "I'll be with you every step of the way."

"How is this possible? I don't remember doing any of this," Robin said. "How can he say I did it?"

"According to the evidence, you did," Sandra said. "However, it doesn't look like the first one was on purpose. It does look like the second was on purpose. And the third looks like Liam was part of it."

Robin shook her head. "I-I don't understand. I don't understand this at all."

"We're going to go with you to turn yourself in," Alyssa explained.

Robin's eyes widened. "T-to *what*? T-turn m-myself in? For what?"

"For setting the warehouse fires," Sandra explained. "I'll help you as your lawyer."

"I don't have the money for that." Her heart raced so fast that her face pulsated, giving her a massive headache. "I don't understand this."

"Ian's covering my expenses in this. Don't worry about that," Sandra explained. "I'm good at my job. We'll get you a psychological evaluation first."

"For what? I have Alyssa."

"It's part of the defense strategy. We have to do it with an independent psychiatrist. Trust me. I know what I'm doing."

"I-I don't know what to do."

"Trust us," Alyssa assured her. "Are you ready to come with us?"

"Where?"

"To the police station."

"I-I...I don't...I'm sorry. I don't understand."

"You have to turn yourself in. I'll work with the prosecutor to figure this out. I really wish you could remember what happened exactly. At this point, we're letting the evidence speak for you."

"Did I really burn those warehouses down?" Robin asked. "That doesn't sound like me. I feel like I'm in a nightmare. You're telling me I committed felonies. That *really* doesn't sound like me."

Ian and Nate were arguing in the kitchen, their voices carrying out into the living room.

"I really don't understand. I feel like I've been blindsided. I feel like I've been framed. What's...what do I do?" Robin asked, grabbing her head in pain.

"You come with us," Sandra said. "We'll walk you through this. When we get there, you don't say a word. You let me handle everything. Can you do that?"

Robin nodded.

"Nate! You two quit yelling at each other, and come give this girl a kiss and hug. It may be a while before you see her," Sandra yelled to him in the kitchen.

The yelling ceased immediately. Nate appeared in the doorway of the kitchen with tears in his eyes. "I'm sorry," he said, running over to her. He wrapped his arms around her. "I hate this for you." He leaned back and brushed her hair out of her face. "I'm here for you through this whole thing. The good and the bad. Don't worry about me. I am standing beside you."

Robin shook her head. "It's a felony. If I'm convicted, it could be years in prison. Please just move on. You deserve to have a family and a life."

"Honey, you don't know what's going to happen. Sandra's good. She'll be there through the whole thing."

"If I'm convicted and have to go to jail, there's no telling how long I'll be there or what I'll be like afterward. Please. If I get convicted, please move forward with your life."

He placed his hands on both sides of her face. "Robin, I love you. I know we have only been together for a few months, but these months have been the happiest of my life. However long you are in jail for, I am yours. I will be here for you."

"I need to know that you'll be happy. If you find someone, I want you to be happy." She was having difficulty catching her breath as her heart continued to race faster than it should. "Please sell my house."

"No," Nate said. "I'll maintain it for you. You already have it paid off. There is no reason to sell it or anything. This is temporary. Just let Sandra do her thing. Let Alyssa help you through this. Let me stand beside you during this. Please?"

"I don't understand why you love me. I don't understand why

you want to stand beside me...an arsonist. That goes against everything you believe in."

"I love you for you. A long time ago, I told you that you needed to learn your true value. Your heart is pure. I don't know your reasoning behind what you did, but knowing you, your intentions were pure. I will stand by you because I know you better than you know yourself right now. I don't know if I will ever forgive Dad for this," he said and glanced back at him before looking back toward Robin, "but I know this...I know I love you. I know I will be with you through all of this."

"I don't want you to be angry with your dad. Ian did the right thing."

"Robin! He's making you turn yourself in. He has to testify against you."

"He's doing the right thing. He's doing what I would do if I knew I did it."

"If it's any consolation, I don't think the first one was on purpose," Ian said.

"Dad," Nate said sternly, "you *really* need to stop talking."

Ian put his hands up in surrender. "Shutting up."

Nate turned back to Robin. "I love you." He looked at Sandra, "Can I go with you?"

"Probably not a good idea." Alyssa shook her head. "She has to separate from herself for a bit. She needs to mentally prepare for walking into the police station."

He turned back to Robin and kissed her. Robin felt what he was feeling in the kiss. She wrapped her arms around him as the tears fell down her cheeks. She pulled slightly away and whispered, "I love you, Nathan Mitchell. Someday I may see what you see. Until then, I will love you with everything I have."

"Hold onto that love. Know you deserve it."

"Thank you." She kissed him again and then looked up at Sandra and Alyssa. "I'm ready."

When she stood, she went over to Ian and gave him a hug. "I know why you're doing this. It's the right thing. Forgive yourself."

When she let him go, he said, "I know it's the right thing, but I feel horrible."

"You should," Nate said under his breath.

"Nate, he is doing his job. He's doing the right thing," Robin said. She turned to Ian, and said, "I forgive you."

He took a deep breath and slowly let the air out. Forcing himself not to cry, the tears still formed. "I'm sorry, Robin. I really am."

"It's fine. I'm fine. Everything's going to be fine. Just watch. It will be fine."

"No. It won't. You will be charged with a felony. This will follow you for the rest of your life," Nate said. "I can't believe you're doing this to her," he said to his dad. "After everything she's been through in this life, you are doing *this* to her!"

"Nate, I'm sorry," Ian said. "I know this isn't what you want."

"It's not what anyone wants," Nate shot.

"It's part of the job."

Nate turned back to Robin. "I love you. I need to not be here right now."

"Here's my key," she said, picking up her key chain. Handing it to Nate, she asked, "Since you won't sell it, would you please look after it?"

"I will. If you end up going to jail, I'll move in here if that's okay."

"Definitely!" she agreed. "Someone should enjoy it." She shook her head. "I can't believe I'm going to jail for something I can't even remember doing. Is there a precedence for this?"

"There is. There was a man who killed his wife in his sleep," Sandra said. "He doesn't remember it, but there were witnesses. He's serving life in prison."

"For a crime he doesn't remember? How is that a thing?"

"Honestly? If a person doesn't remember doing it, it doesn't mean he or she just gets off. They still did the crime. This was a couple who were wholeheartedly in love. There were no marriage issues. For some reason, he killed her while he was sleepwalking. It is a thing. It happens."

Robin shook her head. "Okay. I have to do what I have to do. Let's just go get it done."

Nate grabbed her in a hug. "I love you."

"I love you, too," she said and kissed him before they left out the door. She turned to see him and his dad standing on the porch.

Ian put his arm around Nate. Nate let him. For that, she would be grateful. She did not want to come between them. She took one last look at Nate before she got into the car. She watched him as they drove away, memorizing his face, not knowing when she would see him again.

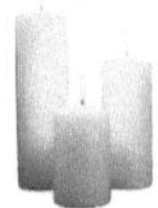

Feeling like an emotionless robot, she went through the motions. They took her fingerprints, and had her stand for the mugshot. Afterward, they escorted her back to a holding cell, where she sat down on a bench. Anytime another woman tried to talk to her in the holding cell, she turned away and faced the wall with tears crawling down her cheeks in a slow stream.

There was no changing this scenario. She had no idea why she did it. Ian said the evidence said she did. Evidence doesn't lie. She wracked her brain to figure out how it happened.

After a few hours, one of the officers came into the cell area. "Robin Flynn?"

"Me," she said as she stood.

"Come to the door. Everyone else stand back," he ordered. He unlocked the door, and she stepped out. He locked it, and they headed out of the area.

"Where are we going?" she asked.

"Just follow me."

They walked down the hall, up a set of stairs, and then he took her to a hall of rooms. He opened a door and gestured for her to enter.

She walked into a room with a big mirror on one wall and a table in the center with three chairs. Sandra was sitting in the chair next to an empty chair. There was a detective sitting across the table from her and another detective leaning against the wall with his hands in his pockets.

As soon as she stepped through the door, the officer closed it behind her with him on the outside. She took the chair beside her lawyer.

"Hi, Robin. I'm Detective Diego Torres, and this is my partner, Detective Justin Callahan."

Robin just nodded her head. She toyed with the bottom of her shirt. It was a habit she picked up as a kid.

"Can you tell us why you're here?"

She looked at Sandra, who answered for her. "She is here because she is responsible for three arson fires in the warehouse district."

"The ones that were pretty much fire hazards themselves?" Justin asked.

"Those very ones," Sandra confirmed.

"Wait a minute," Diego said. "Were you the one they found in the third one? The one Simms is working with regarding the stalker that killed those hikers?"

"Yes," Sandra said. "She was. She was also the one who was not convicted for killing him because he kidnapped her and shot the hikers in front of her. Yes. This is her."

Diego turned a tablet toward her with a pen on it. "Feel free to write your confession."

"That won't happen," Sandra said. "She has amnesia."

Diego shook his head. "I don't understand."

"In the last fire, Liam Rogers knocked her down the stairs. That fall took her memory away. She doesn't remember much of her life before the fall. She gets flashes here and there. Fire Marshal Ian Mitchell has the evidence. Feel free to contact him."

"Wait a minute," Justin said, coming off the wall. "Are you saying she doesn't remember committing the crime? For real? I mean, we've had people claim it, but you are saying she sincerely doesn't remember it?"

"Yes. It is on her medical record. She has been working with Dr. Alyssa Morrison since she got out of the hospital to piece what she can of her life together."

"Wow. Okay. We'll advise the District Attorney of the situation," Justin said. As he walked out, under his breath, he added, "This is going to be a fun one."

Robin looked at Sandra. Sandra sighed and then looked at Diego. "Seriously?"

"He needs to blow off a little steam. We just got done with a particularly rough case."

"And now?" Sandra asked.

"It's a little tricky," he said, writing a few things down on the notepad. "I'll get ahold of Ian and get back to you. In the meantime, we'll keep her in holding."

"That's not right. You're leaving her in a holding tank with drunks?"

"Would you rather we put her in an actual jail?"

"I would *rather* she be released on bail."

"C'mon, Sandra. You know how this works. It's a process."

"Can you process it a bit differently? She's a special case. You can release her, investigate, and then when you're ready to charge her, bring her in for processing," Sandra suggested. "She's under psychiatric care. I don't think she'll be able to get what she needs here. She's also still on shaky ground regarding her mental stability. She hasn't slept much for weeks."

"Sandra," Diego said and then sighed. "She's already been

processed. She *has* been charged. You are the one who told us she did it. You confessed for her. You're welcome to petition the judge for a faster arraignment due to special circumstances," he suggested.

"I will. In the meantime, can she have her own room for holding?"

"Nope. No room for that. She gets no special treatment unless you can get the judge to order it. I can go ahead and put her in a cell if you want? That way, she is in her own space," he offered. "She's already charged. I can't change that."

"Okay. Robin, go with him. I'll see what I can do on my end," Sandra said to her.

"Thank you," Robin said and then followed Diego out of the room back to holding.

Robin's nights were bad before, but now they were downright brutal. She knew Sandra was doing her best, but not knowing what was going on was killing her on the inside. For the first time in her life, she prayed. She got down on her knees in the middle of the cell in the middle of the night and prayed.

"God? Are you there? I know You may not know me, but I need Your help. I know I probably shouldn't come to You only when I need help, but I really need it here. You know what's going on. You know what I've been going through. You know what happened. Even if I don't, You do. According to Nate, You know everything. He said You see everything and You are all-powerful. If that's the case, then You are the only One who can help me. I'm asking for help."

"How can God help you in here?" she heard a voice in the cell next to her. "This place is God-forsaken."

"If He knows everything and sees everything, then nowhere can be God-forsaken," Robin reasoned.

There was silence for a moment before she heard, "I used to be a Christian."

"Used to be?"

"I grew up in church. I was in youth group all through high school. I went to college to be a teacher. I wanted to be a teacher in the mission field. I wanted to teach the kids."

"What happened?" Robin asked.

"I was in college, walking back to the dorm after a night class, when I was raped."

Robin gasped.

"I got pregnant. They tend to not want women who had children out of wedlock on the mission field," she finished.

"I'm so sorry."

"Thank you."

"Did you end up being a teacher?"

"No. I couldn't finish college. As for the mission field, I was angry. I ended up giving my kid up for adoption. What kind of God would let this happen to a person who was supposed to do His work in the field?"

"I'm so sorry." When Robin didn't hear anything for a bit, she said, "My name is Robin."

"I'm Maya."

"Why are you here? How did you go from wanting to be a school teacher to here?"

"My life spiraled after I gave up my baby for adoption. I fell into a deep depression. I know it was the best thing for him, but I went from being angry to furious with God."

"I'm sorry, Maya."

"It's not okay, but there's nothing I can do about it. When I went into depression, I started drugs in an attempt to forget the entire thing. I took them so I wouldn't have to feel the pain of having to deliver a baby and have nothing to show for it. I wanted to forget the fear I had whenever I was out at night walking. I cursed the sun in the winter. I hated that it went down so early. Anytime I was walking around and a guy was anywhere near me, I would almost jump at my own shadow. I would have panic attacks. I wanted to forget it all. The drugs took those feelings away."

"Was it worth it?"

"Absolutely not. Counseling would have been a lot less expensive. It would have also not landed me here. I was so desperate. I wanted to keep that euphoric feeling I got from the drugs. I wanted to forget the first part of my life ever happened. In order to do so, I needed money. In exchange for the drugs, I ran errands."

"What kind of errands?"

"Drug running," a voice from another cell said. "Just tell her the truth."

"Shut up, Julia," Maya snapped.

"Tell her the truth," Julia pushed.

"What am I missing?" Robin asked.

"My dealer, Leo, had been holding out on me," Maya said. "He wanted more than just a delivery. He wanted me. Because I wouldn't give myself to him, he was withholding the drugs. Then, one day I snapped. I was so desperate for heroin that I..." her voice faded.

"Maya?" Robin asked. "What did you do?"

"I held a gun to his head. He went to try to get it away from me, and the gun went off."

Robin gulped. "You-you killed him?"

"I did. Well, it was an accident, but I did."

"You held a gun to the man's head. You had the intention of killing him," Julia said. "Don't delude yourself."

"I only wanted to scare him."

"Welcome to reality," Julia said.

"What did *you* do, Julia?" Robin asked.

"Oh! I own what I did."

"Which was?" Robin asked.

"My guy was cheating on me...in my own house...with our baby in the other room."

"What?" Robin exclaimed, jaw-dropped.

"I killed him."

"What? Wait! What?"

"I did it. CPS took my kid. She's somewhere in the system. When I get out, I'll get her back."

"No, you won't," Maya said. "Don't delude *your*self. You admitted that you killed her daddy. That's not gonna happen. You are not gettin' her back when you get out of here. That is *if* you get out of here."

"What did you do, Robin?" Julia asked.

"I guess I set three abandoned warehouses on fire," Robin said. "It sounds weird to say out loud."

"You guess?" Maya asked. "You don't know?"

"I don't. I have amnesia."

"Oh! I could claim that!" Julia said. "That would make a great defense."

"I really do have amnesia. I guess with the third warehouse, my ex tackled me, and we went down a flight of stairs. I hit my head multiple times and went unconscious. The firefighters basically got me out before I died from smoke inhalation. When I woke up, I couldn't remember anything."

"Wow! And now?" Maya asked.

"Now, I have very few memories. Only the intense ones. The fires are not among them," Robin said.

"Wait. You set fires to warehouses, and those aren't intense memories?" Julia asked. "What kind of life have you lived? What do the intense ones look like?"

"When my entire family died in a fire when I was eight."

"What?" both girls asked, stunned.

"They died in a fire when I was eight. I was the only survivor," Robin said. "From that point, my grandparents raised me. At least that's the story anyway. They died in a car accident a few months back. That memory is there too."

"Ouch! I'm sorry, Robin," Maya said.

"But you don't remember the fires?" Julia asked.

"No," Robin said. "I wish I could. If I could, I would be able to explain to my firefighter boyfriend why I set the fires...which is against everything he believes in. I tried to tell him to move on. I cannot imagine this is easy for him. He says he loves me, and he isn't leaving me through this."

"Time will tell," Maya said. "Sometimes guys can be flakey."

"In their defense, sometimes girls can be, too," Julia pointed out. "My family said they would stand by me. They haven't. I haven't heard a single thing. Here I am, awaiting trial, and I haven't heard a word."

Robin sighed. "I don't have family except Kent and Logan."

"Who are Kent and Logan?"

"Kent's my best friend, and Logan was my ex's brother. Logan's family hated him, and there wasn't anyone left in his family. As for Kent, he's gay, so his family disowned him. Both are amazing guys. Since none of us have actual family, we decided to create one of our own."

"That's actually pretty cool," Maya said.

"Yeah. Wish someone would do that for me," Julia said. "Can't imagine this is going to get any better for me. My trial is supposed to start next week."

"Mine's in a month," Maya said.

"Sandra is supposed to be coming tomorrow to let me know when my arraignment is. I'm hoping to get bail," Robin explained.

"A good girl like you?" Julia clicked her tongue. "I'll bet you'll get probation."

"Especially due to the circumstances," Maya said. "You've never been arrested before now, right?"

"No," Robin said. "Well, I don't think so. I don't know for sure."

"That would be a definite twist if you were!" Julia said.

"You sounded a little too excited about that," Robin said, tongue in cheek.

"You a twisted chick!" Maya said with a chuckle.

"I've heard that before," Julia said.

Robin sighed. "I want to know, but I don't want to know. I have no idea what's happening. I feel horribly lost."

"Robin, remember when I said I was in youth group?" Maya asked.

"Yes."

"There are a few verses I have memorized. They come to mind when I need them. I think you need this one. It's from Isaiah. I think it's chapter 31, verses 10-13. It says, *'Fear not, for I am with you; be not dismayed, for I am your God; I will strengthen you, I will help you, I will uphold you with my righteous right hand. Behold, all who are incensed against you shall be put to shame and confounded; those who strive against you shall be as nothing and shall perish. You shall seek those who contend with you, but you shall not find them; those who war against you shall be as nothing at all. For I, the Lord your God, hold your right hand; it is I who say to you, "Fear not, I am the one who helps you.'*I know that was a long one, but that one helped me when I was confused and lost. It helped me figure out things while I sat in here during those first few weeks. It helped me realize that even though I felt alone, I wasn't."

"Great! Are you turning into a Bible thumper now?" Julia grumbled.

"Just because I am starting to find my way, is no reason to be derogatory."

"I'm not being derogatory. I'm being serious."

"You're being rude."

"You're being fake," Julia accused.

"Enough!" Robin snapped. "Thank you, Maya. The words from the verse helped. I wish I could talk to Nate about them. Julia, thank you for chatting. I think I'm going to go to bed now."

"So, the queen has spoken?" Julia asked.

"Shut up, Julia!" Maya growled.

"Knock it off in there!" an officer shouted.

Silence reigned the rest of the night. For Robin, it was a blissful silence. While Robin enjoyed the conversation, the bickering at the end did not make her happy. If this was what her life had turned into, there would be a lot of long nights ahead of her.

CHAPTER 20

SET THE WORLD ON FIRE

Robin was arraigned two days later and released on bail until her trial. During the next few months, she continued to work with Alyssa. They were unable to connect any more memories, so they worked on helping Robin reconcile that she would never get those memories back. To lose some of them were good, but she also lost the memories of all those years with her grandparents.

In the meantime, she went to church with Nate when he was off work on Sunday. While she enjoyed the stories and the way the pastor used the stories to apply to her current life, she wasn't sure about the giving her life to Jesus part. She didn't feel He had been looking after her, or she may not have landed in the position she was currently in at the time.

The trial was horrible for Robin. They dug up everything from her past. Situations that did not even pertain to the case. They brought up her relationship with Nate. The prosecuting attorney talked about her upbringing, saying she did it for attention. The prosecutor even said she was faking the amnesia. There were many accusations thrown around the courtroom against her.

The day she was called to the stand was the worst day for her.

"Ms. Flynn, can I call you Robin?" Sandra asked.

"Yes, ma'am. That's fine," Robin responded.

"All through this trial, your name and actions have been slandered. I know you have a medical condition. Would you mind sharing that with the jury?"

Robin nervously cleared her throat. "Um, I guess during the third fire, my ex-boyfriend –"

"Who has already been mentioned. That was Liam Rogers," Sandra cut her off.

"Yes. He tackled me, and we went down a flight of stairs. I guess I hit my head multiple times. The firefighters rescued me before I died of smoke inhalation. When I woke up in the hospital, I had amnesia."

"I see. And do you still have amnesia?"

"Yes, ma'am."

"How much of your memory has been recovered?"

"Objection," Prosecutor Carl Metcalf stood. "We are all already aware of her current state of mind. That's not in question. What is in question is her innocence or guilt regarding the fires."

"Agreed. Objection sustained. Please move forward with your questioning."

"Robin, did you set the fires in question?"

"I honestly don't know. I don't remember the fires."

"You don't remember?"

"There are very few events I remember before the amnesia."

After a few more questions, Sandra sat down, and Carl got up. "Robin, I can call you that, too, right?"

"Yes, sir."

"Robin, you stated earlier that there are few memories you have retained."

"Correct."

"You also stated that you do not remember the fires?"

"Correct."

"Convenient."

"Objection!" Sandra stood.

"Sustained," the judge responded.

The lawyer cleared his throat. "You stated there were a few memories that you *do* remember. What are those?"

"Objection," Sandra shouted.

"Sustained," the judge said and then looked at the prosecutor. "Mr. Metcalf, no more theatrics. Do you have actual questions pertaining to this case at this time?"

"Yes, sir."

"Then please proceed. Be warned, though, you're skating on thin ice."

"Do you like fire?" he asked Robin.

Robin cocked her head to the side. "Excuse me?"

"Well, in high school, you were an artist. Many of your pictures were of fire. Do you like fire?"

"I enjoy working with welding, and I like candles. They relax me. Fire has also been a big part of my life. Between welding and what happened to my family –"

"Yes. Please explain to the jury what exactly happened with your family."

"Your Honor!" Sandra jumped up.

"Counselor?" the judge said in a warning tone.

"It's relevant, your honor. I beg the court's indulgence for a few moments."

"Proceed."

"Robin, please share with the jury what happened to your family."

"They," she cleared her throat, "they, um, died in a fire."

"A fire that *you* were responsible for at the young age of eight."

"Excuse me?" Robin asked, wide-eyed.

He went back to the table and picked up a report. "This was already entered into as evidence. Robin, would you please take a look at this and tell me what it is and what it says?"

Robin took the pages and scanned them. "It looks like a fire report."

"What does it say?" he pushed.

"That the, um," she cleared her throat, "the fire started in my room with a candle."

"So, you *are* responsible for your family's death."

Sandra jumped up. "Your honor! Objection!"

"Agreed. Counselor, you are finished," the judge said.

"Your honor!" the prosecuting attorney snapped.

"Thank you for your testimony, Ms. Flynn. You may step down," the judge said. Then to the jury, he instructed, "The jury is to disregard the prosecuting attorney's last statements."

Robin got down from the stand and went over to the table with Sandra. "That's not good. Is it?" she whispered.

"Time will tell," Sandra whispered back.

The rest of the trial did not seem to be going her way. She groaned as Ian, being the last witness, stepped down.

The judge charged the jury, who left for deliberation. Once they cleared the room and the judge left, Robin sat down on the chair and dropped her head into her hands. "Why do I feel like this has gone badly?"

"Don't worry." Sandra rested a hand on her shoulder. "It's up to the jury now. Once they come up with a verdict, we'll go from there. You can't worry about what has already taken place. I can honestly say I have seen worse."

"What if they say I'm guilty? I mean, I guess I am. I just don't remember it."

"If they say you're guilty, then it is up to the judge to decide your fate."

"That sounds ominous."

"I don't mean to sound so rough. I've come to know you over the last few months and know you don't like to beat around the bush. You like things just said."

"I do."

"Robin, we're with you," Kent said from behind her. He sat with Nate, Ian, Erin (Ian's wife), and Logan.

"Thank you. I'm afraid if this turns out how I feel, y'all may not be seeing me for a while," Robin admitted.

"We'll just take it one day at a time," Kent said.

"I feel like my world is burning around me."

"Poor choice of words," Sandra said, writing a few things down on the tablet in front of her.

"You're probably right," Robin said. "I apologize."

"No apologies necessary. If it's what you're feeling, it's what you're feeling."

"I just feel like everything is collapsing all around me."

"It's not," Nate said. "We're here. You're here."

"I may soon be behind bars," Robin said.

"Can we take her out to lunch?" Ian asked.

"You can come with us," Erin offered.

"Thank you," Sandra said.

They went out to lunch. Then, they sat after they ate, talking and drinking their drinks. Robin felt like she was going to throw up, so she didn't eat very much.

After about two hours of them sitting and talking, Sandra's phone rang.

"Hello?" she answered it. After a few moments of silence, she said, "I see. We'll be right there." After she hung up, she said, "We have to get back to the courtroom. The jury is ready with their verdict."

"Already?" Erin asked, wide-eyed.

"Um, is it a good sign if it's quick, or bad?" Robin asked, tucking a portion of her hair behind her ear.

"It's not normally good. Usually when it comes quickly, it's because they don't have to deliberate long," Sandra admitted. "Come on."

When Robin stood, Nate wrapped her arms around her. He kissed her head. "We'll be right there with you. I'll visit you whenever I can. I'll write you when I can't be there. We *will* be together when you are out. I love you, Robin."

Tears crawled down her cheeks. She sniffed. "I love you, too." She looked up at him. When she did, he wiped her tears. "Please. If I get sent to jail. Please find someone else to move on with."

"No. You are the one I am supposed to be with. You go with Sandra and be that strong young lady I fell in love with."

Robin nodded and then followed Sandra out of the restaurant. The others followed behind in Ian's vehicle.

Robin felt like it took forever before the judge and jury came back into the courtroom. She took a deep breath while she stood, and then slowly let it out. With her hands behind her, she dug her fingernails into the palm of her hand. She took a couple more deep breaths while she looked toward the ceiling. Struggling to keep the tears back, she bit her lip.

"Has the jury reached a verdict?" the judge asked.

Robin looked toward the jury, trying to gauge their verdict by their faces. They gave nothing away.

The chairman stood. "We have, your honor."

"Proceed," the judge said.

"We find the defendant guilty of three counts of arson in the second degree. We ask the judge to consider the extenuating circumstances, though, when it comes to sentencing. We came to the unanimous verdict due to the evidence. The struggle ensued due to the circumstances."

"Thank you for your service," the judge said, and the juror sat down.

The tears freely flowed down Robin's cheeks. She really couldn't hear much after they said she was guilty.

The judge asked the prosecutor for their recommendation regarding a sentence. He suggested a light one due to the circumstances as well. After a few more minutes, the judge asked Robin to stand. She and Sandra stood up.

"The jury has found you guilty of three counts of arson in the second degree. I feel that due to the status of those buildings, the charges are dropped down to three counts of arson in the third degree."

Robin wiped her face with her sleeve. She really couldn't focus. His words sounded like mumbles.

"No one was harmed during the course of the incidents except you. This is also your first offense. I would appreciate it if it were your last."

"Yes, your honor," she said and wiped her face again.

"With the extenuating circumstances, along with the other two factors, this is what the court is willing to do. You have ten years of probation with a fifteen-thousand-dollar fine. You will also serve a thousand hours of community service to be served with the fire department, Fire Marshal Ian Mitchell in particular. I have spoken with him, and he feels that your fire interpretation is invaluable. I also feel if you continue to see what damage fire creates, it will deter you from further destruction via fire. It is the opinion of this court that if, during those ten years, you do not violate the terms of your parole, your record will be sealed. However, should you choose to violate your parole, you will serve a two-year sentence in prison for each of the violations, totaling six years without probation. Do you understand the terms and conditions?"

"Y-yes, sir," Robin stammered.

"Then, do not violate your parole, and your sentence stands," he said and banged his gavel.

With that, he dismissed the jury first and then excused himself.

Robin stood there trembling. "I-I don't understand what happened," she said as Ian, Erin, Nate, Logan, and Kent came rushing toward her. Nate was the first to wrap his arms around her. "What just happened?" she asked.

"You got lucky," Sandra said, shaking the prosecutor's hand.

"Actually, you both did," the prosecutor said. "Well done."

"Pretty sure your recommendation helped," Sandra pointed out.

"Actually, I think it was Mr. Mitchell's conversation with both me and the judge that helped. I would have been fine with the six years. See you at the next round," he said and left.

Robin turned to Ian and asked, "What did you do?"

"I, well," he rubbed the back of his neck, "I met with both of them a few days ago and explained everything. I recommended she work with me for her community service. I was thinking, if you're interested, that maybe you should go to college to get your Fire Science degree. Then, work your way up to Fire Marshal or Arson Investigator. I think you would do an amazing job at either of those."

"Will the fire department hire me?" Robin asked. "I'm currently a convicted felon...for arson."

"Be honest with them when they ask regarding your background. That, along with a letter of reference from me, should help."

"You would do that?"

"Take the win," Sandra said quietly to her.

"Got it. Okay. Thank you," Robin said, shaking Ian's hand.

"This is a semi-fresh start for you," Ian pointed out. "You have to work off your community service hours and pay your fine. But after that, head into college, and you will do amazing things."

"Just keep your nose clean and make sure you and your probation officer are besties," Sandra said.

"I'll catch up with you tomorrow and handle everything then if that works for you?" Ian asked Sandra.

"Sounds good. Ian," Sandra shook his hand. "Erin," she gave her a hug. "Until next time." Then she turned to Robin and said, "Here is the number for your parole officer. Contact him first thing in the morning and set up a time to meet. Don't make him chase you down. He's used to hardened criminals and doesn't take excuses. While you got a break regarding the sentencing, you got the toughest of the bunch regarding parole officers."

"Who is it?" Ian asked.

"Randy Kendrick."

"Ooo!" Ian cringed. "He *is* tough. Don't mess around with him. He is not a flexible guy."

"Agreed," Sandra said. "Keep your nose clean. Ian gave you a fair shot."

"I cannot thank you enough for all your help," Robin said to Ian.

"You had a rough start in this life, with not a lot of direction. Take the win and follow the path before you."

"I will. Thank you."

"Report to Kendrick first thing tomorrow morning," Sandra cautioned. "Like nine o'clock."

Robin accepted the card. "I will."

"Okay. My work here is done," Sandra said and left.

"Our turn to vacate," Ian said. He and Erin gave Robin a hug as well and then left.

Nate put his arm around Robin, "See? And you thought I should see other women. What is wrong with you? You're the only woman for me."

"See! Why can't I find someone like that for me?" Kent asked. "You have that sweet girl, Emma," he said to Logan. "Robin, you have Nate. Where's mine?"

"Someday," Robin said. "However, I don't feel your prospects are very high if you stay in your new realm of modeling. I haven't seen any that aren't stuck on themselves or starving themselves. You should really look outside of that world."

"I am. I have made some friends, but even those are a *keep your friends close and your enemies closer* situations," Kent explained. "I like my Hemlock family better, but I can't turn down the money."

"I don't blame you," Robin said as they walked out of the courtroom.

"Kara still wants you," Kent hinted.

"I don't know the terms of my probation yet. I also don't think that world is for me," she said.

"Just think about it. It will get you out of that new ten-thousand-dollar hole you just found yourself in."

"True. I'll think about it. It may also help pay for college."

"Don't forget your thousand hours of community service with Dad," Nate said. "You're going to have to learn to be flexible in your schedule with him. He doesn't give an inch either."

"There is a lot I have to figure out. Your dad has helped me at least get a good jumping-off point."

"Considering he put you in the position in the first place, I'm not giving him all the kudos y'all are," Nate said, irritated. "He's coming off the hero when he's the one who had you turn yourself in."

"Nate," Robin said, stopping, facing him, and grabbing his hands, "according to the evidence, I did it. There had to be some penalty for what I did. I'm sure y'all didn't care for getting up in the middle of the night to go to a fully-engulfed structure fire."

"Those nights weren't fun, but still."

"He helped ease my sentence. They could have kept it a second-degree felony. If so, each count could have garnered me two-to-twenty years. By him talking to the judge and prosecutor, it got knocked down to a third degree. That's a huge difference. Somehow the judge also graced me with a good boss in him for the community service hours. Yes, he had me turn myself in, but he helped me in the long run. Maybe fire needs to be my path in life. I wouldn't have known that if this whole thing didn't happen."

Nate sighed, shaking his head. "All right. I see your point. Do you realize how amazing you are?"

Robin blushed. "I'm definitely not that. As a matter of fact, I am now a criminal. I'm legally an arsonist."

"Who is using that part of herself to go into the fire service. You are taking things that would normally break another and turning it around for the good."

"Part of that is Ian," Robin said. "If your dad –"

"Look," he cut her off, "you're beautiful, sweet, and unapologetically you. You live your life each day, despite what has happened to you. One of these days, you will figure out your true value. Until then, will you please let me love you?"

Robin nodded.

"He's got a point," Kent said. "We wouldn't be a family without you. If you had to go to jail, Logan and I would make it together, but we are better off with you beside us."

"Agreed," Logan said. "You are the one who brought us together. Don't you see that? You could have thrown me to the curb for what my brother did to you."

"That's not your fault," Robin said.

"Exactly. You are choosing to look beyond my circumstances and see me. You do that for everyone. You see our hearts. We are trying to show you yours."

Robin nodded. "I get it. Thank you."

Nate lifted her chin with the tips of his fingers. "I hope you do get it. You are an incredible pearl of great price. I see that, and so do these guys. Liam, in his own way, saw it, too, and knew what he was losing. I'm choosing to cherish that and not control that fiery flame within you. I hope to show you what I see in you."

"Okay. Enough sappiness. Let's get out of here," Robin said. "I don't want to be in this place any longer than I have to."

"Let's get you home," Kent said, and they left.

CHAPTER 21

FIRED UP

Through the next few years, Robin's life changed in many ways. First off, she served her community service under the watchful eye of Ian. He taught her and Nate at the same time as they combed through fire scenes in his district. After a few years, Nate moved into his Fire Marshal position in a neighboring city. This posed a logistical obstacle for the pair for a time.

Finally, after her community service hours were finished and she paid off her fine. Then, she moved cities to be with Nate. She sold her house to Logan and Emma, who married a year after the trial. She then proceeded to go to college for Fire Science. She also got her EMS degree for her paramedic license while she was at it in order to help her be in a better position when she finished to get hired by a fire department.

About six long years after the trial, with the help of a letter of reference from both Nate and Ian, she was hired on to the fire department in the city where she and Nate now lived. Pinebrook was a nice city, nestled in the pineywoods about a half hour from Hemlock. This allowed Nate and Robin to stay close to Kent and Logan. It also allowed those friendships that Nate formed over the years to continue.

At year seven after the trial, Nate and Robin got married.

With everything they faced, they faced it together and came through stronger. By uniting their families, it allowed everyone to benefit from the family experience. For holidays, Logan and Emma, along with Kent, would join Robin and Nate, and head over to Nate's family's house. Ian and Erin, along with Nate's siblings, their spouses, and children, showed Robin, Logan, and Kent what a real family looked like. What love looked like. This shaped the trio in more ways than they ever knew.

No, the road to this point was not fun for Robin. She had some hard lessons to learn. Most of those lessons, she learned the hard way on her own. Through it all, Nate was there in the background. Even when she didn't know it, he was praying for her. He prayed for her since the day he met her back in high school. At the same time, so were Ian and Erin. As a matter of fact, they prayed for her since the day her family's home burned down. God somehow brought them all along separate paths until they united.

As Robin worked toward her desired Arson Investigator position, she found out she was pregnant. Nate was with her, holding her hair while she had her morning and night sickness. He was there during the scares and during the frustration when she had to quit working due to the intensity of her job. He was there through it all.

"One more push, Robin," the doctor encouraged.

Robin screamed as she gave one final push, bringing her and Nate's son into the world.

"It's a boy," the doctor announced.

"Robin, he's beautiful," Nate exclaimed.

"We can't wait to see him," Logan chimed from the hallway.

"Knowing you two hotties, he can't help but have great genes," Kent added. "I mean, he also has two hunky uncles, so it runs in the family."

"Give us a few minutes," the doctor said with a chuckle. "Need to clean this little guy up a bit and take care of Mom."

"Mom," Robin said with tears in her eyes. "I'm a mom. I never thought this is where I would be."

"And you are as beautiful today as that first day I met you in my house at Jenny's sleepover," Nate said, wiping the tears off her face.

"Is it here yet?" they heard Jenny in the hallway.

"He just arrived," Kent explained.

"He? It's a boy?" Jenny asked.

"Yes," Nate said from inside the room.

Jenny poked her head into the room. "Do you have a name yet? Mom and Dad are behind me with Drew and the kids."

Nate looked at Robin, who nodded, so he said, "Nicholas Ian Mitchell."

"Awesome! Dad's gonna love that!" Jenny said and disappeared.

"Here you go, Dad," the nurse said, handing the little bundle to Nate.

"Aww," Nate said, looking down at the baby, who wrapped his tiny fingers around Nate's hand. "Welcome to the world, little guy."

It didn't take long for Robin's world to continue to spin in the right direction. As a matter of fact, as far as she was concerned, her world was great. There was just one more thing that would make it perfect.

"Nate, can we talk?" Robin asked after she finally got two-year-old baby Nick down for his nap.

"Sure. What's up?" he asked, muting the race he was watching on the television.

"You have been very patient with me over the years and have loved me for me. You never pushed, outside of stating that we go to church each week."

"Which you have complied with beautifully," he added.

"I've learned a lot. I've been tested a lot. I've done something that I want to tell you about."

"What?"

"Well, a few weeks ago, during my devotions, I, well, I hope I it did it right...."

"What is it?"

"I finally asked Jesus to come into my life and to rule my heart and soul. I asked Him to protect me and to show me the life He has for me."

"Robin! That's great! Why did you wait so long to tell me?" he asked, throwing his arms around her.

"I wasn't sure if I did it right. I'm still not sure. Here's the thing, though. I thought He had abandoned me all of those years. I thought He was ignoring me and leaving me in the breeze. It wasn't until I looked back that I saw His hand. I saw where He brought you into my life in high school. I saw where He brought my grandparents into my life after my family died, and gave them the strength to raise me. I saw where He allowed you to come back in. I also saw where your dad was in all of this. He was there the day my family home burned down. He was there when you guys convinced me to file the restraining order. He was there when we were trying to figure out the whole fire scenario with the warehouses. He was there when I had to turn myself in. He also stepped in when it came to the sentencing. God used Ian to help me through all of that. He also allowed Kent and Logan to come into my life when I felt I had no one. I could look back at my life and say I did it all myself. I could say I handled it, but I would be wrong. I didn't handle it. I wasn't in control of any of it. God was, God is, and God always will be. He is the One who set me on the path. Jesus is the One Who walked beside me. The Spirit is the One who encouraged me to just sit and let it all happen and work itself out."

"I agree wholeheartedly with everything you just said. I am pretty sure you did it right. However, if you're concerned, would you like us to pray together?"

"I would. As a matter of fact, I would like us to do this together, too," she said, pulling a devotional from around her back. "I think it will continue to bring us closer."

He looked at the book. "Agreed. I love it."

"Thank you for not pushing."

"Anytime," he said and kissed her cheek. "You are my love. I know you well enough to know that you will come to whatever conclusion is necessary on your own. Not gonna lie, it was frustrating but worth it."

"I know. I guess you could say I was tested by fire and won."

"You were. Fire is an ugly beast. You went through it all."

"And with my record getting sealed next week, me accepting Christ as my Savior, and me getting accepted into the Arson Investigator program, there is only one more piece of news that will top it all."

"What's that?"

"Well, we have another Mitchell on the way," she said, resting her hand on her stomach.

"Another one?" Nate asked, wide-eyed. "You're pregnant again?"

"Yep!"

"You're serious? That's great! You walked through all the flames life tried to throw at you and came through stronger on the other end. Robin," he took her hands into his, "you are the strongest person I know. When metal is forged in flame, it makes it tougher. You went through each step of the forging process with Jesus by your side, even when you didn't know it. There were days when I held you while you screamed after waking from a nightmare. There were days when you were exhausted, but pushed through. There are days now when I cannot believe you are my wife. Today is one of them. I am doubly blessed by all the news. Thank you for choosing me to do life with. I wouldn't have it any other way."

"Me neither," Robin agreed. "Me neither."

Life has a way of showing us its ugly side. That is where the forging process begins. None of us come through this life without walking through life's fires. Are you walking through it alone? Do you have the blessed love of God watching over you during that process so you don't burn completely?

Isaiah 54:16-17 – "Behold, I have created the blacksmith who blows the coals in the fire, who brings forth an instrument for his work; And I have created the spoiler to destroy. No weapon formed against you shall prosper, and every tongue which rises against you in judgment you shall condemn. This is the heritage of the servants of the LORD, and their righteousness is from Me," says the LORD.

Do not worry. He will not let you fall.

Isaiah 40:31 – "But they that wait upon the LORD shall renew their strength; they shall mount up with wings as eagles; they shall not run, and not be weary; and they shall walk, and not faint.

But the most important thing to remember while you are in the flames of life is that God has a plan for you!

1 Peter 1:7 - "These trials will show that your faith is genuine. It is being tested as fire tests and purifies gold--though your faith is far more precious than mere gold. So, when your faith remains strong through many trials, it will bring you much praise and glory and honor on the day when Jesus Christ is revealed to the whole world."

Jeremiah 29:11 – "For I know the plans I have for you," declared the LORD, "plans to prosper you and not to harm you, plans to give you hope and a future."

About the Author

C.J. Peterson is a ten-time award-winning, multi-genre published author since 2012. She is also a podcaster, blogger, and publisher who knows how to relate well to folks of all ages.

Grace Restored Series, *The Holy Flame Trilogy*, and the *Divine Legacy Series* have the characters crossing over storylines. In these books, the spiritual realm crosses into the physical. This adventurous journey will have you holding onto the pages for dear life!

The Sands of Time Trilogy (Appointed Time, Race Against Time, & Out of Time) is **an exciting sci-fi series that will have you on the edge of your seat!** This series follows a group of teens with abilities as they go through the US to rescue their siblings. The challenger is their sadistic creator who has the money & power to win at any cost.

Chain Reaction follows Trip and Tori as they go through time guiding their ancestors to change crucial decisions. In changing their past to save future generations, will Trip and Tori cease to exist? Take a wild ride through time in ***Chain Reaction!*** In **Tested By Fire**, Robin's life has been one firestorm after another. But what happens when a fire marshal falls in love with an arsonist? Find out in ***Tested By Fire!*** Don't miss any of these adventures.

C.J. has a children's book series based on the real-life ***Adventures of Chief and Sarge***! She and her husband (lovingly known as Super Hubby) take Chief (stuffed koala) and Sarge (stuffed monkey) on real-life adventures in order to share them with your little one! People have fallen in love with Chief and Sarge, as they follow along on these adventures on their social media and web page! Many have even taken advantage of photo opportunities with the little guys. Check them out under the tab on C.J.'s website with the same name.

The Adventures of Chief and Sarge: Every day is an adventure with these two!

https://cjpetersonwrites.com/

"While the stories are fiction, the journey is real."

Books By C.J. Peterson:

Grace Restored Series:
https://cjpetersonwrites.com/team-angel-series-books

Holy Flame Trilogy:
https://cjpetersonwrites.com/team-angel-series-books

Divine Legacy Series:
https://cjpetersonwrites.com/team-angel-series-books

Stand-Alone Books:
https://cjpetersonwrites.com/stand-alone-books

Sands of Time Trilogy:
https://cjpetersonwrites.com/sands-of-time-trilogy

Anthologies Where C.J. Peterson Is A Participating Author:
https://cjpetersonwrites.com/anthologies

Adventures of Chief & Sarge:
https://cjpetersonwrites.com/chief-and-sarge

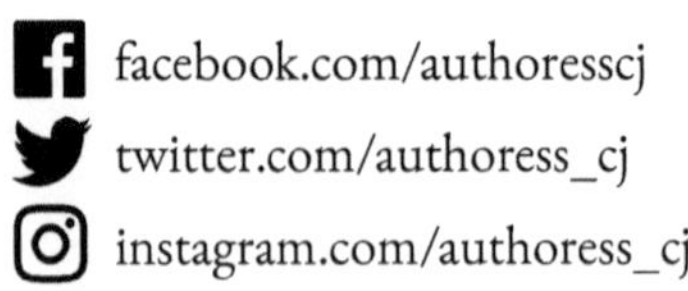

facebook.com/authresscj

twitter.com/authoress_cj

instagram.com/authoress_cj